IN THE BEGINNING WAS THE WORD . . .

This god of letters fellow who would later call himself Mercury handed me a tankard and said, "Have one for the Road." As I accepted, I suddenly felt myself falling . . .

It was a sobering experience. When I came to, I was sitting around a campfire in a buckskin breech-clout somewhere in old Mesopotamia and listening to an earlier version of this same heavenly bloke working hard at the chore of giving the Cosmos shape and character. Still later, I, a humble shepherd, and my campfire companions, would-be poets all, would witness the miracle of reed marker put to mud—the birth of the written word.

"But who'd keep a hunk of mud around for fifty years?" one of my companions objected.

The first literary critic had spoken.

Ace Fantasy Books by John Myers Myers

THE MOON'S FIRE-EATING DAUGHTER
SILVERLOCK

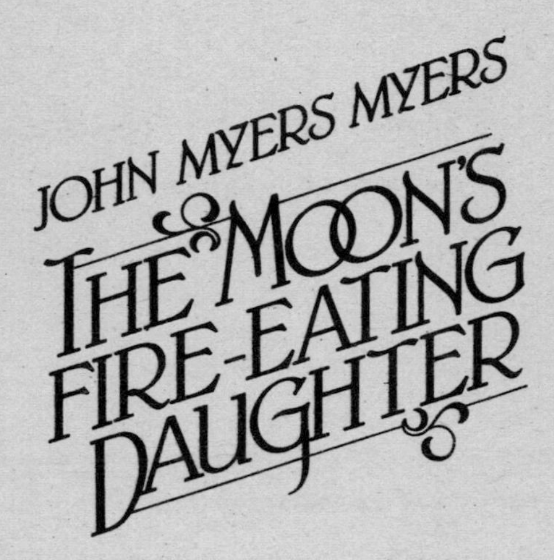
JOHN MYERS MYERS
THE MOON'S
FIRE-EATING
DAUGHTER

ACE FANTASY BOOKS
NEW YORK

This Ace Fantasy Book contains the complete
text of the original trade edition.
It has been completely reset in a typeface
designed for easy reading, and was printed
from new film.

THE MOON'S FIRE-EATING DAUGHTER

An Ace Fantasy Book/published by arrangement with
Starblaze Editions of The Donning Company/Publishers

PRINTING HISTORY
Donning edition/1981
Ace edition/October 1984

Cover art by Walter Velez

For information address: The Donning Company/Publishers,
5041 Admiral Wright Road,
Virginia Beach, Virginia 23462.

ISBN: 0-441-54172-0

Ace Fantasy Books are published by The Berkley Publishing Group,
200 Madison Avenue, New York, New York 10016.
PRINTED IN THE UNITED STATES OF AMERICA

TO—
Anne Caldwell and Celia
from their admiring old man.

Contents

1. Coffee at the Crossroads 1
2. On to Aldebaran 15
3. The Bash at Nebo's Lodge 29
4. The Universe of Mummu 43
5. Doings at a Seaport 55
6. The Drowning of the First World 70
7. Boatless in the Goof Stream 78
8. A Dilettante Goes to Sea 92
9. The Rescued Whale Tenant 103
10. Action in the Critical Woods 113
11. A Night at Eldorado 125
12. The Lake Where the Lady Lived 135
13. The Transmitted Humagram 146
14. A Surge Through Helicarnassus 156
15. That Second Trip to Mercury 171
16. A Map of the Literary World 179
17. A New University Discipline 184
18. Love Is Like the Road 195

Coffee at the Crossroads

This flying fish muscled into the dive I was already in. But the fact is that my story got off to a sort of practice start several hours before.

Then I was in bed, and trying to have a dream, only a girl I couldn't see very well was heckling me. "You're a glum crumb, George."

She should have called me Dr. Puttenham, but I let it go. "It's all in knowing how to get yourself in a bind," I explained.

"You need advice from out of this world," she told my tin ear, but I curled a cynical lip.

"Let's stick to the same old track we're always going to run on. Got any cure for a sore eye?"

She jumped at that like a frog of Calaveras County. "Fixing men up is my specialty. I'm busy now, but meet me at the—"

Dreams have a way of fizzling out at the most interesting parts, and this one quit me before she could name whatever rendezvous she had in mind. Still I found out what had been bothering my eye, when I woke up. Day had broken enough to shine up Venus, which was shooting all the gleam it had straight through my bedroom window.

Irritated by this impudence, I told it off as only a scientist could: "Morning Star, Bertha's big foot!" Why one of the large dogs of Charlemagne's mother should have rushed to mind, as I reached for the cord and jerked the blind down, is a bit I refuse to be psychoanalyzed on, but my point was this pest had no real claim to stellar rank. "You're no more than a circuit rider around the sun," I further put a planet in its place, "and I daily match that myself, courtesy of Earth."

After that I tried for sleep again, but I hadn't simmered down quite enough to be ready for it when the mynah bird in the apartment below misquoted *Caesar's Gallic Wars*. Normally the squawks of this feathered linguist were heard faintly, if at all. But spring mildness had prompted its owner to set the cage by an open window, whence rose words that could not but grate on a scholar. Ever since I had ridden a pony through the second year of high school Latin, I had known that Gaiius Julius had begun by stating that the country he and his legions had jobbed was split into three parts. But this knave of an ave declared, "All Gaul is divided into sweethearts."

Conceding that might be true of Gallia then and France, its modern upshot, I was sure that other conditions governed New Stonehenge, in the cold United States of artless letters, where I dwelt. I likewise deemed that as the mynah bird's error could hardly have stemmed from its own faulty translation of Caesar, it must have been purposely misguided by its owner.

This was an instructress in the Speech and Drama Department of our university whom somebody that cared enough should have advised to shake the racket and go wherever she belonged. With looks that could have been put up for auction, she failed to dress or act in ways that suggested she was a qualified academic cannibal.

If she belonged in any jungle, it was not the one in which I lone-wolfed and meant to share the blood I drank with no one. She should not have been allowed, besides, to rent a cave in the same cliff as an associate professor. For it lowered the flag of standards to have a mere master of arts click high heels into the same entry or elevator I used.

"Peter Piper packs a pickled puss when passing Pippa." That was the Audubonian upstart playing a new and worse record. Certain it wasn't the author of a garbled tongue twister, I scowled to think who was. For no more veiled than Salome, when she'd shed seven wisps, was a jibe detected by solid cues. There was, to be sure, a Dr. Piper, but he denned elsewhere, and he pushed Hydraulic Engineering at a campus joss house distant from that for would-be public speakers. Near that one, however, was where I hustled my own discipline (nobody in the trade said "subject"), of Economic Geography. My home and work zone thus forced me to pass often a satirist whose epigram about me I didn't find deserved. The implied charge that I marched sourly by her was as false as Marmion's forged letter. An instinctive democrat, I always said what the time of day demanded to one for whom "Pippa" was as simply pierced a *nom de guerre* as the hoot she had pinned on me. Both the university catalogue and the card above her mail box pledged that her taxpayer's name was Lalage FitzHorace.

Routed from rest earlier than planned by her nagging pawn, I returned from breaking cafeteria fast with the goal of faking a paper for *The Economic Geographer: A Magazine for People Who Think about the World's Chemical Make-up*. As few others did, I counted palming off a hash of knowledge to save my life again in the "print or perish" war which only greenhorns dreaded.

Old timer enough to snap fun out of seeing how much guff I could dress up as true learning, I was just hitting my stride when the forgotten mynah bird overstepped all former indecencies by turning the tenderest couplet in Shakespeare's sonnets to a poisoned dart:

> *"Farewell! Thou art too dull for my possessing,*
> *and like enough thou know'st thy dead estate."*

I saw more than red or a feathered enemy either. Behind that ostensible carver of my epitaph lurked the sinuous figure and long-lashed eyes of one I didn't care to hear from again that morning.

My chosen refuge was the university library. Being found there by scouts of the administration was good business; and if there was nobody to impress, I could hide in a booth and catch some of the sleep stolen from me.

For years I'd always taken the same short-cut to both the library and the geography building, but as I started to retrace everyday steps, I saw a certain Master of Arts and mistress of others lugging a sack of groceries in my direction. Wherefore I turned west toward Main Street, distasteful though I found it. Walking to work was in itself no unusuality, as it was part of my fitness program; but I objected to mix, as one of them, with the town's simple folk.

Next I regretted that Lalage's outspoken pet had chased me from home in such dudgeon that I hadn't armed myself with the umbrella recommended by April's shifty weather. When rain abruptly made shelter a need, I was midway between two havens, both out of joint with my dignity. To starboard was the door of "Lillian the Palmist: Fortunes Tailored While You Wait." To port loomed corner premises thus lettered in gold: "The Crossroads, Tim O'Lucian, Prop. Ladies will be served at the bar only when squired by heroes with the cash to foot the bill."

As a scientist couldn't have truck with a chiromancer, Lillian was out. On the other hand the bar didn't seem the house for genteel refreshment that a faculty member could be found patronizing. And the odds in favor of being seen and snitched on were here tall, as Main Street bulled through Oak but two or three blocks from ivied acres where spying was a way of life.

But while I was hesitating, the rain was getting more positive. With a shrug I fled thickening drops by skipping below the lintel of the Crossroads. I didn't have to pause to fight either of double doors, for both were swung in and pinned back to invite spring freshness as well as thirsts. Ducking far enough back to miss being spotted by stoolies, I passed a name-plaque noting that Tim himself was the tapster. An eye corner told me he was ready for commerce, but I studied the list of beers, bent upon deciding which brand was least likely to sell me to the nose of any sneak met in the library. Next to the names of breath-freighting malts, though, I was glad to find a sketch of a china mug, freighted with a blameless whipped cream. "Order Coffee," the slogan below it counseled, "like Finn McCool's mother used to make."

"Java, please," I told the waiting house. "But keep the sugar to cast before yaks." Always with a fat wallet on the principle that the sight of it squeezed the best from hucksters, I fed the mahogany a sawbuck, while speaking.

While O'Lucian strode toward his caffeine department, I gazed with gentle nostalgia about a scene that once would have been as standard for me as tundra for barren-ground caribou. Coffee hadn't been offered in honest to Gambrinus joints like this in days I'd sold down Career River; but all else mirrored a time summed in my favorite song of that forfeit season. A dozen years had filched the words, but as I glanced along a line of Bourbon soldiers dressing right before a vertical lake of plate glass, the ditty sashayed back to mind:

My ledger's page is flaming
With ink that's Falstaff jolly,
But now there's choral claiming
That the beauteous hue is black.
Prosperity's in mourning,
The mule of melancholy,
And I was bare aborning
Of wailing willow's knack.

Unlike other bars I'd been in since becoming a status steeplejack, this one was rimmed by a rail as glowing as the fleece for which Argonauts had dared the seaway to Colchis. My right foot ceased to itch when I rested it there, while evoking the second stanza:

They'll never sell the drinker
My merry sire engendered
The flam that gold's a clinker

A gryphon wouldn't miss;
That stars were not for shooting
Unless the rats surrendered
And blue nose not for booting
In his hypostasis.

Gryphons? I had to think to recall that Herodotus nominated them guardians of Asia Minor's goldfields. And 'hypostasis' wasn't just a pussyfooting term for the nock; it defined an officious ass's underlying reality.

Tim returned with my order, as I finished working that semantic problem, and after putting my ten skins through his cash wringer, he returned with the surviving nine. His price for coffee would have drawn an extortion beef but for two stoppers. I couldn't afford a huff until the cloudfall quit. Besides I'd tasted what honesty couldn't booh.

"This clobbers the spot," I therefore said.

Although the phrase was stock, it drew a hearty rejoinder. "The lad whose spot that doesn't wallop is already paralyzed, or the doc that was trying to circumcise him whacked off the wrong article, Squire."

As a call from down the bar yanked him there, I didn't challenge him as to the title he'd spiked me with. Instead I looked to see who else might be profiting from the coffee-making genius of Finn McCool's old lady. The brooder up by the bar's elbow was piecing himself together with a whiskey sour. Between him and me, two were bracing to meet a future sea of troubles with boiler makers. Down near the back room were a pair of beers or ales. There didn't seem to be any others delighting in coffee, but as I turned my head to make doubly sure, my left eye caught the storm in the act of coughing up a flying fish.

Had I been elsewhere I would have called attention to it, but as one doesn't do that in a genuine joint, I sopped my drink and watched for the varmint's next move. It didn't keep me in suspense long. Getting its bearings, it left a small puddle near the door, and made a brief flight which proved to be its last. Landing an estimated five feet to my right, it achieved two-way stretch that gave the Crossroads another client.

Of yore with saloon good breeding, I didn't stare, but the figure examined by means of the mirror puzzled me. As buckskin kilts go, there was no flaw in his, but I wasn't used to a uniform including a cape but not a shirt, sandals and the sheath knife snugged to him by a belt. Hair the length of the hamadryad baboon's was no food for surprise in a university town, on the other hand, nor was a bramble patch of a beard, which half the professors were trying to equal.

As I watched him above the reflections of three in the rear Bourbon rank, he peered for the house and gave tongue. "Hi, Tim; I made it here in three swoops after leaving the team at Teal Inlet." Having named a body of water favored by the students for canoodling and other water sports, he explained his choice of metamorphosis. "I could have come faster as a seagull, but that would have been no challenge. Is this It?"

His nod, as they locked fists, showed he meant me. But though I huffed at being named as some game's goat, I gulped the insult as tamely as I had the mynah bird's slurs. My least wish was to give the New Stonehenge *Megalith* a chance to run an item about me scareheaded PROF AT LOCAL U. HAULED TO HOOSEGOW FOR DECKING EX-FLYING FISH IN MAIN STREET BOOZE SINK.

Caution also held me on leash when O'Lucian replied, "I've been watching for half baked ones ever since you telepathed, and he's the only one that looks as if the treatment might bring him to. Tell me how she happened to zip this way while I flush a glass with stingo for you, Ninshubur."

"Well, we'd only been back a day from visiting the Kid and Psyche, when one of her secret service cupidos checked in with word that janes belonging to We Want Liberation from the Feminine Gender were here, fixing to hold a convention on the New Stonehenge campus today."

"That bunch would naturally drive her up a wall twice as high as China's is long," Tim grinned. "Keep talking."

"Her plan for wrecking the squawking jills was to buzz among them and get herself named as an after luncheon speaker." Ninshubur drank and smacked approving lips. "Before she started she had me swing Lucifer lower than usual, so she could case the town for other business; and she noticed some platypus, if this isn't the one, that looked down in the mouth."

Ordering another coffee, I moved out of hearing with it. If not a platypus, I both didn't like my lot and was afraid of being separated from it.

Letting go of a happy-go-lucky life, I had fled to scholarship for anchoring iron realities. And I had embraced science as it chanced, at the crest of the USAL academic wave, giving Ph.D.'s the cush to buck the stock market at the very season when a sadly shrunken workload had made how to fill idle time a problem. I hadn't first understood that covering up the fact of being a semi-drone is full time slavery. But I knew it now as clearly as I understood that I was panicked by the thought of leading a less plush-lined life.

Looking to see if the downdrench was likely to free me for library shulking, I saw a hairy figure collapse his parasquawl inside Tim's trap. Stepping around the half absent taker of the whiskey sour cure, he ducked under the gate at the wall end of the bar's elbow and vanished behind the mahogany. I was reasoning that this must be the Perpetual Undergrad, as students dubbed the U's gorilla mascot when O'Lucian strolled near and betrayed a disguise.

"It's your colleague, Doc Hornspoon, here for a bomb or so to give him the guts to face a certain class, Squire. He's got a hang-up like Frank Villon's raven-pecked men; and you'll hear him bleat, if you stick around."

Just then a siren bansheed near, and in jiffies two campus guards steamed in. "A guy phoned that the college's big monkey is on the loose and was seen hauling his mangy freight this way," one said. "He ain't used to being on the town, and he might get in with the wrong kind of characters."

"At fourteen that gorilla's a minor," O'Lucian pointed

out, "and I wouldn't serve him without being promised amnesty by Congress."

"Nobody's making changes that you'd serve a goozle with no credit rating," the second law limb soothed. "But no son of a Darwin bitch is going to throw up a soft job which only asks him to strut his stuff at six home games and Baccalaureate Sunday without he's got a good reason. Now I ain't had no dealings with him, but it looks to me like the only gripe he could have is that the U. don't pay him. So he makes a break for where he can anyhow earn some walking around dough."

"There's no 'Help Wanted' sign in my window," Tim declared.

"Well, the big monkey wouldn't have no future with Lillian, and they likely wouldn't take him on as massager at Nadina's Parlor for cuter Body Contours across from you," watchman one said. "Nor he couldn't cut the mustard at the bookstore next to it, as I got it from the grapevine that he ain't a birdseed better at reading than half the students, for cripe's sake. But he could figure on holding down a job as swamper in a dive like this, so I think he quit his good thing to hit you up for at least part time work, Tim. How about it, you other guys?"

In answer the whiskey sour looked through the guard like he was maybe seeing an armed hoop snake, and the two boiler makers blinked indifference to outside trifles. But these were townies untouchable by campus cops, while Ninshubur—wild and fresh from Lucifer—signified that he neither knew nor cared about a gorilla's search for a better deal by picking up his glass and sauntering down the bar.

"But you're a prof or measles can't be told by spots, and I expect you to help us." With that statement the second officer brought me to man or mouse taw. "Did this barrel house baboon come in here or didn't he?"

The day before I would have claimed ignorance and let it go at that, but from this feeble out I now shrank because of a word laid vicariously on me by Lalage. To say only we had not seen the man, quivering within a few feet of me behind the bar, would have but added one more dull lie to the slag heaps piled up daily in the national capital of Cutthroatia and westaway for untold mean miles. Wherefore I raised a voice I hadn't heard since brass raildom ceased to be my normal habitat.

"I didn't want to volunteer what I know, because I didn't wish to sic braves like you two onto window-making dangers, officer. Are those pug-nosed .38 revolvers your only armament?"

"Yeah," one fidgeted, "if you mean is that all we're heeled with."

"A pity." I led the way to the front window with its view of Main Street looking toward the campus before I said more. "Whoever told you of the Perpetual Undergrad's break to get square with his enemies mentioned he was hiding a deadly something under his umbrella, I assume?"

"Well, I've been a bull long enough to know that a throwback on the lam had better be watched by a hawk, if you can find one that ain't ascared, Doc."

"You'll go far," I admired. "Now just as I had caught a whisper of coffee here and was hotfooting it for the library, I gandered up Main and saw him swaggering toward me, close as that 'Claims Paid When Hell Freezes' insurance sign; so I got a good look at his "typewriter"—a caliber .45 Browning it was—and the bandolier slung over his shoulder held tracers as well as ball ammunition."

"Was he out to get them insurance jokers for welching on his Uncle Oscar that time he got amputated on and they only anted enough to cover an aspirin pill?"

"He had somebody's blood on him, but just as I got praying God that this wouldn't be his next murderous stop, he got sucked across Main by a green light and legged it along Oak to join the rest of his mob. Can't you find it in your hearts to let the city police in on this, rather than hogging the glory of rounding them all up?"

"I was thinking of cutting in the national guard," one said. "Thanks for helping us, Doc."

United with my bar spot, I found that Tim had replaced dregs with new coffee. I didn't comment, though, because my hand was shaken by an amateur ape.

"To whom am I indebted for disposing of tyranny's motorized cossacks?"

Most of the faculty I would have brushed off, but Rugby Hornspoon had the name of being one of the back numbers who cared about teaching rather than pantomiming and raking in the returns he'd done nothing for. So I had a smile to shoot back at him as he laid his scowling head on the bar and beamed through gold rimmed gigs.

"Assosh Prof Puttenham," I told the History Department's sachem. "Four morning hours and two P.M. ones in Economic Geography."

"A scientist and with compassion for—? A-a-h!" This last was said to the whisper of water I'd seen Tim sprinkle on a Bourbon bonfire with three logs in it. Hornspoon put it half out with the grace of an old smokeater, then faced me again. "As you were sly to dive between me and dry arrest for impersonating a remote cousin, I suppose you posted on my tragedy."

"I wanted it to come to him pulsing with first person truth," O'Lucian said. "He's nailed to the rail by what I just bought him and cannot choose but hear."

"Excellent." Stamping out the ashes and shoving his glass up for rekindling, my new friend opened his book to me. "You behold in me, Puttenham, a scholar ruined by an insidious magister of the black art of poetry. Having taught Medieval History with acclaim on both sides of the Atlantic Narrows, I could have looked forward to honorable retirement in Chartres, watching the poules mince betwixt my sidewalk café and an also charming cathedral. In an ill-omened hour, however, I reasoned that the fictions of an era would supply insights not rendered by chronicles written in monastic seclusion. Do you ever delve in creative letters yourself?"

Let out of a bag, any campus cat could soon be everybody's; hence I didn't say I had long milked the library for little else. "As an undergrad I was forced to peck crumbs of it."

"But ever since you have done as Apelles bade the shoemaker do, and would that I had been as discreet. It is true that I gained some knowledge at the cost of no damage from certain dignified dreams and romances; but despite the fact that Matthew Arnold had posted him as lost to high seriousness, I at length blundered into Geoffrey Chaucer, his *Canterbury Tales*."

He looked to see if I had ever shot that rapids, but I hid behind a show of dim recollection. "It seems to me there was one about a nice quiet dish called Grisilde—that I wouldn't have minded as a resident of my apartment house—in Group E."

"I never got that far." Hornspoon lowered his glass' table of contents by three fingers. "Robin the Miller laid me a stymie, and I've been unable to make any stroke since."

"He may ride back to me, Doctor, but for now I can't grasp how he could have poured glue in your clock."

"He couldn't have flawed you in a thousand readings, lucky scientist, but in just one he destroyed historically-confident me." He slapped the bar with the woolly mitt of a fake jungle-joe. "Do you know why I don't trust myself to keep whiskey in my office and have to sneak down here incognito for the courage to attend my own 9:40 course in Medieval Monarchy? *He's* the reason, because he taught me that I'm a fraud, ignorant of the Holy Roman Emperors, popes, kings, nobles and bishops I pretend to be an authority on.

"Do I know how Boniface, Margrave of Tuscany, acted when stewed? No! Do I know how far France's Louis the Bruiser or Saxony's Henry the Fowler would go in telling a hot rock of a story in mixed company? Again no; but I can tell you Robin the Miller lost his hat while getting so blotto he could hardly hold his saddle, when leaving Southwark for Canterbury on April 18, 1375—exactly six hundred years ago today. And do you know of what I'm in mortal dread?"

As his shoulders had begun to quake, I was afraid his buttons were about to snap and hurried out a psychiatric folk cure, "Hold nothing back!"

"Rest assured I can't. For every year as April readies to deal the anniversary of that pilgrimage, I get to thinking how Robin told about that—that—and with the prioress listening, you see!"

In gleeful tears by then he raised eyes that begged Heaven for the strength to go on; and fearing he wouldn't, I whacked breath back into him. "That what?" I begged.

"That pretty little naked rascal y-yielding to a k-kiss applicant by h-hanging her st-stern sheets out a window in the dark. And then N-Nicholas. Do you remember him?"

"The picture's clearing up with you as developer. He found out the deceivers can't always be gay, didn't he?"

"After he took Alison's p-place, when Absalon r-returned to the amourous fray with a red h-hot tit for her t-tat! There. That's what possesses me so powerfully that I dread breaking out in roars of applause right in class unless given containing force by Bourbon just beforehand." By heroic effort Hornspoon mastered his tremors, downed the rest of his blast and smiled sadly. "Now you know how a nigromancing poet can devise realities where poor investors in fact leave unconvincing shadows."

Scooping his papier mâché head and his umbrella from the bar, he bowed to Tim and then me. "Until another April, good friend. May Fortune be your slave, kind ally. Now I go to leave protective coloring in the back room, which I'll quit through the tavern's postern, suspected of none but my broken self."

"That's a funny thing he said about poets inventing facts." I'd said that to O'Lucian, but another's voice picked me up.

"It ain't funny if you know anything about how everything got started, It."

Said to a scientist by a shirtless swipe, this was calculated to raise heat. I looked Ninshuber over, while trying to think of a crack at once dirty and not too complex for a slow mind to catch.

"I suppose you know just the word slinger who invented the winds and the waves."

"Sure; don't you?" Reading my flabbergasted look, he put the matter up to Tim. "Puttenham doesn't savvy who yanked Creation out of chaos."

What had scandalized Ninshubur failed to make a dent in Lucian's careless good humor. "Considering that Puttenham's about to meet the wild card in Nebo's deck," he said to the bottle he was pouring from, "he ought to be coached. Yet all I've got time to point out now is that when Nebo pulled the universe out of his back pocket, it was found that Nanna—the moon to you, Squire—had two mismatched daughters, of which the fire-eating one—"

"There's a rainbow!" I broke in to announce. "It's flush with the door, but don't bother to look for a pot of gold, as Government hijackers have already grabbed it. Anyhow its message for me is to walk my dogs to the campus, as soon as I've lapped this java."

While I was attending to that, Tim breezed back from rushing two more boiler makers. "The rainbow's left a deposit the Government ain't about to touch," he called while rapping the cash register, "and it's for you, Squire. When April that swished it down was rolling it up again, that moon's daughter that I was telling you about skated in."

On to Aldebaran

Whoever her father, a female now stood below a stirring painting of Custer's last moment. From this position she was eyeing the street through the window whose lettering warned that lone women could not hope for bar service. Should any man wish to play "squire," as the house chose to dignify the ancient sport of picking up, four stools were available between the dart board and a dwarf bowling alley. But whoever might lug one of these seats to the mahogany, it was no task for a doctor of philosophy who'd never have been in the joint, if he hadn't been pushed around more than enough by womanhood that morning.

"Live it up after you get back to Hickville." After so advising Ninshubur, I called farewell to Tim and strode downward. It was natural to glance at a person said to have lunar connections, though, and as I did so, she looked at me over her shoulder.

The effect was like that of my first bout with scientific research. Not having taken hearsay's word that a hot wire was bad news, when five, I had seized one that shook me so that I had never forgiven Ben Franklin for letting the electrical genie out of its bottle.

This time, nevertheless, I bore the volts that raced through me no grudge. Before I could have repeated Lucretius' maternoster—"Of gods and men the delight, oh you Venus!"—I was vis-a-vis with her babbling as I bowed. "Allow me to introduce George P-P-Puttenham, Bachelor of Science, Dulcarbon, Master of Science, Shandygaff, and Doctor of Philosophy, New Stonehenge." Then I sneaked in propaganda via a nickname I'd never had but thought might help. "Lasses that know me well call me 'Torpedo.'"

"That will be proofread but not at the moment." The voice was the same one that had slanged me in my dream that morning but it was not now hostile. "You are troubled by other matters now, and I'll want to hear more about—"

Before she could finish, a hawker of the *Megalith* bustled in, noisy because of the old grads that would be drawn to the U. the next day, it being sacred to the Founders. The headline he bellowed accordingly ran "ALMA MATER TO HUG HOMING TOTS; THOUSANDS DUE."

Not scoring with that word at the Crossroads, the fellow left, seeming not to notice that by touching one of the bundle of sheets under his arm, she had acquired it. "Thousands—the poor little partridge," she murmured, while conning what she had stolen. "Who is this dear mother of a brigade?"

"Alma Mater's just shorthand for all remembered aspects of a university: the bored faculty advisers, the deadhead student drifters passed to keep from losing Government educational aid, the sports fatcatted by shifting library funds, and—" I didn't mean to bleat what followed but some magnetic force sucked it out of me. "And even some prized courses, though no old grad dreams of the good old days when I spell-tied him, damn it!"

"I'll see what I can do about that." She tapped the paper, which rolled itself into sausage shape and sailed into a trash can twenty feet away. "What's this shiny box?"

"It hands out cigarettes to any one who feeds it the asking price for any particular brand."

She had a better idea. Petted by one of her fingers, the usually surly gizmo hicked a pack which drew a smile of praise from her. "A knowing machine." She paused for me to do the lighting honors. "Will you situate me now, sugar?"

Sauntering with her toward the stool quartette, I fished for small talk. "Er—are you indeed of the moon's kin?"

"Just on Daddy's side of the family. Mother was well connected, too—especially with Daddy whenever she felt like it—but she was mainly wrapped up in her children; at least the two who took more after her."

There was a hint of the bleak background the Twentieth Century was used to. "You mean your mother didn't understand your father?"

"Well, Nanna's the shoot the wad kind, which is why he and I have always got along. Ningal—that's mother—liked unadventurous types; my brother Utu, for instance. Being the sun, with nothing better to do but glitter in the same groove all day summed his brain range and Mother's as well. Then she could understand Sis—that's Erishkegal—because she was as set on holing up in Kur (Hell to you, I believe) as any other laughless snake. But because I just do what I want to when I feel like doing it, she called me Daddy's Girl, which was the worst thing she could think of, except when he'd got her under the spell of his—penumbra. I've always loved tactful old Latin."

But I was thinking of her other problems. "Utu had the sun to ride around in, Erishkegal had Kur to take out her frustrations in; and you were given nothing?"

"Just the bitsy Evening Star, when it's not the morning one; but I think it was good for me, because it encouraged me to branch out and not depend on material things. The red stool goes best with my earrings, pet."

By the time I'd toted it to the bar, Tim was setting down another coffee and a glass of something golden for her. "Sorry I'm late in saying Heaven's here when you are," he cheered, "but it's morning break time for toilers hereabouts, and I've been busy as Argus's oculist."

They swapped a little more of the inside baseball of old friends and then she turned to me. "You're a professor of what and how do you go about it?"

"Economic Geography takes in all the basic prizes in Earth's Jack Horner pie: Lanthanum, Krypton, Tantalum—the whole crowd of elements. How I promote them is to show on maps where the various ones hole up and what has come of rooting them out. That ought to be as exciting as calling spirits from the deep that actually come, but I've found no way to shoot life into it.

"Molybdenum is a dandy element for making barbed wire, I'll tell the suburban-set that never snagged their pants on a strand and had the point rammed home. Or I might point out that the twin presence of iron and coal made England's Birmingham the sparkplug of the Industrial Revolution. Then I watch the kids' faces fall when I go on to confess that the key product of this inventive metropolis was the anagram 'Brummagem," symbol of everything gimcrack. Result? With all the makings of all the civilizations that have ever freckled the face of the world at my command, I can only sum up the whole by 'so what?' "

"So much I telerealized, if in more general terms than yours; and that my giant is only sulking like a soured pigmy, because he is not achieving yet aspires to." She put her hand on my non-drinking one. "So you can be pointed out with awe, lamb?"

"No," I whispered, when I could bear the impact of her stare no longer. "If this gets back to the administrative goons, I'll be lucky if I live to get railroaded to a junior college, where profs think nothing of working for their pay. But all right if it's just between us, Venus; I'd like to make a worthwhile pitch to raise my stock not only with my mirror but with a certain mynah bird. And that's every bit of what I'm going to say."

She fell for that stall with less question than I thought she would. "I'm sure you picked out a feathered echo that does credit to your taste, bee-tree. I'm also sure that you'd better get out of your routine and help yourself to infinite variety." It seemed to me that her golden snort hissed when she tossed it down, but she didn't blink. "How'd you like to make a survey of the Road for me?"

"I haven't been trained in that field of geography," I objected.

"All I need is a cove to give me a clear, objective report based on first hand observation. None of the others I've commissioned have lived long enough to do that."

I allowed that clause the freedom to enter one ear and exit by its mate. "What was the matter with them except being dead?"

"They got all tangled up, because they didn't know how to look at things; I don't know why I never thought of turning the job over to a scientist before."

"It's a mistake the voters make, too," I comforted her. "Any scientist could make a respectable whited sepulchre out of Casa Blanca, but they keep turning it over to amateurs."

"It only takes one vote to appoint you, honey, and that's mine. Are you on? There's no fee, but I've already thought of a suitable reward."

I sipped my coffee to keep her from seeing I could think of one, too. "When would you wish me to start my survey?"

"Right away's never too soon for me."

She'd left her perch and was in evident eagerness to go somewhere, but I put my hand on her arm. "This will be a cinch for me," I said, visualizing her road as the private one leading to some estate. "But I wouldn't want to lose my job by muffing my one-forty class today, and I can't get a sub because there's not another E.G. cackler around."

"You'll make your class. If you don't get drowned in space, chewed up on land or sea, mobbed or what not." She ran a hand through her hair. "But do, for my sake, be careful, pet."

"For you, sure." I tried out a laugh, but it didn't fit. "What's scheduled now?"

"A phone call to Nebo, but that won't take much time." Patting my cheek, she made for the phone booth next to the cigarette machine she'd bamboozled.

The castanets of her heels clicked the same tune as Lalage's until she stepped into the glass-doored box. I watched her long enough to be sure she wasn't sparing the phone outfit any coins either.

"Do you think you can stand foreign travel?" A hairy fist setting down his ale glass was notice that the ever restless Ninshubur was pitching barroom camp next to me.

Not bothering to wonder what had prompted the query, I gave him the icicled shoulder. "I've already been up the crick and down. Doesn't it show?"

"Yeah," he said, "but don't wash it off just for me."

I was still looking for a lofty reply to that when her heels clicked the message that she was coming back. "He's within one step of being ready for the Road, so will you get the team please, Nin?"

I didn't have to worry about him any more, for he turned into some sort of pony express bird and zipped through the door. She did bother me, though, by reminding me of the Fitz Horace danger zone, and not only facially. When Lalage shifted any of her gang of conscienceless parts, the rest all smoothly adjusted, keeping the picture always in balance. Now Venus did the same thing when climbing back on the earring matching stool and turning to me. "Nebo's ready to put you on the Road, and he's prepared to answer any questions you may have."

"Will I need any equipment?"

"Only enough to track me through C. and report with scientific accuracy that history's only in form when telling of my accomplishments. That isn't too much to ask, is it?"

As she was staring at me, I didn't feel that it was, but a doubt was nagging me, nevertheless. "What's C.?"

"Oh, just civilization; you meet quite a few phases of it on the R." She turned. "Deal with the shenaniganite yam, so I won't have to mess up Tim's premises by striking him dead."

That was said with reference to a guy who an instant later undertook to muscle between us and bark at her, "Let's see your age card!"

"That's a bizarre idea," she said. "Why would you want a thing like that?"

"Because I work for the State Liquor Control Department, that's why, and you can't be twenty-one," he snarled.

"How do you explain that to a millennium?" she inquired.

"Huh? What do you want?"

That was because I had grabbed him and swung him my way. "I want you to get lost like the Generation," I told him. "This lady and I don't want you butting in any more."

A flat-faced shark, he flashed his teeth at me. "This lady is a minor that you're steering into the gutter by pouring alky in her. What's your name and place of business?"

That took the wind out of me but not of her. "His name's It, and he's working for me as a road surveyor."

"Quit kidding!" he ordered. "You're a snotty kid, and probably a co-ed to boot. Hey, bartender!"

"Before O'Lucian could get on the scene, she said to me, "I don't like what this helot said to me, hero; he needs manners instructions."

Finding that I was furious, too, I forgot about the U. and the necessity of keeping out of the limelight in dives and let one go at the State Liquor Department john that started way out in left field. Byron's wolf of a Syrian couldn't have come down on that purple and gold cohort with half the force of my mitt when it whacked the guy's button. It should have split him as well organized lightning does an oak that forgets to duck, but he came back with a wallop that staggered me until retreat was cut off by the dart board between the tables for ladies and the three remaining stools.

Hitting the board with the back of my head dropped me, but not for the count. I was charging in for a second crack when Tim vaulted over the bar and jumped between us.

"What did you start a row for?" he demanded of me.

"Sugar did exactly right." After sticking up for me, she fingered my foe. "This said something horrid that hurt my feelings."

"He did, eh?" O'Lucian gave the fellow a swat that crumpled him. "Help me carry him, Squire. If I pitched him out the front door, it'd be just my luck to hit a little dog and bring a lynch mob of animal lovers quicker than Al Swinburn's hounds of spring. So the best we can do with a moke that may feel he needs a new fortune is to carry him out to the alley and leave him at Lillian's back door.

As all of the joint's regulars understood that strife was one of man's conditions, none did more than watch from their respective points along the bar, as we rolled the agent over. But I had hardly lifted his shoulders and lolling head when a voice roared, "Turn that murdered man loose!"

Looking behind me, I found that four law limbs were now of the Crossroads' company. Strangers in blue, a town police couple had reinforced the known two in the khaki of campus guards. It promptly became clear that the latter remembered me.

"You're the bozo that's in cahoots with the big monkey and slipped us a bum steer, so he and his mob could make a getaway," one said, as they all closed in. "Where are you going, Sister?"

Perfectly well while I was drinking with her, she was now tottering away from the bar. "I think I am going to faint unless some strong, kind man helps me to a chair."

All four such, they jostled to be first about her. When they'd helped her to the nearest of the two tables for ladies, she made another appeal to their chivalry.

"Are you sweeties going to arrest that fiend I believed when he said he was going to marry me, so—" How she swiped a lacy handkerchief from the air of that hoochery, I never have figured out. But it looked already soggy when she began dabbing her tear ducts. "So, oh I can't say it," she finished.

When my eyes came back from a search for villainy, I caught her in the act of indexing me. None of the cops wanted to leave for the purpose of collaring me, but one of them thought of a short cut.

"Any clunk who'd murder a guy right in front of the unwed mother of his fatherless child ought to be night-sticked, but she'd probably pass out for keeps then. Come here and be grilled, lifer."

"Don't believe him if he pulls the gag about being a university prof," Tim now sung out. "The reason he swung that bar stool, on a customer I'll have a hard time replacing unless I can get a Government grant, is that he crabbed as a philosophy croaker."

"And he told me that he was George Puttenham, the famous undertaker of Economic Geography," she wailed.

"But I am!" I shouted. "At least I'm as famous as a noncelebrity can settle for in an unfair world I never made—and wouldn't now if it begged me."

"Alibis—all the time alibis!" One of the bulls wrenched

himself far enough away from her to clap a hand on my shoulder. "You never made no world, eh?"

"Look at the big birds!" somebody out on the street commanded, but I was too deep in despair to oblige. I was struggling for freedom with the awful knowledge that I had no place to go if I did succeed in breaking away. Then four swans harnessed to the glider in which Ninshubur sat swept through a doorway they cleared on the downbeat of their wings.

"Let's get on our way to Nebo's hive!" the former flying fish yelled, as his team turned and lighted, facing out and away.

The twin campus cops had by then joined the town one that had first nabbed me, but they might as well have tried to hold back shaken champagne. In all the world there was one hope for me, and nobody was going to block my way to it. I slatted two of the bulls against the bar and scored a sidewinding strike on the bowling alley with the other.

"Good hunting on Alderbaran, Squire!" Tim called as I hopped into a flimsy vehicle that therewith took to the air again. Men shouted, bullets whined and swans trumpeted. Then we whizzed into the hazards of Main Street traffic.

"Damn it!" Ninshubur yelled at the driver of a truck whose cab he barely snuck the team over. "Why don't you go back to mule's butt watching?"

"At least I ain't driving no carrier pigeons, wise guy."

Higher than most of the roof tops by the time of that return fire, I was not as jaunty as a jail dodger had a right to feel. Despite trumpeter swans' fame as crack flyers I didn't fully trust them. I did not see how I was going to meet my one-forty class in the Distribution of Useful Elements. And I was itchy about owing escape to a fellow I'd never so far addressed civilly.

There was a book I had once read, though, in which a character so fixed had paid off the debt with a terse manliness I hastened to imitate. "Awfully good of you to rally when the stake flames were getting chin high. If the snowshoe is ever on the other moccasin, you will learn that a Puttenham out memories an African elephant."

"That's better than the short-term Indian kind." After

showing that he appreciated my sharp distinction, he explained his kindly rescue act. "She wanted the soup cleared of you; and I didn't mind, because anybody who can dive, in the shank of the morning, into as much trouble as you managed to find can't be all bad."

The swans were still beating upward, or rather outward from Earth, but I thought I'd better lash some relationships in place before butting into the future. "Even for a barkeep, Tim has more than the usual number of tentacles. I went in his place simply as a storm refuge, but he seemed to expect me."

"He's too smart to unexpect anything, which is why nothing will be ever sneaked over on that boy." An overtaken swift tried to hitch a ride by perching on the harness connecting the two leaders, but Ninshubur shooed the chiseler with a whip-snap. "It would be a flash idea for you to be open-brained while barn-storming points along the Road, by the way."

Deciding not to turn that rock over, to see what lived under it, I kept the chat local to O'Lucian's. "And you, too; you were laying for me like Scotch reviewers for bellyaching bards."

He sidestepped that with the ease of a soap-dodging flea. "Somebody had to weed 'em out or they'd have been too many for the available grazing to support. The romantiskalds have multiplied, and wherever that happens all the big game dies off or takes to the tall woods. That's a good topic to throw on the table at Nebo's, by the way."

"The cosmic tinker and roadright. And what crossroads does he camp at?"

"Tim didn't wish you luck on Aldebaran—if you have the moxie to get there—just to make a noise, It."

I stuck that irritating name in a pocket where I could easily find it and stayed with the ball. "You probably know more Aldebarans than I do, but the loner of my acquaintance is a star."

"What's odd about stars?" he asked. "You talk like they are seldom, but the last sidereal head count turned up several billion."

* * *

Sulky about walking into that punch, I hung up my conversational gloves. The world was no bigger than a basketball. With nothing else to notice, except when the swans detoured an air pocket, I was drowsed by their pinion rhythm. At length I must have slept, and leaned against my seatmate like a tight subway tick, for he shook me off.

"This is no time to dormouse, for we're coming near the Stratospheric Sirens.

"They're the pom-pom girls of outer space," he went on when I blinked by way of inquiry. "And I can't spell what they're like, for it will be whatever they seem to you."

Not being able to find Earth in back of us, I swung my eyes forward to watch for sky scenery. First there was music waxing louder by the wing-sweep, then I saw the swans were speeding us toward a chorus of wildly prancing girls. As they wore about what Gunga Din did, it was easy to note that they were as gifted with symmetry as with sweetly persuasive voices. Putting the Indian sign on me, too, was their maestro, who hopped back and forth before a spread of glistening globes, by turns striking chords from these with his baton and jabbing it commandingly at the singers. Whatever they had been choiring while I was out of ear range, it was now this:

The death of joy's a fetish, Freudian as a pogo-stick,
That poets bounce with toward an assignation with despair
Upon a plain no longer tempting any knight to prick,
In Spenser's homely word, a rogue or hopeful ladye faire;
For peterless as Echo pipes the quondam gladsome Pan.
So cangs alone will pilgrim to Nebo's Aldebaran.

Charmed as though a bird a snake was dazzling, I was weighing every syncopated syllable. Fools went where I was surging was their message, and to me they seemed sybils.

While they were kicking and skipping through a silent dance routine, in response to their coach's lifted hand, I glanced to see how the man next to me was reacting. Grave as a boneyard, he wagged his dome.

"As I can't name them either deadfall dolls or angels, it must be your vote that will stop you here or blow you where they're warning you not to go. But I will take you where she wants you to climb, if you don't hop overboard."

The sirens were in voice again. And as I was close to them now, they were dearer to eye and ear.

The melody of speech is sold to buy barbaric yawp
Of me-me-me, the only note upon the tonal scale
Of vatic scops who rightly boast the vision of a scaup
And technical equipment of an adolescent snail,
Adroit to coin unerringly caboose before the van;
So cangs alone will pilgrim to Nebo's Aldebaran.

Now I could see corpses floating in the stratosphere lapping around the dancers' feet. But I cared only for the advice being poured down my senses in witching tones:

The mastery of creation's scrapped and flung where junk belongs;
The only ploy for makers is to shrill a shrew's laments
And castigate all flyers in castrated-mudcat songs,
For ordure is the order of his Lordship Impotence,
Who praises but graffiti that his spavined meters span;
So cangs alone will pilgrim to Nebo's Aldebaran.

"Go alone where fools alone go!" I yawned at Ninshubur, rising as I did so. A corpse floated where I would land on him if jumping, but that isn't what kept me from a spatial Brodie. Sirens whose bodies had kept me from caring to look higher had begun by reminding me of Venus. Then as things equal have a Euclidean way of being like each other, as my optics elevated on upward these forms suddenly reminded me of my severest New Stonehenge critic.

As I certainly was not going to stay in that part of the stratosphere if the mynah bird's tutoress and eleven copies were romping all over it, I scouted the phiz of the nearest dancer and sat shakily down.

"No eyes!" I gasped to tooth-flashing Ninshubur, as the swans all trumpeted a banzai for my discovery. "I don't mean they'd been blinded; there are skeleton blanks. And there's nothing to fry in their brain pans, what's more. I could see a star twinkle behind the socket of that last tomato."

"That star would be Alcyone who usually manages to be the first of the Pleiades to scud into view. We haven't far to go, as Aldebaran is always close behind those Tauric outposts." Ninshubur patted a trembling shoulder, "Nectar or Bourbon?"

"I didn't know there was any difference, but which ever's stronger." I needed the whiskey I found on a tray latched to the dashboard a few moments later. "There's nothing like a close shave to cheer you up after you've squeaked by, always provided you've got some bottled help. It's hard to see now what I expected of those floozies, but to do me justice I wasn't—er—prospecting their faces until the last instant."

"You can miss a lot that way and form judgments as false as the bottom of a smoke den's jigger," Ninshubur seemed also relaxed and glad I wasn't a drifting stiff. "Take the Pleiades; there's nothing glittering about them, but they're neat and sweet and wine for a man with an eye for class. I've named Alcyone yonder. Reading from right to left, the others are Taygete, Electra, Asterope, Celaeno, Merope and Maia. She mothered Hermes, incidentally, though she'd be the first to admit she got invaluable help from Zeus."

That was all very well for small talk but something a lot more massive than the Pleiades was shaping up, and I reasoned it was time to put my feet on more solid ground. "Before I start bumping into things in the dark, I want to know the answer to questions you frostbit on the way up."

He crunched a bit of ice. "There was no use in improving the mind of an imminent corpse, which was what old Fifty to One said you were."

"He's a pretty smart fellow." I decided I wouldn't let thought dwell on how many losers Venus had littered the stratosphere with; or how she had implacably trapped them, as she had me, by working them into positions from which the only escape lay in going where she wished. "But now that I've jammed a dunce cap on the odds, what in Tophet's the Road, and whence does it take off?"

"Not hereabouts; Aldebaran's just for indoctrination. The Road, not counting the parts that run through the planet Mercury, is an Earth affair, and what it amounts to is the way blazed by clay scratchers or inkswingers as the centuries skidded by."

"What?" but I lost interest in what I was about to say when the swans squawked and plunged toward water, softly golden from reflecting star-glow.

"It's Aldebaran Lagoon," Ninshubur said. "Half rise and let bent knees cushion the shock or you'll bust your fundamental concern when we wallop the water."

The Bash at Nebo's Lodge

Splash-Down over, I took stellar stock. As we were on a lagoon, a sea was presumably making or ebbing somewhere near, but all I could spot was a thick surrounding woods. Ninshubur was meanwhile unharnessing the swans.

"I always get a kick out of the air here," he looked up to remark.

By tossing off the last of my highball, I got my mind back on track. "What's she got to do with the Road?"

"It wasn't nailed down so she annexed it." He watched the birds glide toward some reeds fifty yards or so away. "She said poetry was habit forming like Napoleon Brandy, only it keeps longer and has the advantage—"

"Yeah, unlike the butter Br'er Rabbit stole, you can swallow it without wearing it away. But who dragged poetry into this conversation?"

"I did, because most of the working stiffs that laid the Road are as metric as the Olympic Games. And to complete your tour of the Road, by the way, Ininni will expect you to make an extension of some kind yourself."

"Ininni?"

"Wise up!" he snorted. "Venus equals Ininni, Ishtar,

Atargatis, Astarte, Anahita, Aphrodite, Lakshmi, Dione, Morgan, Freya, Niam, Nimue and two or three others I missed. Different names for always the same beauty and intelligent devilment, so she's always at home everywhere."

That didn't make sense to me, but I switched topics rather than risk getting more confused. "Why have I got to know Nebo?"

"She proposed you for the Road." Ninshubur was fishing under the seat for what turned out to be a paddle by the time he'd unfolded it. "And he decides whether you know enough to be allowed on it."

He started paddling, but I looked dubiously at that golden water. "Are any sea serpents likely?"

"Don't try to start anything!" he protested. "The world got sphynxes, say, because they were thought up by trouble makers that weren't satisfied with grounded lions but had to have airborne gut gougers. So for An's sake don't drop the idea for jazzing up these waters with monsters in Nebo's suggestion box!"

"Is he that scared of having this lagoon bugged by Loch Ness stuff?"

"You muffed the point that mention of it might be just the bean his nose would like; and then I'd have to answer to her because her swans were guzzled by a sea brute that wasn't in the big game list before today."

Ahead of us, I could hear singing without being able to make out words. "What's he got, or what could he do about a water terror that I couldn't?"

"He's got Mummu, the word of creation—the Logos that he used long before Greek copyright pirates pretended to invent it. This is us."

A rustic landing had loomed ahead, and by the time he'd finished speaking we were alongside. There was nothing to be seen behind it but a dark stand of trees, but a loud chorus announced that glad men were among them.

The skulkers of Kur had aspired to hide,
Like under-rock crawlers in the world's glum gut,
In fear of being bussed by the boons that bide
In the company of mirth for they honed to cut

The throat of joy
To salve their noy;
But bastriches were wrenched from their blind-worm rut.
Ininni dared to laugh in the crypt of doom
The time she picked the lock of the Ganzir hatch
And fingered with her light all the slugs of gloom
That since have ever fled from a stricken match.

Threading a trail through the trees we had come to a cabin with light beams shooting out around blinded windows by the time the chorus ended. But we had to wait for overworked echoes to catch their breaths before Ninshubur could be heard.

"Jar this door, before I have to kick it in, Nebo."

"I'll brook no tart talk from the loafer who's kept Taliesin from beering the Welsh rabbit," the answer came.

My mind's eye hadn't previewed the fellow she'd sent me to meet; but the one who let us in was, of course, two different lads. First was the husky smiler that was glad to see Ninshubur again, and he was easy to get along with as a shot of Bourbon for an eye opener or day closer. The other was the polite, nothing telling gent I linked mitts with.

"This is a great treat for me," I led off with both wrong feet, in an effort to win over the guy I was supposed to shake down for guidance. "Ever since I gained the hang of the Zodiac I've been sorry I wasn't born a bully Taurus boy."

"It's had a rough day," Ninshubur excused me. "He'd never been shanghaied before, and I guessed this is the first star he was ever on."

"You're leaving out a canto." Our host said that loud enough for the other four percent to hear. "Unless the swans found a detour around the Stratospheric Sirens, that is."

"No problem there, Neb. The aerial broads were putting their stuff over as well as I've ever known them to do, but he got by on his own."

"This is what he owns now." I'd have liked the fellow's looks even if he hadn't shoved a tankard at me.

"Mead's a rewarding drink." Blank of brain till I'd dived,

I surfaced a gay two-timer of words. "Got a name besides benefactor?"

"I'm Shot'ha Rust'haveli, and this is cold ham and turkey. Come on." I knew that the craftsman in business at the other end of the table was Taliesin before he was announced, because he was trickling stale beer into a pot of spice doctored cheese.

"Had I one more hand, I'd shake," he vowed when briefly looking up. "But all Wales would fly black flags at half mast, should I bungle."

"Stand to your post," I blessed him. "Men of ideals have been in short supply since the thermometer went down with all hands, and we can't spare another."

Beneath a rack holding rods and fish spears were Arion, who had a dolphin tattooed on one cheek, and Egill Skallagrimson, pricked as to forehead with a battle axe. "It's a broad gauge panel," Ninshubur told our host, when I'd rejoined them.

"What isn't remembered as often as it might be," Nebo replied, "is that a panel can rise no higher than the curiosity of its quizzer."

"I thought you guys were going to pitch me questions," I said.

"What in Kur for?" Ninshubur asked. "You don't know anything."

As the chef then yelled that the rabbit had come of age, nobody said anything for a while but, "Trump my plate with some more, Tal, before I let you have it with my snee." But when mead had flushed a golden bunny out of sight, the man of Mummu brought us to business order.

"Throw the plates and forks outside for the dew-laps of Taurus to lick clean and refill your tankards."

By that time I'd decided to show these ginks that a Ph.D's ignorance was big enough to keep them in a sweat, and I rolled out the first of a series of posers designed to keep 'em from going to sleep. "What's the distinction between science and poetry?"

"The difference between seeing a dolphin and riding one home," Arion picked me up. "Science is the art savvy to find out what the sea's got that's worth keeping, and poetry's the tough business of jumping aboard it and bringing it in alive."

"Whether you bring yourself home alive belongs to the separate business of gambling," Nebo put in as monitor, "and can't be considered now."

"Very well." I was pretzel crisp. "Let's take up the question of why the Original Sin of poetry erupts in some of the descendants of Pithecanthropus and spares the rest of equally liable kin."

"Put that way the question's too general," Nebo ruled, "so I'm going to rephrase it. His good point is that of An knows how many unsuspecting young savages in their teens, poetry crashes into the life of one while leaving the others untouched. Do you remember when and how you were blitzed, Tal?"

"Does an old sailor remember the first time cannibals threw him in the pot?" the rabbit genius wanted to know. "There was this druid back at Caerleon that put all us equally grubby kids through math all the way up to Regularly Connected Polyhedra, though I never did learn how the queers among 'em went at it. But I didn't let that or anything else worry me, for in those idyllic days I'd never dreamed of writing a line, till one day he lectured on the Theory of the Solid State; for he was a scientist like Pliny and you, It. But that didn't bother my tolerant fleas till he snapped me to by saying what I can still quote: "In nature there is no boundary line between substances we think of as ideal solids and those we consider ideal liquids!" That did it, and I was off and gone! Without asking my permission, my stylus began scribbling on the wax dohicky used to take notes, and what emerged was this:

In Beldame Nature's sawdust niche
The cosmic picture's cankered;
She can't tell which is ship and which
The harbor where it's anchored.
And worse than that, the batty bitch,
When tippling mead that's Midas rich
Will drop her every mental stitch
And try and swig the tankard.

Taliesin chuckled. "It's appropriate to remark that none of my schoolmates was moved to do anything. But I was hooked and never recovered."

"That was clarifying; thanks." While separating an ideal liquid from an ideal solid container, I framed my next query. "If poetry takes the turn of drama or epic, how do you go about recruiting characters?"

"Aristotle didn't say anything about comedy, so we'll limit debate to tragedy," Nebo lawed. "Egill, you studied that when straying into the hands of Eric Bloodaxe, after first taking care to kill the favorite whelp of that gore drinking varmint."

"That old kraken sure catharsed me with pity and terror for yours truly." The axe tattooed on Egill's forehead turned from blue to red when he laughed. "He dared me to write a poem he would rather read than chop me up, and after that there was no problem but to wonder if he had good taste."

"Interesting but remote from the point." After throwing at him a response that had been made to me by my examining board at New Stonehenge, I smiled good humoredly, too. "Now let's get back to how tragedies are peopled, Gill."

"Well, the way Sophocles and Aeschylus went about it was to take on the first two or three characters that applied and deal lines on a more or less even-steven basis. Then when the crunch came that left them all dead or crocked, the chorus was always there to tote them or lead them off. And it's important to remember that there was always enough for the chorus stiffs to do to keep them on hand."

Skallagrim's boy jumped up. "Here, It, let me reload your tossing pot, and Arion will tell you how the Mermaid crowd handled a harder proposition."

"The first thing one of those fellows would do," the dolphin buster allowed, "was to figure out how many characters they thought enough of to want to give 'em the business. And it takes six live ones to bear one pall; right?"

"I've never known that count to fail." Then I smiled at my freshened tankard. "Thanks, Gill. Go on, Rye."

"But before I do, jot it in your diary that in those pre-

Women's Lib Days the babes were lads, too—just on stage, I mean—so any character could be drafted to shoulder a box and limp toward one of the wings, while the orchestra played 'Go Tell the Whiffle Tree the Old Grey Mare's Goose Is Cooked.'"

"Conceded," I said, when I'd meaded.

"Now let's say that John Webster had picked six characters to knock off. That would mean that he needed three dozen more for the final mop-up, and as an experienced playwright, he knew that he had to give them a hobby, or in the clutch they'd be off tomcatting or getting obfuscated."

"I might have qualified as an actor under Good Queen Bess," I hazarded.

"That's why they called her that." Arion tabled his tankard with a bang. "Now some of the bearers had always been kept busy in roles supporting the doomed few, but nobody'd thought of a feather and molasses to keep the rest harmlessly occupied till Marlowe crashed through with his play about that Ph. D from Cracow."

"Johann Faustus, and his discipline was magic," Rust'haveli said, "though I don't think he was beans as a wizard compared with Virgil."

"Virgil!" Egill yipped, but Nebo cut him off.

"Rye hasn't yet told what Marlowe did."

"Marlowe?" Arion wondered. "Oh yeah, he came up with what they called his mighty line, which was his underplot scheme that all the other Elizabethans were glad to borrow. Most of the underplots had nothing to do with the main play, but nobody kicked because it gave the audience more for their money, *and* it kept all the pall hustlers on deck."

"To get back to Virgil," Egill smiled at what he was drinking and frowned at what he was thinking, "he couldn't have been too hot as a sorcerer or he never would have cooled his cod all night, dangling in a basket below the window—"

"Of that Naples duchess he planned to deal an inside straight." Taliesin tipped his tankard and snapped its cap shut. "My theory is—"

"How about ditching the side-gab, gang, and fielding It's

question as to picking a cast for an epic," Nebo urged. "Shot, narrative verse is your racket, so I'd like you to lead off."

"The thing you've got to be hawk watchful about is letting your poem be muscled into by a strong character that makes a monkey out of the one picked as your leading joe," Rust'haveli warned me. "I avoided that by screening everyone allowed in *The Man in the Panther Skin* the way blind pig keepers used to do in the USAL; but Virgil—I suppose you know he took time off from wizarding to write poetry?"

"With help from John Dryden's trot, yes," I said, licking an absconding drop of mead from one chop.

"Then I don't have to tell you what a boo-boo old Maro pulled when he let Dido in his *Aeneid*. Every reader of an epic is entitled to a little juicy love making, which both the Homers knew how to handle; and Milton, too, in his own tut-tut fashion. But you've got to know what kind of a girl you can show having the blocks put to her."

"A real queen like Dido was no one that should have been laid on a horse blanket spread in a cave," Arion disapproved. "That's the sort of thing I could josh about in my dithyrambs that Periander angeled at Corinth, but raw stuff like that is out of place in an epic."

"The worst was running out on a swell doll he'd been living on," Egill growled. "And as Shot said, it was all so unnecessary. If Maro had told Dido to find an epic she belonged in and had given Aeneas somebody in his class to shenanigan with the readers wouldn't have minded how he cut up."

"Message received," I said. "Let me do the honors at the keg this time." But while I was cunningly operating the spigot I was framing yet another deep query.

The strain of doing so must have showed, for Nebo called out, "Hold on, It. These large curiosities are all very well, but don't you ever wonder about the small niceties that make the language of poetry a special joy?"

I would have given his question careful consideration, but before I could caution it to mind its own business, the mead answered for me. "That ain't the style of a big thinker.

I don't give a curse in ten Hells for anything small and nice!"

"You ought to be careful about crawling out on a limb that sports a wasp's nest," Ninshubur said.

Knowing him for an ally, I meant to ask what stingarees I might be bumbling toward, but Nebo spoke first. "A man aiming for the Road has a right to fall in any pits of his own digging."

"Skunk cabbage!" the mead scoffed.

"Glug!" Ninshubur groaned, but I barely heard that estimate of trouble to come above the sound of the door being whammed by something big and hard.

The second time it happened, the door flew open, the log that had jolted it was dropped and the dozens of angry little customers who had carried it swarmed inside. Small niceties, Bertha's other big foot! It was a flying wedge of hard boiled egglets that grabbed me.

"You're being had by the verse viceroys!" Ninshubur yelled.

"By Zeus, there's Synecdoche and Onomatopeia!" That was Arion naming the two that yanked my feet from under me. "Nice to have known you, It, in case you turn out to be a gone dolphin."

Whatever my zoological category, I was gone from that cabin in a hurry. Out under a night sky I found Orion watching Castor and Perseus arm wrestle for stakes held by Pollux. Yet I had no more than noticed this than I was dragged from the clearing about the lodge and shagged under trees where I saw nothing but touched much.

"Be careful!" I squawked. "You just made me bark my shin."

"Bark; did you get that?" one of my captors asked another. "He thinks his mother was a dryad like Eurydice."

"I'm not akin to a tree, and you know it," I snarled. "Barking is just a handier and more vivid term than peeling the rind from a man's peg."

"Peg; would you say that was a metaphor, Ignatz?"

"I wouldn't say it was anything," I answered. "I never think about language. I just use it."

"And we won't think a thing of being a set of kangaroos

who lawlessly hopped on you," one of them said. "Bear right a little, fellows."

When they had done that and dropped down a steep bank with me, I was on the edge of Aldebaran Lagoon. "I don't see any rock," one little savage complained.

"Aw, we're not sentencing him to drown, just to soak his head for that rotten thing he blatted."

"A rock about his neck'd sure help his dome to get soaked," the guy pointed out.

"I know," another conceded, "but unless you can coin one, we haven't got a rock, and if we all go looking for one, he'd probably get away. I don't think we ought to trust a rat who said what he did."

"I don't know as we want a rat on our consciences," a third chipped in. "Let's take a vote."

"That's no way to harass a guy successfully," a fourth claimed. "Let's just soak his head and get it over with."

"Now you're talking sense," I said.

"Shut up! Who's asked your opinion?"

"Well, it's my head that's being talked about," I offered.

"Yeah, and we mean business," annoyed voices snapped. "Grab him and swing him, boys."

That time they really meant action, but I wasn't really alarmed when they seized both arms and legs and started rocking me. It was clear that they meant to throw me in the water, but though they would thus doubtless accomplish their purpose of moistening my bean, I didn't expect a long journey first.

Nor did I get one before I hit the water the first time, but those rascals knew things about launching a man in a lagoon that were new to me. For I had hardly bellyflopped amidst enthusiastic cheers than I rose and zipped forward in the manner of, if not the poise, of a pitched flat rock.

It would be idle to claim more than guesswork, but I described a series of parabolas scaling down from a quarter mile to a furlong. Changing to the metric system, next, I skipped a hundred meters, fifty and twenty-five. My momentum then feeble, I bounced no more than ten feet to where I sank.

I didn't see any sea dragons, killer whales, giant cuttlefish or sharks while going down, but they didn't have a chance of lulling me into a false sense of security. Popped up again, I cased all points of the compass for suspicious looking monsters before I let go of a sound that could tell 'em where I was.

"Help," I then whispered. But the situation wasn't desperate as long as I was allowed to stay alone, and I cautiously trod water while reviewing my options. A guessed several hundred yards away a dark bank of trees indicated the nearest shore, but the trouble was that I was ascared of what or who might be laying for me there. In fact the only point on the lagoon's shore that didn't give me the willies was the vicinity of Nebo's shack, which the verse vigilantes had presumably left.

That meant more swimming than I could manage in soaked clothes, though; so I risked the leers of devil fish and whatnot by easing out of everything but my shorts. But while I was shucking my undershirt without splashing, trouble pounced from the one direction I hadn't been watching. Glimpsing a giant outline between me and the stars, I dove too late to do anything better than change the thing's gripping point when it plunged and tore me from the water. In place of being suspended from claws about my shoulders, I had been fundamentally grasped.

That left my arms and legs free to put up a sham battle, yet that isn't all I did. It was no time for pussyfooting—or for a scientist's atheism, either.

"Help!" I howled. "Damn it, Heavenly Powers, don't just loaf on your pampered fannies; *do* something. I just told you all that I need HELP!"

When I got a reply, it came from above all right, but not very far. "Hush your fuss," thirty feet of wing spread advised. "Aid's what you're getting now, because I heard you the first time."

I was too upset to be detented with that easily. "Why don't you learn to keep your snoot out of other people's affairs?"

"Why don't you learn to speak accurately?" the bird cracked back. "I have a beak not a snoot, thanks to a creator whom I'm twice as grateful to for not including me in 'people' like you, whose only genius is for floundering into trouble you have no means of getting out of except by appealing to undeserved charity."

"What trouble?" I wondered. "Enjoying a nocturnal dip, I was swimming calmly and confidently—"

"Pappycock!" he sawed me off, "which is the correct term for male egg layers. You were as afraid as Leander was of meeting a biter that'd snip off his search warrant for Hero."

As he seemed to know more about my affairs than I liked, I switched to a new topic. "What in the name of Aldebaran are you?"

He groaned. "I'm the Simurgh, the biggest, toughest thing the Audubon Society ever sighted on a first magnitude star this early in April; and by rights I ought to be hunting horseradish like you to season the panthers and walruses I bring home for my little ones. But in practice I'm a soft headed and hearted oofus that can't think of anything better to do than to salvage human puddingpates like you because that's how somebody saw me."

I hadn't been hitting the mead at Nebo's with four of that kind for nothing. "Who you think you're spoofing by saying you were seen by 'somebody,' ave? It was your poet or maker, so why pretend you can't read his label?"

"O.K.; I was created by Firdaussi or Firdousi—slice it whichever way, it meant the Paradisiac—no akin to Aphro. Anyhow it was the *nom de plume*—that's French for pen name, in case you were wondering—of Abul Kasim Mansur, who made up *The Shanama*. Well, I was leading a nice contented nonexistence till one day Abul got a human meatball in a jam he didn't know how to ease him out of until he called me out of the aether. It wouldn't have been so bad if I'd been assigned to other bit parts, but when he used me again, it was always the same way, so being a nice old scout is the only damned thing I've got knowhow for."

Before he began that last sentence I could make out Nebo's landing with Ninshubur's car-canoe beside it. "Well, you're a good tamale anyhow," I told the bird on finding I was no longer in his talons, and if I ever meet Firdousi—"

"Forget it," the Simurgh said, "which is what I propose to do about you, as soon as I find another stupid chestnut to keep from being scorched."

After it nearly blew me down when it flapped off, I began picking my barefoot way along the tree-darkened trail to the lodge. I'd been half afraid the mead had blown taps and sent the lads to the bunks; but then I heard their joint voices:

"Throw the monkey overboard!" roared the pirate skipper,
And over Arion was throwed;
But a dolphin fast as a Baltimore clipper
Cut in and off he rode.

"Actually," I heard Rye say, as I stepped on the porch, "there was nothing accidental about it, the comic that made that ballad notwithstanding. That dolphin recognized my whistle."

"Well, here's something besides sea water to wet it with now," Gill chuckled.

Taking that as my entrance cue, I cuffed the latch and strode in. "If you maltworms haven't sucked the keg dry, I demand a drink."

From their stares I gathered that I'd not been expected to survive the Verse Viceroys any more than the Stratospheric Sirens. Nebo was the only one with words for me, though.

"I can't tell a man who's only in his skivvies to keep his shirt on, but I can say you look ready to retreat to first causes. Do I read you right?"

The understanding that I'd beaten odds none of them had thought I could acted on me like the Wild West Wind on Buffalo Bysshe Shelley, "I'm ready for anything the little old stars can throw at me."

"That's a remarkable statement." He passed me the full tankard that Taliesin had just drawn. "And what do you say to that?"

"Damned be he that cannot hold enough," I said after I pitched the mead down the hatch. "Mynah birds should watch my style, Nebo."

"Sure, they should, It." He handed me another loaded tankard and caught hold of my free hand. "Have this one for the Road."

The Universe of Mummu

I meant to point out to Nebo that you only said what he did to a lad that's bound somewhere else, but when I wrapped myself around the drink he'd given me, I started falling. But I didn't know I was dropping into the Pit of Time, because I blacked out like a glow worm a night hawk has just bolted. So it wasn't the mead that kept me from inkling what the trip to old Mesopotamia was like; it was tumbling down the stairs of five chiliads.

It was a sobering experience because, when I came to there was nothing on my breath but the smell of the hot sheepshank I was gnawing; just as there was nothing on me but the buckskin breech-clout which had replaced my shorts. But I knew where I was: on a ridge between the Euphrates and Tigris rivers; and I knew I was there to keep sheep from being ruined as roast mutton by lions, leopards and wolves.

I also knew who I was proud to be avant-garding with, when the situation allowed time for culture, in place of sticking big cats with spears and plugging lupine raiders with slung rocks. Nebo was the bull baboon of our campfire ringing crowd and he was talking as I munched and digested his words, too.

"We've made a pretty good go of stretching language far enough to reach around a fish yarn, but if we're going to own word gazelles fast enough for fiction with a purpose—"

"Is that when you snow a girl you want to join you in a navel engagement?" That was Hesiod, a flapjack with a practical side, though when you flipped him over you found he was a man of visions, too.

"Fiction's making, and maybe some day we'll glide about it like swallows, but we're still in the crowlike wing flopping stage." I didn't know that Nebo was about to wear his Mummu hat for the first time, but I did ken that nobody could throw a switch strong enough to sidetrack him when an idea was driving him. "The purpose of serious fiction is to make room for the mind to jump to new and more exciting conclusions in."

"And room for wilder gales to blow," Amergin said, "which is what I always wanted when I was a storm wind."

"Yes," Nebo said. But I covered up my growl by tackling my sheep bone again. Amergin was a good enough fellow, yet it bothered me when he brought up old unhappy days as a vulture or battles long ago as a wild boar.

"Empty your conk, Nebo," I urged. "Before other jaws flapped, you were about to say we need what?"

"Frame of reference yardsticks: how can you tell how tall the dragon, Kur, is until you know how he stacks up compared to An?"

Hesiod, Amergin and I said nothing of names we hadn't heard before, but they made Thjodolph happy. The worm in that otherwise easygoing apple was that he was on jolly terms with all sorts of deadheads. The sling that he slang and the spear that he flang had names that he coached them with, and though I couldn't tell them sexually apart, the Tigris was always 'she' and the Euphrates 'he' to him. Smelling that he was about to add to his army of friends, this joiner chuckled as he fed the fire. "Who's this tall guy, An, a palm tree pal of yours?"

Now that he'd harnessed all our attentions, Nebo was ready to make. "An is both sky and the god that runs the universe caboodle. First wedding Spacette, An fathered Ki, the earth goddess and earth substance, below which lives Kur, the dragon of death, in Kur, the lair of death."

The man of Mummu was sweating at the chore of giving the Cosmos shape and character but having such creative fun he didn't care. "Now Spacette died in childbirth, which is likely why Ki has remained an old maid. Anyhow An picked Autun as his new wedding belle and begot Enlil, god of air, and Enki, ditto of water; though I'm sorry to say there was a scandal—"

"B-a-a!" bleated about a grand of sheep.

Faithful to our lamb chop trust, we left culture hanging fire, grabbed our weapons and rushed, five strong, toward rescue or revenge.

The villain, a tom lion, was bounding away with a half-grown ewe as we charged within spear-throwing range. Wrenched from making too abruptly, Nebo made a wild fling. Not allowing for windage enough, Hesiod grazed the cat. I had the right line but was short as a Mexican hairless that aspires to a St. Bernardess, while Amergin overthrew.

As for Thjodolph, he infuriated me by pausing to have a chat with his spear. "Staying pat, bust a slat and gut the cat, Rastus!" he yelped, not lunging to pitch until he'd named his sticker.

Thus appealed to, his spear shifted twice to keep on target, but when it arrived, it bashed in a rib and finished the varmint. "Why don't you always click?" Amergin asked, when we were all looking the lion over. "Lots of times you flub as if you couldn't guess whether game was backing or bulling."

"I know," Thjodolph had yanked his spear out and was patting it by the time he'd found an explanation. "But I can't always read Rastus' mind."

To keep vultures from taking over, we dragged the beast to the fire. While we were skinning it with copper knives that often buckled like rubber ones, Hesiod restored us to intellectual order. "What was that scandal about Enlil and Enki you were just about to spill, Nebo?"

"I don't want you to think Enki was tarred with it." Silent since having his creative style crimped, Nebo got back in his lively voice. "But Enlil, that's straightened up since, jazzed Ninlil without mentioning matrimony and nearly made a bastard of Nanna."

Amergin stopped peeling the pelt from a hind leg. "I never met Nanna," he complained.

"Sure you have, only I forgot to tell you he's the moon. Now as Ninlil got sprung from Kur in time to bear him honestly in the sky, Nanna led a normal life and in due course sired Utu, the sun, and two daughters with opposite destinies."

"I was afraid of that," Thjodolph said, "on account of Enlil cutting up a couple of generations back. It always happens."

"Nergal, a kissing cousin who didn't know where to stop, ruined the younger daughter, Erishkegal," Nebo said, when he'd brought his eyes back from far horizons. "But as she turned out to be the kind of hop he couldn't get off, they wound up as King and Queen of the Dead, troubled only by a visit from Nanna's unruined daughter."

"Unruined?" Amergin was shocked. "What did she do for a living?"

"Ininni's the morning and evening star among other things. But she told An it didn't fit her style to be local to any skylight as she intended to be known as the Lady of the Whole Welkin Shebang, when she wasn't on earth managing the two liveliest pieces of action."

"You mean she laid claim to goddessing love and war both?"

"Right, Hesiod; and as that would entail a lot of commuting between her planet and Sumer here, she told An he'd have to supply her with a combination flying and sailing yacht that could maneuver under water, if she felt like it."

"The Nergal she did!" Amergin was working the pelt free of the skull. "And what did An say?"

"I don't know what he allowed under his breath but over it he told Enki, who doubled as the djinn of invention as well as water god, to fix her up with a cat-rigged beauty known as—"

* * *

He broke off to stare at something or other just as Thjodolph yammered a beef about unrequited scholarship: "Here we've been doing all this research on the Universe, and winning the best reference frame in all Summer; and the hang-up is that there isn't a way to make a record of it."

"Tell it to somebody who can do something about it." Nebo took his eyes from space. "Here comes a pelican, and as there's no reason for a water fowl to fall afoul of water in favor of a dry run like this ridge, it must be Enki, flying to share with us of the avant-garde his matchless creative wisdom."

The sheep bleated, and I jumped up, but Hesiod pulled me down again. "Take it easy, It. Wild beasts we've got all the time, but how often does a god come to call?"

"I ain't never seen one before unless all pelicans are gods hiding out in disguise." I waved my spear in frustration. "How're you gonna tell which bastard is which?"

"Don't call no bird a bastard till you're sure he's gonna keep shape, see?"

This one didn't. While I anxiously watched, he plopped down beside Nebo and began shedding his feathers. It was then easy to see why Enki had chosen to arrive as a pelican. He, too, was pot-bellied, with bright quizzical eyes above a long, pointed beard which suggested a beak.

"I was making my watery rounds and got the telemessage that you were worried about something, Nebo," he said. "Unlike certain other gods—though I'll name no names—I'm always happy to serve the author of my being."

"That's warmly appreciated, yet it doesn't astonish me, as I was always sure I could count on you," Nebo answered. "To brief our situation, all here wish to be artists with words, but it's harder than you'd think."

"Word artist," Enki mused. "You're pretty young to be writers; but if you grab time by the forelock and hang on, no matter how he kicks and squeals, there won't be any problem about getting older. What have you accomplished so far?"

I cleared my throat. "To kind of put pazazz in our styles,

we've made a reliable guide to the Universe, Lord Water and Invention God."

"Never mind the formality. In an intellectual forum it isn't status but the spirit that counts; and as mine isn't so old that I wouldn't yoo-hoo if a lively enough idea was to flirt by, just call me Enki. But as I was about to say, what remains to be seen is whether you belong to the talking or doing branch of the trade. Talking is more popular but acting is more demanding, as this pig with different wings requires a means of recording what comes to mind, don't you know."

"That's precisely what we do not know, because you haven't devised any such system," Nebo reminded him, "or at least you haven't made it available."

"Haven't I? Well, has any woman of the tribe mastered, or perhaps I should say madonnaed, the art of alphabet soup?"

"No, sir," Thjodolph said. "That is no, Enki."

"Then it doesn't matter that there are no papyrus plantations. The available stationery is Euphrates mud, and a river reed will serve for marker or stylus. Gather around and let me show you, literary primates."

There was a slab of wet clay in his left hand when we sprang to watch his demonstration. "Will it hold any kind of animal or fish?" Amergin whispered.

"It will hold earth, sea or sky, singly or all at once; but let's begin with a good, simple subject like a rain squawll." Enki made several quick passes at the clay with his bit of reed. "There."

I had been counting on anyhow a sprinkle of water. When nothing showed up on the mud slab but what looked like a cluster of small bird tracks, I frowned. "That's not much of a shower."

"How much thunder rolls or wetness falls when you say 'storm'?" Enki fired back. "You're thinking it, and you're counting on your readers to copy you, eh? This is Mummu with the difference that it keeps; so that if somebody I've never met was to see this fifty years from now he'd be forced to see a grey sky and hear the splash of drops falling from it."

"Who'd keep a hunk of mud fifty years?" Hesiod asked.

"Stick mud like this in the sun or an oven, and it will be a hard record, holding on to what a dead man says like he'd never kicked off." Happy as a kid that's just caught a big fish, Enki beamed from one to the other of us. "I'll sum it up for you in a way that'll make it easy to explain to others what a grand invention I've come up with to help you young fellows succeed. The form I'm using is also brand new, by the way, so listen carefully."

Egged to dream a scheme of writing,
Enki scorned to hesitate;
In the challenge hurled delighting,
He was lightning to create.

Others might have pled for paper,
Called for keyboards, oiled for speed;
He of moistened clay but shaper,
Pecked it with a river reed.

Wits and fist, in union nimble,
Form a code of graphic sounds,
Each a hushed but heeded symbol
Of the speech his skill expounds.

The old boy needn't have asked us to follow him with careful ears. He was chanting to men who'd never known the spell of voiced rhythm entwined with meaning before. As charmed with himself as we were with him, he was swaying and gesturing passionately as he went on.

Swift and simple its incising,
Stands the ageless, talking clay,
All its sage soliloquizing
Saved for ever, fire its stay.

Time, no longer androphagic,
Floats the maker with his word;
Enki coined a mighty magic,
Bygones now no silent bird.

Tears of delight at his triumph trickled down into his beard as he ended, holding out both hands to us, nor were we slow to press them and thump his back.

At first we spoke only of cuneiform, as he called his writing code. But when that topic had been chewed over, Nebo asked what was on all minds. "Do we get to keep the other; I mean will we be able to write like that, too, after a while?"

But at that reference to song, Enki's face registered a canny coyness. "I wouldn't counsel holding your breath until the end of that while. Eridu wasn't built in a day; in fact nobody's settled on the site of that seaport yet, so let's think of another comparison. Oh yes; ostriches have to learn how to walk before they can run. Come around and ask me about poetry when you've built up some mileage in prose, and I might reconsider. But right now my reaction is that a rooster shouldn't try to crow until he's learned how to cluck convincingly. Now how many prose yarns are you ready to tell the clay about, as soon as you've scooped some from along the Euphrates?"

"So far," I said, "we've been pretty busy organizing the language and getting oriented generally. You see, we're new at invention and haven't got your knack."

"Creative mastery, you chump!" Amergin whispered. "Don't you know enough to butter a god?"

I coughed. "Not having your creative mastery, we haven't glimpsed a way to begin a tale, so we're hoping you will show us what must be as easy as turning into a pelican for you."

"Heh, heh." Enki held up an instructing finger. "Of course, I don't have to do this myself, but you youngsters should appeal to the god of writing for inspiration."

"But there is no special spirit in charge of writ—"

"Ba-a-a!" the sheep interrupted Hesiod.

"Our practical side's in trouble," Nebo explained as we all dove for our weapons. "Would you wait a few minutes, Enki?"

"It's raiders from the Elam hills this time," Thjodolph yelled; so I dropped my spear and dug in my sack of rocks for one to stick in my sling.

* * *

Squat, shaggy fellows with vulture feathers twined in their hair, the Elamites were driving fifty or so woolies east toward the Tigris. "Up, Sumer, and bash the heathens in the name of An!" Hesiod roared.

Having the top god going for us sure helped. I wasn't usually a nifty slinger but, as he said 'An,' I let go of a stone that made for a guy's dome like a lonesome homing pigeon. You could hear the 'bong!' of that beautiful shot as it lit on the poor lunk's dome, and he went to Kur without any back talk.

"That's my head!" I whooped. "I just naturally drawed back and calamitied him!"

That was the fight, as it turned out. When the three with him saw him drop good and dead, that was all they wanted to know about Sumerian slingers; and to my delight they squawlled and ran.

"They'd better have scatted; I'd have got 'em all," I said below my breath. But what I yacked over it was, "Just a minute, fellows; it won't take me long to get what's coming to me."

Nobody said anything, as I sawed through the Elamite's neck with my copper knife, but I didn't mind jealousy. "I'm going to like strolling past my patootie's tent, nonchalantly swinging this curlylocks with one hand."

"You can't do that, It." You'd think I'd messed up a point of grammar from the way Nebo spoke. "It's not done by civilized man."

As a reaped head had up to that day been the great tribal status symbol, I felt I had grounds for arguing. "Why, Kur," I growled, "everybody that's lucky enough to win one brings in the potato of his human kill, and this will go over big with my girl."

"You're still living in yesterdays," he accused. "We're a literate people now, and that sort of barbarity is passé."

Glancing from one friend to another, I met the same disapproving frowns and resignedly caved. "Everything happens to me," I beefed. "It's the first crack at a head I've had since I began rushing that torrid zone."

"She'd be horrified now," Hesiod said. "Don't you want to be a writer?"

"Sure," I said, kicking the cabbage and watching it rattle

down hill. "And, say, now I could turn out a book on 'Wicked Old Sumer Days and Customs' and sign it 'Reformed Desperado' or something, so my toots would know what a tough character hung up his socks all on account of her and civilization."

So I was cheerful again, when we all trotted back to where Enki was waiting. "At the time of interruption," culture's god led off, "I had been reminded that no deity presiding over the written word exists, though admittedly one was in order; and a moment's reflection showed me that a conflict of interests made it improper for me to assume that post myself."

"That's too bad," I said. "But there must be some qualified god."

"Unfortunately they're all meatheads except for Ininni, and she's not underweening enough."

"What's underweening?" Amergin asked.

"Well, if I said she was overweening, she might sic a fatal passion on me or have me star-mobbed, she having the portfolios of love and war." Enki looked behind him and lowered his voice. "She'd be likely to take a man's idea away from him and make something different out of it."

"This is awful," Thjodolph said. "Are we going to be the only kind of people that have to get along without a god?"

"No, because I can reach outside of Heaven for the brains and understanding of the problems involved and fix my selection up with godhead." Enki then turned to Nebo. "It will be my very great pleasure, progenitor, to return the compliment and make a deity of you."

"But I don't want to advise anybody else," Nebo protested. "I want to write stuff myself!"

"Tut, tut; that's not the attitude which cements creation. You shouldn't be worrying about the odds and ends you'll have to sacrifice. Rather you should be asking 'what can I do the Universe out of?'"

"Well, what can I do the Universe out of, boss?"

Enki thought for a jiffy, then brightened.

"A planet I now rename Nebo (but to be known as Mercury by ignorant later ages) will at all times be the official seat of the guardian of writing and learning." But having made that solemn pronouncement, he twinkled. "Moreover, as the Heavenly establishment recognizes that hard working cosmic servants must have a sphere where they can relax, the star Aldebaran, up in Taurus, will be your private preserve for kicking the gong around."

It was such a stunning bestowal that even the man of Mummu was stumped for expressive words. "Jeez, kicking the gong around on my own star," he said to nobody in particular. "I'm going to like public service."

If he was awed, his phrase brought the rest of us alert by reminding us that we had a stake in his promotion that we had better learn how to exploit. "Where's the best way to get help from Nebo?" Hesiod asked. "And how do we get in touch with him?"

"I think the procedure will be for him to get in touch with you, if you ever deserve it; but those details haven't been worked out yet." Enki then caught Nebo's arm. "Come, son. While your planet and Aldebaran will be your listening posts for such beseechers of your goodwill as you may in the future desire to notice, you're now due for orientation at my headquarters. Wing after me."

Two pelicans then flew off towards the Euphrates, and we couldn't even tell which was our former friend and leader of our councils. "Well, at least he left us the Universe to stay in," Thjodolph said. "But what's the program now?"

"I can't go back to being a wild boar or a salmon after being in the avant-garde," Amergin came in. "So I guess there's nothing for it but to write something."

"We could start an art colony," Hesiod suggested, "only nobody but professionals like us can join. Will you watch the baa-baas, while the rest of us hike to the Euphrates for a mud supply, It?"

"You'll have to step, if you want to be back before Utu takes a powder," I warned.

So they cleared out to scoop stationery, and I walked higher up the ridge, where I could see all the sheep better. Then I leaned on my spear and thought deep thoughts the way a professional author does. The next day I'd wow my tootsie roll by telling her I was going to write a book which began—er—It took me a while to work out a blood-dripping opening sentence, and before I'd finished polishing it, Utu did slide out of sight.

After that I started blinking on account of something shining in my eyes, but as I turned away, Ininni spoke. "That's not in the direction of Eridu."

"Eridu ain't been started yet, according to Enki, and anyhow I've settled down as a member of this art colony. You see, I'm part way through a marvelous book."

"I know you're going to write something when the time comes and never mind how marvelous it is. But the Road doesn't start at any pokey art colony, honey. It always starts at some raring, tearing city, and now that's primordial Eridu."

"Primordial rats," I said. "And even they can't get along there, if it ain't been started."

"Don't let a little thing like that worry you," she laughed. "Get moving."

"Not a chance," I snapped. "When I say something, that's all there is to it."

"Well, if you won't do anything else for me, may I suggest that you get out of the way of those leopards crowding in from the north and east? There must be about a thousand."

I chuckled. Leopards weren't gang runners; the most I'd ever seen together were three. But I did turn my head to humor her—and almost lost the jaw I dropped. There were hundreds of those mean cats loping south and west.

Right then I turned in my resignation as shepherd and forfeited my franchise as an art colonist. Breaking the Sumerian record for the five mile dash, I hit the Euphrates and jumped upon the raft I found waiting. The leading ten leopard also-rans stood on the bank and snarled as I floated out of reach.

Behind them was a big slab of wet clay and an arrow pointing downstream. "This Way to New and Booming Eridu," cuneiform jabs said.

Doings at a Seaport

As crocodiles started convoying that raft, I changed my mind about swimming ashore and walking upstream to where the tribe was camped. Instead I stretched out to think up a few more brilliant sentences of my book, and when I waked up there was Kur to pay. The sea was bound and bedamned that it would climb into the river's bed, which the old Euphrates wasn't about to stand for.

I tried to calm 'em down, but you know what happens to innocent bystanders. Finally I was pitched overboard and got ashore by kicking in the teeth of the crocodile that had grabbed my breech clout in the mistaken conviction that it was part of me. When I'd made sure I still had all my toes and both halves of my fanny, I studied a sign upreared a few feet away. "Welcome to Friendly, Progressive Eridu," it chuckled.

The sound of a saurian being publicly sick told me my breech clout was rejected, but as I didn't want it either by then, I merely looked disapproving. It seemed a hard thing for an author to have to visit his first metropolis in no braver show than his own pelt, but buoyed by the thought that nobody would realize who I was, I went where the sign pointed.

First there was a sandy path, then there was a beach with four horse-shoe crabs and three men on it. Neither seemed to know or care what they were doing, so after a while I strolled along the wet sand myself.

"How about a double shot of bouncing and butting milk from the liveliest, sassiest and don't give a damndest goat this side of the blue blazing zodiac?" a voice called.

Right where the wet sand left off and the dry stuff began there was a booth shading a big grin and a goat which didn't look so cheerful. Not having had anything since that mutton bone I'd gnawed before Enki showed up, I walked up the beach but stopped short of the hand the fellow put out.

"It must be clear even to the owner of the most remarkable animal that Capricorn ever kicked out of the family nest that I'm a man of no monetary standing. How do you expect to get paid?"

He tapped a sign indicating that the price of a mug was one clam. "Venus mercenaria, if you haven't got its equivalent in beautiful mercenary metal," he said. "It's the old shell-money system till another gets voted in by the city council."

So I prospected where an ebbing tide made finding riches easy and kidnapped a mollusk, and the guy stuck it in his cash register: a crock where it had company which included a couple of disgruntled crabs. "I hope you'll be one of my regulars," he chatted while using his influence on the nanny.

The milk was welcomed by an empty stomach, but I couldn't find any special qualities in it. "I came here because it was recommended to me as a jumping town, but outside of you I can't find anybody who's got the bounce of a stuffed mud turtle. I met several of those sub-gooseberries while raising the clam wind, and they've got no more boom town swank and mustang style than a plugged sea dollar. On account of a writer not being able to afford letting his genius wither in a dull environment where everybody's out of sympathy with him, I'm scramming the Kur out of here."

"Are you an author, too?" He shoved a hand reeking of

honest toil with capric teats across the counter. "Mit John Mandeville—Jehan de Bourgogne it used to be before I *nom de plumed* myself and shot here yesterday, thinking there'd be a lot of excitement to give my stylus a work-out. Of course, I realize I'm not setting the Euphrates on fire by operating this milkery, but—"

"Look out, below!" somebody yelled. The booth collapsed all around me, and I peered out from under wreckage in time to see the fleeing nanny goat flattened by a huge rolling crockery vat, which thereupon came to a stop, yawning wide-mouthed at the sky which had somehow laid it.

Then there was a voice I recognized. "That was supposed to be delivered to your place, not on it. Are you all right, John?"

"Except for a bad case of astonishment. And that was my sole support your juggernaut flattened."

"Oh, well you're going into a bigger and better business now." Then I was discovered. "Why, It darling; you did decide to go to Eridu after all!"

I was still pretty sore about the leopards and crocodiles, but I didn't see any sense in mentioning them. "As soon as I pull all the splinters out of me, I'm going to shake this dead hole before the vultures stake out a claim on me, too."

"Before you do that, you and John had better go fishing, so you won't be in town when the barley squawll hits it. But be sure and be back in three weeks, sugar."

"What's a barley storm?" I asked, as a couple of guys with two heads and a tail began to run me down the beach toward a boat. "And why three weeks?"

"A barley storm's like a sand storm only more likeable," she said. "And three weeks because Daddy says it takes that long for a homemade wolf to learn to bite you back."

Remembering her old man was the moon, and figuring he might know some games I hadn't played yet, I let myself be picked up and tossed in the boat they shoved in the water. "I'd always wanted to go sea fishing," I said to John, after I'd pulled a squid out of one ear and got an eyeful of black juice, "but the sheep'd never give me a day off."

"My nanny goat was the same way." He picked up an

oar by its blade. "What do you suppose this is, a lee rail?"

"Naw," I said. "It's the niftiest starboard I ever set eyes on. This is a pukeworthy sea, John."

"Don't try to keep anything back," he counseled. "It's bad for the psyche."

"At least it ain't deluging like it is ashore. That barley storm's going to get its feet wet, if it ever gets here."

"It don't seem to be going anywhere's but in that vat, It," he said after a while. "How do you con an oyster into grabbing a hook?"

Well, it was three weeks before we'd mastered all the fine points of seamanship, and when we got back to Eridu, the first thing we noticed was that the vat had a collar of foam a yard high. The second thing we noticed was that those two-headed gazooks were standing guard over it. Now there was nobody else to tell about our fishing trip, so, of course, we swaggered near to give them an earful. That's when we noticed the third thing, which was that they picked us up and threw us on top of that foam.

That collar wasn't as stiff as it looked. In no time at all I had plopped through it and was fighting to keep afloat in the liquor below. "Help!" I hollered. And as I got a big mouthful when I did, I tried it again. "Help! Help!"

Then I was hanging onto the rim of the vat, and John was beside me. "Do you suppose," he asked, "that if we poke those guys in both noses they'd do it again?"

"I'm going to sneak a couple of more swallows anyhow," I told him, "which I wouldn't do if they throwed me in goat's milk."

"Say, I bet I could sell this stuff, if I could figure out a way to put teats on this fat, It."

"Roof the vat over, and sink a pump through it, John. Cut me in as full partner and you can have that idea."

"Suits," he said, taking a couple of more gulps of the stuff. "Let's get down and poke those ginks anyhow."

They'd gone and didn't show up again; but that was how the Inspiration Bar got started. "If you're not a stinking yak, ask for ale," was the cuneiform slogan in the back of the mahogany. John thought of that, because he said nobody was going to admit being a yak, and we had to call the stuff something, and every other name was spoken for by some varmint or other, while ale wasn't copyrighted. Well, a few didn't buy—and we weren't asking for clam shells, either, for the city council had voted in a system of metal coins—but there were always enough non-stinkers to run them out, so we always had a good friendly clientele.

It remade Eridu where there were no more foot dragging wet smacks. Everybody hustled so he could afford his daily load of ale. And the quietness that had bothered me went out a one-way door. Air waves that had been out of work now carried guffaws at salty jokes, sea-going lies, the patter of con men, the cheers of cock fight fans and challenges for duels with knives or slings.

Even before girlie shows began breaking up the united stag front, Eridu was more than a one-bar city. I've often thought that by patenting the ale formula and opening branches John and I could have cornered a world wide monopoly; but we were dogooders who thought nothing of telling anybody that the first thing to do was to go fishing and let a barley storm do the rest; and by and by there was competition all along the water front.

But we were never hurting for business; and the Inspiration's regulars included some of the prize apples of Eridu. Walter Map was another writer, and one who started thinking where Barnum left off. "It," he once said, "there's a fish called 'remora' which isn't half as long as your arm or my jib-boom that can latch on to a keel and stop a ship dead in its tracks, though a forty-mile gale is blowing its lungs out trying to get action from the sails."

But Walter was the best company you'd want to meet, and he'd even researched the truth sometimes like he did in the case of Nicholas Pipe. He told me, "Nick has got so used to staying under water—which he managed by lashing copper ingots to his ankles—that he can only stick being on land for two or three hours at a crack."

I laughed, but damned if he didn't bring the old hermit crab around. Pipe got to be a regular of the bar himself until once he got so canned that he overstayed his shore leave. Right in the midst of telling how he'd laid a sea-tart on the blubber hump of a whale—which had offered that convenience because Nick had once saved it from sharks, when the sperm was down with the epizootic—the bawdy hank of seaweed dropped to the floor gasping. And he would have hicked his ghost if Walter and I hadn't strapped his ballast back on and rushed to pitch him off the nearest wharf.

Joe Baldwin was another bar fixture of the Inspiration that I took to. He was an author, only the boom town rather than the seaside phase of Eridu was his racket. "I bet if they'd all stop lying for a split second all these guys would chirp the names of babes they were hiding out from settling down to good and useful lives with. You, for instance, you'd be a moral coward if you had any morals."

"Yeah, I know," I moaned, "but I ain't all to blame. I couldn't stand the way her bird was all the time slanging me."

He said that over to himself, then he drawled. "Tell me as a friend that never betrayed a confidence unless there was something in it for me, did you ever get next to a wall-eyed seacow?"

I put my bar rag down and stared into the distance. "I had a close shot at one once, but she was mighty young and came of good family, so I couldn't square it with my better self."

"Answer me, eel."

"When we said good-bye, she gave me a wild rose which I always keep under my pillow, Joe."

"An damn it! Did you or didn't you?"

"No; I guess when you come right down to it, I never did."

"Well, you said one thing I can believe, so maybe I'll learn to swallow that talking bird."

"Maybe you can learn to swallow a drink on the house, too," I said, as I stopped mopping the bar and reached for his ale mug.

But the good, laughing days didn't last at Eridu, for one night while I was counting up the wampum take after closing time I looked up to find Nebo had sifted through a locked door. He looked as well groomed as a prize county fair pig and had that sophisticated look I suppose you get from being a regular of Heaven, but I was glad to see him; yet he upstaged the hand I shoved toward him.

"I've come to find out about your progress with master piecing, since I haven't had any appeals for me to split divine afflatus with you."

"That's because I'm a careful craftsman, old man; I mean old god. Not wanting to boot my genius out of the nest until it's ready to fly, I'm still in the stage of taking careful notes."

He helped himself to ale. "First you were going to deal with savage, pre-cuneiform Sumer, and next you were going to let everybody in on the mysteries of seamanship; yet neither work has materialized."

"That's true, but only because I outgrew both those ideas and now I've one that does justice to my talents. I'm storing up anecdotes for *The Uproarious Memories Of A Waterfront Mahoganist*."

"If I thought you were ever going to author the work, I'd advise leaving 'Uproarious' for the publisher to blat in a blurb." Nebo pulled at his ale. "Have you heard of the medicine men who claim that—for compensation—they can arrange for An, Enlil, Enki and so on to take favorable action on the wishes of humans?"

"Sure, and I laugh to think how you with your power of Mummu brought them into being to serve our needs back in the old avant-garde days."

"As part of a reference frame designed to shoot light rays to all corners of the cosmos," he nodded, "so writers wouldn't be ascared of the dark any more."

"Shucks, you can't be afraid of a rascal you can whistle the name of." I raised my ale in salute. "It was a handsome job, Nebo."

"It *was* a handsome job." He made a slate wiping gesture, "This new organization is changing the role of the gods from cultural to moral, It. For those who don't toe the priestly mark by paying off, there will be withering curses while they're on Ki here and punishments down in Kur later. There's been crime before but there hasn't been sin—

which will be whatever the priests say it is at any given time, and which most of the gods will form a united front against, if I know immortal nature."

"What the Kur will they care what the priests, as you call them, beef against?" I wondered.

Nebo drank as though he suspected I'd dropped an unfriendly bug in his suds. "My colleagues haven't previously worried about what was expected of them, because nobody but writers trying to jazz up their styles ever thought about them; but they'll start worrying about their images when this union stampedes all of the people against sin into its camp. When a god that wasn't noticed much before finds temples, incense and prayers raised all over the lot in his honor, he's going to get a new picture of himself that he doesn't want to lose."

"Well, how about you and Ininni, Nebo?"

"Nobody's going to draft her for any game she can't find sense or fun in; but what she can do to rescue yours truly from writers that have nothing on the ball but ruses to get in good with me, I can't now glimpse." Putting down his stein he began sifting back through the door. "Ill fares the god, to ruthless men a prey," I heard him sigh, "who turn to night what he had planned as day."

Things turned black for me, too. A week or so later John Mandeville, Walter Map and Joe Baldwin went fishing; and I suppose the squawll the south wind spat that afternoon capsized their dory, for they never came back. So I didn't have those friends to cry in my ale with, when the priests turned a moral crusade into a power grab with a sweet tooth for real estate.

I lost the Inspiration Bar because Enki as water god had become worshipped as Eridu's tutelary one. Mine was one of several sea-fronting properties swept away without so much as a grunt of thanks to make room for a temple sacred to the city's patron.

Up the Euphrates younger towns named Lagash, Sippar, Akshak and Shurrupak had been dedicated to this or that god by the all devouring cuttlefish. Although I was swallowed, too, I escaped being sent to the salt mines through being able to do wrangle with cuneiform. As the priests couldn't make the clay talk, they put up with writers that could, so I ground out ritual dullness in a temple tablet factory at so much an inscribed clay slab.

With that drudgery and my scheduled class at New Stonehenge both in mind, I might have pecked some such distich as the following:

Ininni, I am woeful, me ignoring minx;
The Road is blocked and every day my hope
of homing shrinks.

But Enki still sat on verse like a snudge of dragon on gold, and though he might let Nebo borrow the use of it, a human could do no better than write: "You wanted me to do a job for you, but I'm stuck here by a flock of pocket picking holy joes." And I never mailed that, because a writer drifted down from Shurrupak and told what priest-prince Ziusudra was up to.

"The cluck's building an ark, which is a boat that looks like a mountain and a barn. There's no water handy, It; but he thinks the world's going to be drowned."

Concentrating on a curse guaranteed to straighten up grain guzzling rats, I wrote 'If a one of you rodent polecats takes so much as another mouthful, may Enlil give the whole wretched gang a thousand years searching Kur for cheese that you can smell but never find.' "Where's Ziusudra figuring on going, with the world washed out?" I then asked.

"Maybe the Milky Way to take the beauty baths. Who knows what prophets see at the bottom of their drinking cans?"

Although I grinned back at him, his news made me think of consulting Nebo, who could be reached only by going through religious channels now. As god of writing, he had a shrine adjacent to the tablet house where I drudged; but as I'd tired of his negative growls, when I asked if there was any chance of the Road opening, it had been months since I'd shelled out for the incense necessary to get him on the line.

To make up for the neglect I burned a double dose and

got the desired quick contact. "For An's sake, put out that stinking smudge; it gives me hay fever!" He coughed a few times while I was complying, and I thought I heard the gurgle of the throat clearer he poured himself. "Well?"

"Is this dope about Ziusudra for real?" I asked. "I wouldn't want to chase a wild goose."

"Why not?" he wanted to know. "It's a lot more interesting than a tame one. Or have you sat around adding lard to your bum so long that you're not game to cover the best story that's broken since Etana flew Chaucer's eagle to Heaven; or was it the other way around?"

"It was Etana's bird, but Chaucer got the best ride out of it, Nebo."

"I'd have remembered that myself, if I hadn't got peeved when you half asphyxiated me," he replied. "Hustle up to Shurrupak, for something worth being in on is about to break."

Leaving Eridu that afternoon, I found myself trailed by a scorpio-nine, one of Darwin's experiments that he didn't breed many of because he never could get it to look natural. At first I tried to shoo the ugly little pooch away; but he insisted on sticking with me, and he turned out to be a good companion during my hike along the river. Spindly-legged, he didn't look to be a match for the hefty sentry hounds that rushed out to heckle me. But Vinegaroon, as I called him, would flick the nose of a would-be man-eater with the stinger he sported where his tail belonged, thus closing the incident.

I walked by the way, because the river boats only gave passage to members of the establishment. But footing it was no hardship in April, on the seventeenth of which I strode through the south gate of Shurrupak. Pausing only to find an inn where Vinegaroon could be left, I sought the bistro of Al Cofribas, which was where I'd been told that local writers irrigated. Al turned out to be a fellow who'd called himself Frank Rabelais when he'd hung out at the old Inspiration joint for a couple of weeks; but as it was no business of mine if he changed monickers, I deadpanned as I hooked his bar's rail with a dusty boot and sluiced a dusty gullet.

"What," I then asked, "is the square root of the apple that thinks the world's going to get lost like a diving mud turtle?"

"He just might be less than half dotty." Al slid some salted nuts within reach. "Up in the mountains there's the makings of a prime flash flood."

"And if the gods wanted one, they could turn this valley into a lake that's damp enough to be real." I washed some pecans down my sluiceway. "Is there any reason why they should?"

"About three thousand mouthy priests practicing quantum mechanics. Their only plain mathematics is fitting their positrons in women they lay without somehow ever becoming laymen themselves; but in their spare time they're apostles of negative energy, reminding me of how other sacred cods were acting when I was riding the ridge between Medieval and Renaissance France."

"I've never been in that space and time hookup so far. What happened, Al?"

"There was a Pope who was going to barbecue me at the stake on account of a little book of mine which he might have thought was funny if he'd read it with one eye on the rest of the period's zeitgeist. His nibs hadn't found out that a serious minded Dutchman named Luther was about to give more trouble than my spoofing; but anyhow I took French leave from that continuum and slid into this one, courtesy of Venus—or Ininni, I should say, as long as I'm hiding out in Sumer." Al ran a short one out of the tap and tossed it down. "If I'd had my druthers, I would have opted for that bar Anacreon hung out in before Lycurgus sold Sparta to the prohibition dogs; but of course she could only switch me to another set-up steered by holy howler monkeys."

"Including one named Ziusudra."

"I heard you slanging the world's greatest benefactor!" A big guy with a bigger spear had grabbed me and was bringing the point of his sticker into line with my ticker.

"Only by implication," I argued.

"That's the worst kind of cation there is!" he shouted. "I'm going to send you to Kur before you turn it loose on anybody else."

I was reflecting that a well placed bolt of lightning was my only hope of rescue, when the fellow dropped at my feet anyhow. "There's no pacifier like a bung starter," Al said, as he tucked the mallet under the bar again. "Help me carry him to The Pass-Out Room."

After I'd obliged, I resumed our dialogue. "Who's Ziusudra going to save from the terrors of the deep outside of his fellow priests?"

"Oh, he loathes their guts as much as they do his, which is why none of them believes in the need for his ark. But he won't lack for lots of the kind of company he enjoys."

"Such as?"

"Well, I shouldn't have to tell you where Achilles was unfortified, or where the booted Dragon of Wantley was short of armor, but I will inform you where Shurrupak's king and high priest of the goddess Ninlil leaks his short change of brains." Up to then only the quaking of Al's stomach told of the laughter he was holding prisoner. Now he threw back his head and let the happy captive out. "Inin—Ininni—b-bless her—f-found out that this toughnut—too flinty for the worm Schamir to bore through on any other count—is a muling, puling does-oo-like-me animal doter!"

I goggled. "You really mean that this monstrous hooker he's building is just to save varmints from having to swim for it, if the gods wring out enough rain clouds to turn the world into a puddle?"

"Yeah, but he can't expect the gods to act as keepers of his zoo, so he'll have to take some folks along. Good afternoon, gents."

The party he greeted lined up at the far end of the bar, but I gave them no more than a sideswiping glance until Cofribas rejoined me, after bringing them four steins. "That's Ininni's head wrangler, Ninshubur," he whispered. "The buttons with him are some of the freaks I hope he'll get Ziusudra to take on as menagerie busboys."

Although eager to greet a friend I hadn't seen since that

brawl on Aldebaran, I asked Al for one more information bit. "Assuming there actually will be a bigtime squawll, what will happen to you?"

"As I'm not the back-to-the-soil type that will be wanted, if and when the world gets its second wind, I'll take a chance that the Pope has forgotten about me rather than stick with the funny business here," Al replied. "Let me put a head on your ale, if you're going to answer Nin's come hither wave, It."

"Hi, Ninshubur," I beamed, as I set down the drink Al had undecapitated and footed the rail at a new spot. "Nebo told me to hightail up here from Eridu, but I didn't look to have the luck to cut your trail."

"I came here to wave good-bye to you when the First World does its dying swan act." He flipped a hand toward his bar companions. "These will be among your shipmates, by the way."

I was wrestling with two of the worst kind of cations—[a] that he believed the world really was going to be a wash-out and [b] that he expected me to be on Ziusudra's floating monstrosity—as he introduced his drinking partners. "This seer with one dewy eye and one horny one is Jean Jacques Rousseau; that sage with a nose for the moo-cowiest anecdotes ever impressed on annoyed clay is William, whose words are worth a pocket full of rye every third leap year, nevertheless, and that cyst of sapience coyly nesting in a copse of silver whiskers is known to biographers who never met him as Faultless Walt."

"Only after I got old enough to sprout this benevolent looking beaver," that fellow was careful to point out. "When we used to have oyster fries on old Paumanok I was a coquin—or rascal, in case you don't lapse into French with my cosmopolitan grace—that the boys—ha, ha!—were even more afraid of than the girls."

"As long as one's vision is pure," Jean J. assured him, "one can safely forget about morals. That was what I always told all the countesses, duchesses and empresses I was so often called upon to comfort; and I didn't use apples to bring joy to the pippins either. It was a frightful disruption of my quest for the good life, but it would have been selfish of me to put my happiness above that of all the dear little well-heeled creatures."

"You can get away with liberated love in Gaul," William congratulated him, "and I did myself when there. But *par bleu,* when I tried it in Albion, I had no more than mentioned *amour* to the perfidious girl than she ran to tell mama and papa she was getting married; so it turned out that I was, too." He dipped his beak moodily into his stein. "You can't say I didn't learn though. Nowadays when I get a sexy urge, I just tell it to the daffodils."

Jean J. hadn't listened. "You can read all about my trials in *My Brags* which is how the Sumerians translate *My Confessions*. In a way I brought them on myself, because I've always known that primitive folks make the best associates; but my stars never allowed me the luck to be loved by a savage without a stultifying *centime* to her name."

"Well, we'll be emancipated from effete females," William comforted him, "when all the cities on earth are slushed from the map, and only mother nature in the buxom raw is left to be gandered at."

"It will take me back to rugged old times along the Delaware," Walt enthused from deep in his good grey spinach. "Why once when I was in Camden, I sprang aboard a ferry whose commander I ordered to stop at nothing short of Philadelphia. Nor did I lose my exploratory fire at the dock. I pressed on west to the main drag, and there in front of a trading post I found a full blooded cigar store Indian, peering under his hand at horizons which might have lured me toward sundown regions as they did Daniel Boone, only I had the character not to push a good thing too far."

"To ring in the real wilds or the Lake Country," William said, "it was there and in no lesser wilderness that I hardened my famous idiot boy style."

"There's no such thing as style; ask any bullfrog." As nonchalantly as any mill-pond serenader, Walt snapped his fingers. "Once you hit on a subject, kind of, you just close your mind, open your ego and let it run like a faucet with a busted washer. Fortunately *ego mio excels*—see how in three words I exploit three languages, me cultural hot dog!—all others."

"What!" There was a scowl on William's face as well as in his tone. "Am I to understand that you're exalting the ego of a mere USAL colonial above mine?"

Walt was unmoved. "Compared with my own, yours is as a pussy cat to the lion of the mountain wilds where oft I was too cagy to wander."

"Damme, I'll brook no contempt from an upstart!" William was reaching for his rival, when Al intervened.

"Settle it in The Pass-Out Room," he ordered. "The boy that's in there won't take sides."

Jean J. went along to referee, but I was glad of a chance to quiz Ninshubur about a bothersome point. "I know Ininni uses rough tactics to get her own way, but is she actually party to a scheme to murder the world?"

"Partly!" he snorted. "Once she found a geezer willing and able to build a craft big enough to hold all the life forms needed for a new global set-up, she wouldn't let An rest until he agreed to smear the present one."

"But she's the goddess of love!" I protested.

"And war," he reminded me. "She loves everything that's worth standing up for, but she's got her knife out for bones and mudsills. Look: would you like for the current religious ant hill to be permanent?"

"To sum up my position in a well chosen word, no."

"Well, did you bring the mutt she arranged to waylay you?"

"As he wouldn't be left behind, sure. Why?"

"That kyoodle's your passport to the Second World, It."

The Drowning of the First World

It was all very well to tell me I was going to make it into the Second World, but I didn't know what it was going to be like. After a while the terror of my ignorance must have shown in my eyes, for Ninshubur gave me a reassuring back-slap.

"Don't worry; there'll be plenty of ale there."

So I was in first-rate fettle when the gladiators came out of The Pass-Out Room. There was a blue bulge under one of Walt's eyes. But he was happy, and his antagonist was smiling while wiping blood from his proboscis. "We've thrashed it out nicely," William announced. "With forty-nine years of seniority, mine is recognized as the ranking ego, but I've yielded the admission that his has even flimsier grounds to strut on and is therefore the purer vanity."

Whether that peace treaty was broken I don't know, for I started shooting bar dice with Al and was still at it when they cleared out. The next morning, with Vinegaroon at heel, I walked to where Ziusudra's ark had been assembled and stocked with supplies. No greyhound of the so far invisible waters, it had about the length and beam of the New

Stonehenge football stadium, and from keel to roofridge the height of a ten-story office lodge.

When hearing that this animal loving gooseberry was for rescuing all the world's dumb species, I thought of only those native to Sumer. Herders I took to be Annunaki, or gods with no particular function, were herding up the gangplank such foreigners as bison, kangaroos and scaly ant eaters. However, when I reached a scene that was panstinky as well as pandemoniac, there was nobody else around but an unknown jumping jack with a wild light in his eyes. I soon forgot about him, though, upon hearing the voice of someone I did know.

"Why, pudding, how rewarding to meet you again!"

I should have cut her off with an icy crack. But unluckily for sophistication, she whipped Lalage to mind, so I could only give her the eye a moth saves for the one and only lamp in his life.

"I—er—Look out!"

Tired of waiting in line, a white rhinoceros had begun charging toward us, in spite of several protesting Annunaki, two of whom he knocked for ungodlike gools. It didn't seem to me that we could escape trampling by furious tonnage; but when Ininni stretched a hand toward it, the brute put on the brakes so well that he ploughed furrows with all four hooves.

I'd never seen a bull rhinoceros simper before. Yet that one did, and wagged his tail when she scratched spots behind his ears he couldn't get at himself.

"Poor old boy;" she crooned, "you know you aren't cut out for sailing. But you don't want to drown, and there'll be plenty to eat aboard, so come along."

Getting the message, the lummox followed her back to his line. When she rejoined me, she took note of the smaller beast in my own custody. "And here's the rare little dog you weren't too busy to take care of when readying to move into the next world. Ziusudra will be so happy to—Oh, there he is!"

After plucking something from a tuft of grass, a bulky seven footer strode toward us. The cat o' nine tails dangling from his belt made him look like a graduate of Blackbeard's Spanish Main School. But only until he opened his fist to show what it cradled, at which point his iron phiz turned to custard.

"See the poor frightened itsy-bitsies that almost got left behind," he said of a pair of locusts that looked full of pazazz to me.

Although I'd never been a pet's patsy, I had friends at New Stonehenge that were, and knew the proper patter. "Those bugs have class cuneiformed all over them."

"And I have one more human for you to preserve," Ininni told a stone that wasn't listening until she sweetened the pot. "And guess what he's brought you! Remember Vinegarette, that precious little scorpio-nine you couldn't locate a mate for?"

"He didn't truly find one!" His face all junket, the big galoot crouched to hug a pooch I was afraid would slap him with his stinger. But either Ziusudra had a way with animals or Vinegaroon had more political savvy than I'd thought; for he put up with being slobbered over and called "a handsome-lancesome doggie."

"He's got a cock flea and a hen in heat somewhere in his wool, in case your regulars get rubbed out," I built the mutt up.

"Good, good!" Ziusudra was still cuddling the pooch as he rose. "Now how do you want to help out when we're aboard?"

"You're engaged in a very important mission which future do-gooders to animals have a right to know about," Ininni put in. "So you'll want talented It here to keep a log on which to base his official report."

"That's fine, for the other men I've agreed to take along will be amply occupied—Ah, here are the three that Ninshubur recommended earlier in the day."

Jean J., William and Walt were nearing, and hastened to join us. The former drew a deep breath of air that couldn't have been more loaded if it hung out in a glue factory.

"It smells nice and primitive."

"I'll do the talking, *humans*." Ziusudra touched the scourge at his belt but didn't unhook it. "Now which one told me that he was an expert on hay?"

"Feuilles, foolscapia or leaves of grass," Walt said. "Me polylingual when it comes to deep subjects."

"Don't quibble with me, my man. When grass is cut, and dried so that it won't get moldy when stored, it's hay; and I want you to see that chewers of it get plenty. You other two can clean the stalls; and if they don't pass inspection, you'll be keelhauled. Yes?"

"What part of the ship can I be lonely as a cloud in?" William asked.

"Try the bilges. Meanwhile you'd better stand ready to jump for the gangplank when I yell 'all aboard', or the non-lonely clouds rubbing their bellies on the ark's roof will open up and swallow you." Here Ziusudra glanced at the restless, yellow-eyed hoverer I'd noticed. "How long can I wait for any stragglers to show up?"

"Just till Ininni's in the clear," the fellow answered. "And here comes Ninshubur to pick her up now."

A gaff-rigged cat boat was skimming the grass. With a nod to me, Ninshubur brought a yacht labelled Belle of Heaven into the wind just long enough for Ininni to vault to a seat beside him. As the sail next filled and the craft's flukes changed their pitch, the boat started to climb.

We waved farewells at each other, as the ark's skipper strode toward the gangplank, cracking his cat o'nine tails. "All aboard that don't want to stay with or in the fishes," he bellowed.

"You can't persuade me it's going to rain," William declared. "Up in the Lake Country they called me the Bull Fiddle, I was so in tune with nature; and I don't get any ominous vibrations from that cloud that's come to roost right above us like a skylark, only kind of friendly."

Then from amidst that same mass of chummy vapor came a cry from Ininni. "Pour it on the world now, Ishkur!"

The loiterer whom I'd been unable to place was thus revealed as the storm god. Swinging his clenched fist, he split the cloud with a jagged lance of lightning which hit the ground close enough to William to make him jig with two hot feet. But I didn't laugh, for the stroke was followed not only by a local Niagara but by the roar of rushing waters rushing out of storage in the hills above lowland Sumer.

Trailing William a half a length and dodging rain columns that were like inverted oil gushers, I was the last to cross the gangplank. Aboard I found a grimly satisfied Ziusudra.

"Come with me, chronicler, for you will wish to overhear the dialogue when we steer close to the drowning city of Shurrupak; so I can give the bird or raspberry to the priests who laughed when I prophecied a deluge."

Unluckily for his dirty purpose, the visibility was too bad to allow the mean skate to crow over doomed colleagues. Besides the ark began rolling like the amateurishly built tub she was, and I don't think the skipper held back even his spite.

I've got to hand it to Walt for hitting it right; she was sure "a cradle endlessly rocking," which is all I could think of when I crawled to the small cabin high up in the hooker, and what little was left of me died there. That was only one of the things that blighted my hope of writing an imperishable work on the demise of a world. Cuneiform was kaput; I couldn't scratch anything on the clay which seemed to have any meaning.

"What's going on, Nebo?" I finally croaked. "Can't you at least fill me in on the bad news?"

When a puffin landed on the sill of my glassless window, and thence hopped to the floor, I thought that my god had arrived in answer to my groan. But the figure which unfolded was that of Enki.

"Nebo asked me to explain that he's going to retire to his planet—Mercury, to the Second World—until I make up my mind what I'm going to do about the Mes." He looked like a shirt that was plenty stuffed rather than the jovial chap that had dropped by to enlighten the avant-garde in my old sheep-tending days; and he let me know the name of his fleas. "It was nice of me to stand in for him, in as much as you didn't go through the regular channels of prayers and incense burning."

Working in a tablet house, I'd acquired a degree of religious cunning. "I'd never expected to be able to deal ceremonially with a god as important as you. What are Mes?"

"They're all the properties of civilization acquired since I began teaching men how to graduate from baboonery. When the First World died they all reverted to me, which is why you can't make cuneiform work."

I wasn't liking this gink any better than a thorn in my foot, but it didn't seem the time to point that out. "But, of course, good old Enki will restore them when the Second World is started?"

"On the contrary," he smugged, "I came to warn you that I'll let men rest in savagery, since they did so ill with the advantages of civilization that An was prompted to destroy the whole depraved push."

That tore my temper loose from what moorings it still had. "Depraved men, you sick hiccough of heaven! Who knocked up Ki outside of wedlock? It wasn't a man that seduced virgin Spacette—who died when her bastard was born, by the way. It was An, the head morality prune of Heaven. Who raped Ninlil, the mother of Nanna, the moon? Oh, he covered up by marrying her, when the other gods decided the scandal was too rank for public relations to stand; but the stoat was Enlil, An's son. And it wasn't a man that swiped the cherry of Erishkegal, so she could only get Nergal to make an honest goddess of her by inviting him to be King of Kur. Do you want me to tell you of any more musk roses sprouting from Heaven's family tree?"

He responded to my rage by smiling. "Do you recall an invention of mine called poetry, which I refused to turn over to Nebo for distribution to men?"

"Yes, but what's that got to do with the fact Heaven stinks like a dead mule too lazy to take a bath?"

"Well, as I have decided never to let a second rate class of sinners enjoy the most divine of all the Mes, you will be the last mortal to experience a hint of its virtues, when I regale you with *The Ballade of Double Standards,* It:"

If ever you venture to gamble, my boy
Eschew as the grave any innocent games

Where nothing's at stake but the fun of the ploy,
Such trifling with riches society blames
As heinous, while leaping to honor the names
Of felon endeavorers, clever to throw
Their ropes upon juicy imperial aims,
For power's as pure as impeccable snow.

Looking him grumpily over, I found that one of his feet was now a claw. In spite of this evidence that he was on his way back to puffinhood, he continued with his metrical homily.

Be chary of stealing, if needing the loot;
That's vulgar, and rightly a gallows offense.
But wealth is a touchstone adept to transmute
Despicable crimes to proceedings of sense:
Historians purr when a theft is immense
Who'd scorn to applaud if the winnings are low;
For poverty's granted no moral pretense
While power's as pure as impeccable snow.

With both legs feathered, Enki shrank in proportion to their shortness. He was thus looking up at me when he swung into the third stanza.

The chasm that yawns between maker and man
Is simple for any inquirer to spell:
For gods there exists no morality ban
On following purposes selfish as fell.
They'll fry you alive for thier joy in your yell
(All torts they perform without menace of woe),
And lose of their holiness never a del,
Since power's as pure as impeccable snow.

All puffin now as far as his wings, he flapped to the window sill. From there he hurriedly delivered the envoi while he still had a mouth to shoot off.

You're cooked, if you're mortal and minus the pelf
To bail out your soul with a temple or so,

For this is the dictum on deity's shelf:
"Yea, power's as pure as impeccable snow."

When Enki signed off with a raspberry you could have dished a quart of jam out of and flew away, I felt closer to Hannibal than I had for a long time. After his old man talked to him about Rome he had a feeling of serious purpose that he hadn't had before; and it was the same way with me now. Enki was one god I was going to get square with somehow; and I began to look for signs that the ark was no longer aimlessly drifting.

Boatless in the Goof Stream

Vinegaroon didn't make it into the second world. "It was a case of jumping to the right conclusion at the wrong time," Ziusudra summed up, when coming to tell me of the disaster. "That small heap of hay would have tempted any small dog to nap on it, but when the hippopotamus who was the rightful tenant of the stall decided to indulge in a delightful roll, he didn't trouble about minutiae; he just up and did it. I wouldn't wish you to think there was any malice involved—for the horse of the river is the soul of sunny good nature—but accidents don't take good intentions into—"

"I'll call on the hippo and let him know there's no hard feelings," I said, "but not now. You won't need me on the hay pitching squad, will you?"

"No, my poor friend; stay here and steel your heart against grief."

Malingering was dull but better than playing waiter or janitor to animals, and after the water began to drop, I had the hobby of watching the new world begin to show itself. I've since scanned malarkey about a raven or a dove beating back to the ark with news of land. Actually what happened was that a muddy ridge snagged the keel of the slowly settling scow and held it there until Ininni's brother, Utu, could dry the vicinity out and make setting forth to look around possible.

That wasn't safe, though, until the Annunaki drove off to suitable points all the animals not native to Mesopotamia. On account of the Mes being missing, nobody knew anything about setting up a town as a base of future operations, but I remembered a primitive dodge for supplying us with fresh fish as a badly needed change of diet from First World leftovers and went off by myself to activate it. But, while I was fashioning a two-pronged willow spear with which to stab carp locked in shallow pools left by the dwindling flood, talons closed on both arms.

Aloft I went, wrying my neck to see what was taking me for a ride. But having looked, I wished I had stayed blissed by ignorance. Etana, King of Kish, was borne to heavenly heights by a grateful eagle he had once rescued from a double-crossing snake. Chaucer, Prince of Pilgrims, was carried skyward by probably the same obliging bird, as the odds swear there couldn't have been two such aquiline good fellow. I myself had once been given a lift by a kind, if grumpy, Simurgh. Now, however, I found myself in the clutch of a lion-headed Imdugud or Zu bird, never known to have any but deadly intentions toward men.

I tried an appeal to its better feelings anyhow. "You don't want to hurt good old Ziusudra, who built the ark that saved you and your lovely better half from the flood, do you?"

"Don't make me laugh; I might drop you," my captor cautioned.

Held between sky and earth by a snare, Br'er Rabbit had been both afraid he would fall and that he would not, and I both longed for the ground and feared joining it too hurriedly. "Fly carefully," I backseat drove, while still hoping for release. "Did you know that I have the pip?" Then, as I guessed that might lead to being dropped, I revoked. "Forget that; I was just kidding. But if you set me down gently, I'll spear you fish lots tastier than I am."

"You're a bird yourself," my kidnapper chuckled, "An Imdugud could snap forty carp from a pool while you were trying to stab one. To save you from inventing any more funny stories, I'll tell you that if my voice hadn't been warped by a lion's larynx, you would have recognized me as Nebo."

I was so relieved that I forgot to be sore at the scare he'd given me. Besides I was now busy trying to figure out where he was taking me, which the sun said was south along the unrecognizably swollen Euphrates.

Finally I reopened the conversation by telling of Enki's visit. "The old pelican, or puffin as he was then, threatened to hog all the Mes indefinitely."

"I know; but they can and will be pried loose from him somehow, It. That won't be a pressing problem for a couple of repopulating centuries, though and as Ininni doesn't wish you rusticating for such an interval, I'm going to put you in the one place where it will be possible for you to broaden your outlook pending civilization's full second coming. If it kills you, we can comfort ourselves that we did the best a bleak set of circumstances allowed."

"Um," I non-committed myself.

"Do you remember Amergin mentioning adventures in other than human forms of life?" Nebo wanted to know.

"Yeah." My laugh sounded rusty, so I tried it again. "If you want my vote, old Am was off his rocker."

"Not a bit of it. Now other types of authors can afford to bypass this experience, but scientific ones—"

We had reached the sea, which was a bigger deal than it had been when I had lived at Eridu. Not locating a trace of a town the deluge had apparently had the effect of turning over to the horseshoe crabs, I picked up a sentence which had hung fire.

"What about scientific ones, Nebo?"

"They should learn, among other things, that there's a marine equivalent for every form of life found ashore, e.g. sea-butterfly and sea-dive."

"The sub-world of the sea sounds fascinating," I said, peering out over open reaches of it and wondering when he was going to turn back.

"I hope you'll retain that enthusiasm," Nebo replied. Plunging toward the water as he spoke, he released his grip on me. "Tell me of that, if we meet again; but for now it may be of interest to know that you'll be washed about the world by the Goof Stream, swimmer."

I didn't answer, for as my god had implied, it was not in human form that I'd been mixed with the sea. I was, in fact, a fish of the order adopes, or an eel.

My first observation was the satisfied one that I was skilled at weaving through the Goof Stream with a *je ne sais quoi* which set me apart from swimmers dependent on overdeveloped fins and tail. Secondly I was glad of habits that were neither too much of the herd or anti-social. The members of some fish tribes felt such a compulsion to be near each other that there were always two or three fighting for the same sea-quail or sea-bottle. But eels slithered midway between aloofness and overdoing the brotherhood of gills bit.

So I was reserved but pleasant when a sawfish drew near the second or third day out. My years as a bar philosopher told me he wished to spill aggrieved guts all over the coral grove below us, while the same advanced course in psychology warned me that he would be snooty, if I spoke first. Wherefore I peered into the marine distance until he asked, "What led you to seek these waters?"

"Oh," I said, "as a reporter, I had hoped to meet important figures to interview here, but alas!" And with that I gazed ahead anew.

"The local situation isn't as barren as all that," he declared, when able to be ignored no longer. "I was almost a statesman, though I had to settle for being a writer."

"I've heard good things of that profession," I admitted, "but what's a statesman?"

That staggered him so he sawed a tentacle off a cuttlefish that paused to snarl, "Watch what you're doing, slob!" before it started sprouting a replacement.

"He never would have dared to flay me with that epithet, if destiny had been dutiful to me," my saw-snouted companion moaned as we swam on. "What's your name, sir?"

"It."

"In your, of course, feverish quest for renown, Master

It, have you ever heard of that whipping boy of Fortune, Jonathan Swift?"

"Maybe not the same one as you're thinking of," I mumbled, having just made a bonne bouche of a sea-cockroach. "The only one I know of had the luck to be a crackajack author."

"Yes, but I was smart enough to have been a statesman or even a bishop."

"What's a bishop?" I wondered. "Outside of a chessboard and away from the derriere of a Victorian dowager, that is."

"If there was anybody else to confide in, I wouldn't tell you that a bishop is a dignitary that the in-crowd asks to all its cocktail parties, which is where policies of state are formulated, by the way. But people jealous of my brains froze me out where the best I could do was write and sop it up with pals at my club."

Having met quite a few farers of the Road by then, I didn't feel that the qualities which shaped an author were the same as those needed to keep a ship of state from crashing on the rocks. Nor could I grieve for my companion on the score of missing out on cocktail parties, which I suspected of being as sticky and short of anything worth drinking in Queen Anne's court as in the New Stonehenge Faculty Club.

Yet of these things I said nothing, while not ignoring his cried-in beer either. What I had discovered the brass rail way was that at a certain point the sharer of griefs wishes to be reminded of his virtues and strengths.

"Jonathan," I said accordingly, "you may not have had all the best breaks in the world, but doesn't it sometimes cheer you up to think that nobody remembers any of the in-crowd doodlebugs that gave you the business, while every year you get more column inches of swell publicity than all the royal houses of the world, except the Bourbon one?"

As I knew it would, that tickled him, though, as I likewise knew, he was both sure of it, too, and was going to act as if it was a surprise to him. "Is that really your considered opinion, It?"

"You bet; you can always depend on an eel to give it to you straight from the shoulder, pal."

Yet in spite of his moping fits, Jonathan was rattling good company; and I would have stayed with him longer than I did but for a shocking accident. Yes, I hadn't meant anything by it, other than to give a Goof Stream girlie a laughable memory of a relaxed visiting professor, when the world blew up in my face.

I should have looked at her more carefully, but it was sundown when this little trick frisked by and almost as a reflex, as it were, I slipped her a friendly ell-feel. Talk about the chair at Sing-sing, if you want to. There's no red hot mamma like the female of the Gymnotus electricus species and I got every volt this one had to dish out.

When composed again who knows how many years later, I found I had slid down Darwin's ladder as far as the oyster rung; and perhaps as punishment for my ungallant behavior the last time at bat, I had been assigned to the monastic camp of Ostrea virginicus.

Although it has been maintained by some specialists that the refusal to have any fun out of procreation has been due to the Oysterettes' Liberation Front, it has been pointed out with equal probability that the absence of joy is owing to the fact that this species of Lamellibranchia is without cranial development.

And I noticed that all the oysters of our branch of the family were leftists, swelling out on the portside only. When we were all lined up in our communal bed, it made for a uniformity that might have depressed me, had I been mentally equipped to give the matter thought.

Yet there was one member of the gang that couldn't remember from day to day whether he was pleased with his lot or against it, so when the luck of the tidal draw put me next to him one day, I braced him. "How come you're such an amused case of the dumps, seesaw?"

He spat out a pearl and scrounged for the makings of another. "That's no way to talk to the only Oxonian Litt. D. that ever piloted a Mississippi stern wheeler."

"Don't try to pull your temperamental airs on me, cake-eater that loves to act as if it was hard tack," I flared. "Of all the Road travelers that ever lived, nobody ever came nearer to having everything he wanted—and I won't go into whether you knew what you were doing most of the time when it came to writing."

"You're just an insensitive plant that doesn't understand what authors suffer while serving humanity throughout their tragically lonely and unappreciated lives," he hauteured. "Haven't you read *The Ordeal of Mark Twain,* which I personally can never examine with a dry eye?"

"Ordeal, Bertha's billowing big fanny! You had a boyhood you delighted in more than was good for you. Every kid then wanted to be a professional river jockey, but you actually did it. You got away with running out on a war, because you welched on the losing side. You lammed out West and emerged famous in the East on the strength of one article about a frog that was never authenticated. You caught a good squaw who gave you fine kids. The world then your Ostrea, you made more money out of lectures than Abelard, more cash out of assorted pieces than Plato, and more money out of novels than Fielding. What's more," I tiraded, "you were the only writer in history who got all the dough realizable from most of your books, because you could afford to be your own publisher."

His arrogance a thing of the past, he looked at me with the appealing eye of a stricken doe a bartender has threatened to cut off. "Don't you like my stuff, It?"

"Oh, Kur, Mark, of course I do, in spite of the fact that you never knew whether you had driven down the fairway or had sliced the ball into a water hazard belonging to the next hole. But I don't think anybody else ever noticed, so who the Nergal cares?"

We got along fine after that, but I lost track of Mark when an undersea volcano got tired of being dormant. What happened to any of the old oyster bar crowd is a closed book to me, as a matter of fact. It was also a matter of indifference, for when I regained personality it was as a gay Goof Stream lobster.

I won't reveal the techniques for cutting up which I had

mastered, for an Ostracod doesn't tell. Suffice it to say that I knew what to do with my claws whenever I stole up behind an alluring bit of temptation.

But ever a conquistador one cannot remain. For years renowned as 'The Lobster Lothario,' I more than met my match at last, and as a scientist, I can do no less than be frank.

Waterloo involved, *ca va sans dire*, a shapely lobsterette. Having observed that she seemed lost in the contemplation of a marine view, I crept near on eight poda and was flexing my claws, as called for in Tactic One of Homarian courtship, when the lovely creature whirled to glare at me.

"I'm George Sand," she snapped, "and when any monkey business is tried I expect to be the simian that's calling the dance."

My temperature dropped like that of a thermometer hit by a Texas northerner, "You got me wrong, George," I croaked. "I was only moving my pincers to get the cramps out of them."

I was backing up, as I said that, but she stayed as close as sticking plaster. "Who are you, Petronius?"

Ordinarily I would have been pleased to be mistaken for a hotshot like Gaius, but I hurriedly handed the idea back to her. "I'm not anybody worth a spot in your memoirs; I'm just It of the little old USAL."

Instead of putting her off, this information was as fish to Don Marquis' Mehitabel. "Oh! the country of great lovers, where all the novelists carry sleeping bags around with them, so as to be ready for life's supreme moment twenty-four hours a day."

"Some of the boys don't seem to have much else on their minds," I admitted. "But I'm not a hot pants Spanish flyer; I'm the cold philosophical kind."

"Je m'en fiche de pantalons chauds d'hommes!" Her stalk mounted eyes now red with passion, she still kept pace with my desperate crawfishing. "When there is any torrid panting to be done, I'll attend to it, *joli coeur.*"

"Oh, An!" I groaned, out of fear that she would back me against a coral reef and there qualify me for a chapter of her autobiography over which pitiless readers of the future would gloat—aye, and do it again when she flung my ruins aside.

"I've dealt with nobodies before who didn't know they were geniuses until they slept with me," La Sand gloated. "Of course, you've never previously felt the glow of creation, *mon petit chou,* but when I ignite you—Come back here, you coward!"

George had chased me clear out of the Goof Stream; and as it wasn't her destiny to leave it yet, she was helpless to follow. Nor could she do more than stamp her pretty pods, when I snapped a nonchalant claw and turned to amble away.

As my own destiny now lay counter to the Stream, the rest of my experience with evolution was brief and uneventful. When a storm smeared shallows into which I wandered with ostracodal confidence, I was tossed roughly ashore; and upon recovering from shock, I found myself a land tortoise. All but indestructible in that armor plated shape, I lingered in it until struck by lightning.

On that account I reached the banks and braes of the Euphrates at long last—and there is no short one, I am glad to be the first to point out—as a gamesome ibex. Not as gamesome as the other male members of the Capra syrica club were, I confess. The memory of confrontation with George—nee Amandine Lucile Aurore—was too vivid to allow me to get out of goathood all the delights promised.

But while I was cagily keeping wide of dangerous temptations, I once more heard the flutter of big wings above me. As a kid every ibex learns that heavy brush is the best defense against airborne peril. Wherefore I bounded toward a copse, only to be pounced on while a few feet short of it.

Starting to bleat, I ended by speaking quietly. For my shape was human once more, and I was sure I knew the true nature of the Zu-bird bearing me south along the river's winding course.

"What's happened since you know when, Nebo?"

"Nothing since you started on your tour many fruitful generations ago but Ki's repopulation."

Gazing along the valley, I could see no sign of a city in which to celebrate my return from a long dry spell. "Am I to understand that the people of Sumer are still being short changed by Enki and have gained back none of the Mes of civilization?"

"Not even the booze you've been storing up a thirst for, It."

"Why the Nergal did the gods schedule the Second World, if they didn't intend to make it habitable?" I demanded. "Have you any plans for correcting this outrage?"

"Until writing's restored, I'm a god without portfolio," Nebo said, "and powerless to move in any large fashion. But when Ininni asked me to locate you, she told me that she has decided to establish a headquarters on earth. And if she is taking that much interest in human affairs," and here he gave me a long and meaningful look, "my bet is that they won't remain asleep long."

Searching the country ahead with renewed zest, I still could find no signs of activity. "And how do I fit into any plot to put a fire under the Second World?"

"All I can tell you, It, is Ininni picked Erech—one of the scratch settlements pioneered by descendants of the ark's crew—as her terrestrial stand, so that's where you'll be deposited."

Erech, at that time, was the only place where I knew the names of all the June bugs. Not counting racing caterpillars, naming j.b.s was all the sport there, and I was going stale on that by the time Ininni and Ninshubur showed up in Belle of Heaven and took me on a raid of Enki's undersea headquarters at Eridu, where I squared accounts with that ornery god by helping steal all the Mes he'd squirreled, including the one for Poetry which men had never had.

But though I'll give a detailed report of that greatest of all fishing trips later, I wasn't so much as able to talk coherently when I got back to Erech. For in order to help me carry out the project she had commissioned me to complete, she had given me what only a god had found not too hot to hold before.

It was like being handed a tidal wave or a volcano with no directions as to how to set it in motion. The wretched container of forces I could neither jettison nor employ, I staggered out of town and fell by the river for vultures to claim if they would.

There Nebo, radiant with renewed godhead, found me and laughed. "What's spooking the world's first human poet?"

"Incompetence," I moaned. "Here I have firsthand knowledge of what she planned, risked and achieved by way of bringing the Second World to life, and I haven't the science to grace it with a line. Oh, I learned enough of the fundamentals from that crew that mobbed me on Aldebaran to handle a lyric—if I ever return to where there's a mynah bird owning target for one. But because I am short of the seasoning it takes, I don't know how to give the flavor of the big whiskey I was actually a part of."

Nebo's eyes gleamed, as he hauled me to my feet. "As bards are distinct from cheese omelets, seasoning cannot be sprinkled on them; they must acquire it the smoked ham way. wouldn't tempering be rather what's required?"

"If you say so." Considering a profitless interview over, I shrugged.

Yet he clapped a hand on my shoulder. "I do say so. And furthermore I'm going to take you up to Mercury and put you through the skaldic shop I rigged, in case Ininni was as successful as I'd hoped."

To that I made no rejoinder, having just been turned into an ingot of pig iron, handier for him to carry than a man while flashing me to his private planet. Mercury had other features which I'll find occasion to describe later; but on this first visit I noticed only the "shop"—a forge manned by a couple of bruising Annunaki.

And bruise me they did, when I had at length been drawn from blue-flamed charcoal and slammed, white-hot on the anvil for shaping. Meanwhile they sang a spell in alternate lines, the odd ones voiced by him of the heavier sledge and even by the wielder of the lighter hammer, who also held me to it with the pincers he clutched.

Proposition: rear a poem,
Plain but scintillating,
Gliding from a gripping proem
To climactic skating;
Sound as careful vintner's barrel,
Never drained of liquor;
Harmony its must apparel,
Heart its tonal ticker.

Having whacked me from a lump into a slab, they tossed me back into flames, a bellows blew to full strength again. While I was turning red and then white once more, Nebo and his smiths exasperated me by smacking lips over ale.

"Do you think he's got any grain?" my deity inquired.

"Maybe," the swinger of the sledge offered. "The most I can swear to now is that he didn't crack while being turned from pig to possibility."

"The next round will tell more about his fibre." Setting down his stein, the speaker caught up his hammer and pincers. "We'll wham him inside out and back again, boss."

Topping centipedes for timing,
Feet, however, hidden;
Able even in subliming
Matters of the midden;
Trafficking in tiers of meaning,
All of them congruent;
Taciturn in proper leanings,
Next, when fitting, fluent.
Milking lexicons as cattle,
Not, however, wordy;
Spinning out of booze or battle
Gossamer that's sturdy;
Gathering for sure recital
Insights stiff to stammer;
Turning shapeless torpor vital
With the metric hammer.

Pounding out the kings deranging
Adamant that's bubble;

Minting comets when exchanging
Light for muck or rubble;
Pinnacles from pits extracted,
Dust recast as slaker—
Such as these are sleights exacted
Daily of the maker.

This time I knew that something had happened to me under the stress of hard walloping. Aware that in place of being broken I had been knit more strongly together, I hit the forge with a defiant grunt.

"He might be good for something better than mule shoes," the smaller of the Annunaki hazarded, when both were drinking with Mercury's master again. "Did you hear him sort of ring, when I got in amongst his spare ribs with my hammer?"

"But will he take a temper?" Nebo asked.

"I'm not sure," the big smith said, when he'd come out of his ale. "He's *got* a temper, though. Have you noticed the way the bastard's been giving us the red eye while we're tippling?"

They kept on enjoying themselves, and I kept on getting hotter than I'd been at other spells in the forge, till a fellow that used to be a close friend of mine yelped an order. "Pitch him in the tank quick! And if that doesn't shiver him—"

Nebo didn't finish, because I spat steam in his eye, as I went under water I boiled. The satisfaction of that gave me a confident glow while I was again in the flames. On the anvil for the last time next, I felt so sure of myself that I jolted both hammerers, this their closing chant:

Air's the soil a maker's planting,
Earth's his sphere for flying;
Fire's the drink for which he's panting,
Water's when he's drying;
Space he darts amongst as swallows,
Death he'll coolly slaughter;
So he'll toe the Road, it follows,
Urged by Nanna's daughter.

"He rang, and good this time, so something might come of him," the sledge swinger allowed. "What do you want done with him now, boss?"

"Nothing you can handle, thanks." As I'd been cooled by a final plunge in a fresh tank, Nebo tucked me under his arm. "He can only be shaped more particularly by what he does with his craftsmanship, so I'll pack him back to Ki and let him be his own molder for a while."

A Dilettante Goes to Sea

My hot tip to philosophy is that there's such a thing as being full of the wrong kind of beans. Look, when I got back from Mercury, I was raring to go places, and I got as far as a fly taking his constitutional through glue, though it seemed that everything was in my favor.

Erech was crackling with doings, for Ininni wanted it to be the top city in Sumer, so it was. There was a prince called Enmerkar—one of the rare combinations of epic and civic talents in the history of the world—that held the reins she'd tossed him; and every day was action day for that live wire. But I never used my in with her to get next to him, and never saw her or Ninshubur. And most especially I never saw Nebo, whom I'd made up my mind to do without.

Yet I was in there pitching after a fashion. Because of the fact that of all squabs, the writer is hatched with the least knowledge of where he wants to fly, I was buzzing my wings backward. So in a gung ho burg I was a moth. Except for the circumstance that Erech stood on the right shore of the Euphrates, I was, in fact, a *rive gauche* Bohemian.

And on a modest scale I was a professional. Erech incubated the first magazines produced in either of the worlds;

and it was as a contributor to such publications as *The Nebonian* and *The New Sumerian* that I settled in a section of town called "The Magpie's Nest." There was a shrine for Nebo in it, but, as I said before, I made a parade of ignoring it.

"He knows where I am, if he's got anything to say to me, but he's sulking because he knows I can get along without him." There was a spot named the Mauve Gryphon where I presided over a group known as the Mock Turtles; and I tossed that remark on the table while pouring myself a slug of date wine. "He resents the light touch I've developed and wants me to write like the muskrats of the Erech Academy."

"You've never needed him," Henry 'Slowcoach' James said, "Having had the prestige to go over his comparatively plebeian head and obtain the Mes for poetry by the direct concession of the Lady of Heaven—meaning as you may properly infer, the goddess Ininni, daughter of the blueblooded Ningal and even more aristocratic moon, himself divinely sprung from the lordly loins of Enlil, who married very little beneath him when taking to his bosom the already samples, as delicacy enjoins me to put it, Ninlil."

Skilled by then at unraveling Henry's verbal labyrinths, I worked back through this one till I came to the point that Ininni, not Nebo, had given me the bardic Mes. "Ha, ha! She sure did."

Yet that was a laugh I had to struggle for, to keep it from sounding lame, because the time had gone when I enjoyed talking about my journey to Enki's undersea stronghold. Still unchronicled, it stood for an unkept promise of something I'd earnestly meant to achieve; but now I again succeeded in kicking it out of mind.

"Oh, when I was getting started, I swapped him enough of the sneezing powder called incense to get a metric tool kit; but you don't want a solemn god brooding over your shoulder, when you're planning Enmerkar's establishment."

"'The sneezing powder called incense;' that's rich!" 'Barnacle Jim' Boswell thought it was rich enough to be jotted down; but 'Kiss and Weep' Hal; as Heine was known in The Magpie's Nest, drooped a sarcastic eye. "Are you standing up to be scriptorially counted or are you sinking to the Academy's level by merely writing against whatever it believes Nebo sanctions?"

"Maybe he sanctions only songs about an interminable array of dying, dead and ghostly lollipops," I hit back.

But Hal had a point I had come to recognize myself. While attacking bores is theoretically a holy war, the author whose only lyre string sneers at the work of others never finds time to declare anything on his own account. If I hadn't left that rut, I had at least varied it by finding a new target; and I now chose to air the fact.

"The Academy is so lacerated by my lampoons that I've turned my lancet from that dead horse to a virgin asininity."

They looked at each other to see who'd bite, but as the conversation was a corpse until somebody did, Marcel 'Saloon boy' Proust sighed: "If the Academy is declared too mortally wounded to be worth stabbing again, you must have discovered some new burgher fatheadedness to be so tickled with yourself."

"Some of our mercantile nabobs have become patrons of song, only they can't abide the singers!" Starting to down a dative bumper, I paused to laugh. "Mark Martial, editor of *The Nebonian*, wised me."

"'Patrons of song that can't abide the singers,'" Boswell repeated, while stamping the phrase on clay. "Just what do you mean by that antithesis, It?"

"Well, one lug endowed a foundation to help writers give of the best that's in them." Leaving the other Mock Turtles cliffhanging, I downed my postponed drink. "So this rich but honest innocent handed a chunk of moolah to Li Po, with directions to retire to quiet rural surroundings for the purpose of putting his collected poems together. And, of course, Li rounded up some pals and blew the donation on the most spacious drunk of his distinguished career as a soak. Another would-be Maecenas decided that a good home environment—meaning gotrocks' own wigwam—would bring out the beauty spots in Frank Villon's soul; but you can guess what happened to the family silver then."

This was the moment I'd been working up to, and I

whisked a tablet out of an inside cape pocket, "With your joy in mind, I've incorporated these dilemmas in the ensuing dactyls."

Weep for the wealthy possessor of literate yearnings
Anxious to squander a quantum of boodle on bards,
Eager to forfeit a mite of his mountainous earnings
Just for the pleasure of meting a metrist the cards
Needed for buttering tablature reams
Gently with dulcet and elegant themes;
Weep!

Mark Martial had discovered of certain disillusioned patrons that they'd had a more prissy concept of poetry than some they'd sought to benefit. Incorporated in my next stanza, too, was the fact that they'd been shocked by the discrepancy between their soft drink concept of what it took to make a poet and the hard liquor reality.

Wince for the evil eruptions from heavenly talents
Shamelessly flaunted by miscreant shapers of verse:
Lecherous belchers of lines that a sorcerous balance
Renders harmonious, making the treachery worse—
Chaucers and Hafizes choosing to bawl
Matters they shouldn't have known of at all;
Wince!

Wail for the chasm dividing desire from the frightful
Fumblings of fate as betrayed by the docket of fact;
Velveteen palpable poets supplanted by blightful
Roarers, but makers in merest creational act—
Jonsons and Villons and kindred gossoons,
Dueling bravos and filchers of spoons;
Wail!

Woe for a world where a poet a patron can stomach
Scribbles as ill as the ways of a qualified cat:
Brawler in taverns or swiller, collapsed to a hummock,

Scraped from the floor and deported to bed like a brat–
Marlowes and Li Pos, disdainful of grace
Crowning the metrically vacuous case;
Woe!

Everybody laughed except Anton "Snowshoe" Chekov, "Poetry wouldn't have satisfied that seagull I found in Uncle Vanya's cherry orchard," he groused. "If he'd ever convinced himself that self expression was worth the effort, that deep bird would have written nothing but good heartbreaking prose, for he grasped the bitter realities of life."

"Then you don't go along with er—" Barnacle Jim was thumbing through his notes. "Then you disagree with the buoyant dictum of William Henley, who unequivocally states that 'Life is good and joy runs high?'"

"The hound that thrives on life instead of being remorselessly destroyed by it," Snowshoe pointed out, above the brisk death rattle of the stalk of caviar-loaded celery he was crunching, "is fresh out of soul. Pass the pickled penguin and gamble a guess as to how that un-Bohemian crashed the gate of our rendez-vous."

He had a right to ask, because no mock turtle had limped through the door. As rugged as a rampike, he wore clothes which looked like they'd been bought at the fire sale held after Gunnar was smoke-cured by a gang of swine. Most battered of all, though, was the harp he unslung from one shoulder.

"I'll ask the favor of your silence," he rasped at a staring crowd of Magpie's Nesters, "while I, Torna sing of what Enmerkar of Erech has just won, north over the roof of the world at Aratta."

"If you're seeing this, too," Hal Heine whispered, "I'm going to sue you for trespassing on my nightmare, It."

Returning from a kitchen visit at this point, the Mauve Gryphon's owner was shocked to find a weathered rooster in his haven for dickey birds. "Hey, hobo, you can't peddle your yowls in—An, save me!"

He had put a hand on Torna that nearly served to open his own bread-basket, for the old chord striker had found a knife he was just too late to rip more than air with. "Stay wide of me, skunk tick," he told a man who'd just won the backward broad jump championship of Sumer, "while I sing of the bucko of a prince the others are glad to honor."

But many there had jumped up, screeching in support of the host; and the poet now saw the pastel puts he'd hoped to entertain with cardinal colors. "As Niall rows where gales rattle reeds at Skeleton's Ford, and as Eormanric rides where Loki's fish-cold daughter is mistress, it isn't either of *my* lords that I walked five hundred miles to sing of—to a herd of barrows too eentsy to miss their stones."

That flare-up finished the fire, though, in an old man who had found himself where his values were as sulk as sugar at a fat people's convention. Hanging his harp on one shoulder, he turned to leave. This that all there watched I did, too, plus a sight exclusively mine. For Lalage's fetch walked a few paces beside Torna before vanishing; and I knew I could not let him limp away alone and comforted of none.

"*I* want to hear the deeds of Enmerkar at Aratta, man of the Road!"

Knowing I'd just tipped myself the black spot as chief of the Mock Turtles, I pitched enough to pay for my share of the booze and food on the table and sprang to join a bard I led to the water front, because its out-reaching vitality stood at the far end of the local gamut from Bohemian bean bag games. "Tell me how you got to Sumer," I invited, when ale steins were in our fists.

"Well, when the Morrigan took nine-hostage Niall, I jumped to England; and what do you think a George—which was their word for king—wanted me to sing about?"

"Birds!" he roared, when I shook my head. "And I don't mean ravens or kites, that have a decent place in battlesong, but tweet-tweet birds with soulful gizzards." After a long pull at his ale, the poet dug farther into revolting memories. "'Can't you get a cloud to leak something about its habits?' one of these kings asked."

"'My name's Torna, not Thor,' I said, which would have earned me a laugh anywhere else in the Western Isles, but this George got sore. 'I don't want any cracks about clouds,' he yelped, 'or mountains, winds, torrents, butterflies, autumn, mist, meres of the Epipsychidion.' What the Kur do you reckon that is, It?"

"That puzzled me, too, for a while," I owned. "But it turned out to be the sympathy Shelley wanted to show a babe who'd been pitied by Romantic poets before and didn't want it to happen again without benefit of clergy. Did this George fire you?"

"Aye, but it was a relief to pull out of his court and take up with Eormanric, the Goth, who was dangerous as the Fenris Wolf but didn't expect me to sing through my hat; so I got along swell with him until he did the Dutch to keep from eating the crow Attila the Hun was cooking for him."

There was a guy at a nearby table that seemed to be following everything Torna said. Thinking it would please the old man to enlarge his audience, I signaled for a fellow to join us who introduced himself as Tusitala Stevenson.

"Proceed with your metric vagabondage," this likable lad urged; and the scop cheerfully complied.

"After Eormanric died, I had no special prince; I just barnstormed. Alexander was a good prince to sing for, except that he couldn't hold his liquor and was poison when potted. Sober, he liked the same kind of poetry Niall and Eormanric did, though, and he had a scroll of it about warring for a town named Troy which I wouldn't mind having made myself. But after Alexander died of D.T.s, there sprang up a fad of singing about sheepkeepers."

Even a swig of ale couldn't keep the old boy from looking sour at that memory. "It was started by Theocritus, though no harm would have come of it if he'd copyrighted the slop. But it was pirated by dozens of baa-baa singers; and when I dodged to Rome, the sheep dip had spread there. Virgil called his cackle about woolies Eclogues, but he wasn't fooling anybody else in the trade."

"And with the Mantuan furnishing the lure of a distinguished example," Tusitala prompted, "I imagine others took it up."

"It spread like the crod or Christianity," Torna nodded. "Things got so bad that I couldn't check in at any court in Europe without finding that the favorite skald was a woofer about sheep tenders and the mawks they tumbled in the hay with."

"How'd you take it," I wanted to know, "when you got back to England and found that 'shepherd' was what they called any poet?"

"Ned Spenser was responsible for that guff." Yet the bard of Niall and Eormanric was now chuckling. "The only shitepoke that dirtynamed me as shepherd swore off when I opened his brisket to let his bad manners out. But as improving the environment turned out to be against the law there, I lammed for Iberia, where a boy whose name I can't give you at the moment was writing about a tall lad called the Cid."

Torna drained his stein and reached for the full one Stevenson had ordered for him. "Well, this fellow had the only good subject on tap there, which was why I was glad to hike for Asia when word blew from there of a king of Erech who recognized his responsibilities to poets and ravens."

At that Tusitala surprised me by taking over as master of ceremonies. "Torna of Erin, known as Widsmith in parts nearer to these, will sing to you, men of river and sea, of our Enmerkar's latest campaign on Ininni's behalf."

Harp in hand the old man took thc floor, and in a water front den he got the glad attention missed at the Mauve Gryphon. His voice wasn't in much better shape than his music-tool, and his words rattled like a landslide. But as they tumbled down hill, they brought in view men on the march who had to lower their spears to keep from gashing the sky, as they crossed the passless, snow-thatched Caucasus range. Next they wound swiftly to the gleaming capital of a mining region, perched on the knee of a mountain overlooking the Caspian—a lake you could put several oceans in without any of them feeling crowded.

The city was Aratta, ruled by a man of two right hands who thought he was salty as Enmerkar and came within a dwarf's hangnail of being right. But the grandest prize won by the victorious prince was the increased esteem of Ininni, whom both Erech and Aratta claimed as patron deity, and who was there to watch the showdown.

The firm establishment of Erech as the number one city in her affections was the note on which the lay ended. Its author was so pleased with the warm applause and modest pence it netted him that he offered a free encore.

"Without again passing the hat, I'd like to tell good fellows about a deed of Ininni's learned while I was passing through Hittite-land. Like Babylonians the Hittites worship her under the name of Ishtar, so—"

"That's right," a burly sailor said. "I don't mean that it's really right, but it's the crazy way foreigners think."

"They're even screwier east of here in Dilmun," another tar said. "They not only call her Lakshmi but swear the sea coughed her up."

"Lets let Torna call her what the Hittites do," Tusitala suggested. "As long as we understand she's really Ininni, what difference does the goofing of gumps from other countries make?"

"You've got something there, professor," a seaman allowed; and the scop proceeded to chant as he could.

A beast of the sea, as the Hittites tell,
Had a gust for the flavor of girls
As pretty as pictures, when painting was well,
And not the idiocy—artistry's knell—
Smeared by zooks with their zigzag curls.
This dragon was not depraved of taste
But favored dainty designs, as graced
With truth to purpose as gems or pearls.

Although the rugged bard sang the above in his usual gravel-gaited voice, I didn't feel that it was what he had meant to spiel. For I hadn't, from him, expected digs at the do funny painters of the Magpie's Nest—which it wasn't hard for me to see as barbs aimed at the matching feebleness of the Mock Turtles. Thus stung, I glanced at Tusitala and surprised him in the act of gazing at Torna hypnotically. Catching my notice of him in this attitude, my new acquaintance turned to peer toward the river instead. Relieved of the pressure which had been imposed on him, Torna sang in his own natural vein again.

But Ishtar, the instant to war on bane,
Stormed when learning of beauty's abuse;
She stooped from her star to the Hittite main
To harpoon a brute with a twisted brain,
Mangling maidens for gourmandic use
That ought to be valued on valid grounds
While bed springs tweeked ecstatic sounds
And shouldn't be treated as charlotterusse.

As those were manly sentiments I could concur with, I nodded while lifting my pot of stingo. And I did so again, when noting that Ininni's rescue of nearly devoured loveliness was an exploit for which Ovid's Perseus, Ariosto's Rogero and An knows who's St. George would later receive the credit.

She pounced on a beast about to reap,
From a rock where his bonne bouche was staked,
A lass that was chosen by lot to keep
The bastritch from sifting a human heap
Till his thirst for an oomph girl was slaked.
But just as his jaws commenced to drool
For fainting charms in a sob-fed pool,
His back by the keel of a ship was raked.

The squawk of the dragon resounded in Kur
Where Erishkegal said to her knight,
"Our pet's in a bind, and his woe is her."
And Nergal allowed, "She's a cockleburr
Evil shouldn't be challenged to fight.
But An is the Lord, and he was wowed
By winsome ways, or by fierceness cowed;
So double's the strength of the Lady of Light."

As the monster's backers had tossed in the towel, the rest of the fight could be guessed. Outraged by having his spine ruffed by Belle of Heaven's keel—which was, as I recalled, really a centerboard—the sea dragon reared up to pluck the craft from the air, opening his mouth the while. So when Ninshubur jibed the yatch he had also lofted by shifting her fins, Ishtar was in the right position to plunge her harpoon down a throat without an appetite for oomph girls thereafter.

Still, if the wind had fluked, the Belle could have been battered down, and the winners would have been Nergal and Erishkegal. All of us were therefore proud of Ininni for taking the chance she did, and everybody wanted to buy Torna a drink for spinning an adventure of hers that hadn't been known in Sumer before.

"Speaking of salt water coups,"Stevenson said, "while Enmerkar has been praised for campaigns ashore, he hasn't been awarded deserved kudos for fathering a merchant marine which has reformed the city's liars."

As sea-going activities had been as out of favor with Mock Turtles as military ones, I hadn't until that day given the trading fleet dead fish notice. "Tell me about that," I suggested.

"They've straightened up, because their best efforts can't match the real news from lands to west and east of us that hadn't been so much as rumors until Enmerkar sent his captains forth." Tusitala smilingly nodded at Rona, whom the combination of ale and a hard day's march had lulled asleep. "While he's dozing, wouldn't you like to visit a ship bound for Dilmun, come dawn?"

"A superb idea," I said, or my load of malt did.

Anyhow I soon met a mariner who was as cordial as a Congressman to a pork barrel. As he gave me a drink, I have no recollection of the Oriental curios he doubtless exhibited. All I do remember is trying to steady myself by stretching a hand toward a wall of his cabin; and as it was farther away than I'd judged, I flopped to the floor. Consciousness was failing me, but I still had enough left when rolling over to stare at faces to find one was known of old.

"I borrowed Tusitala's semblance," Nebo explained. Then he prodded me with a foot. "If you survive it, slug, going down to the sea in this particular ship will wring the dilettante out of you."

I managed one more realization before blacking out, Ininni was a party to my shanghaiing, as she must have been the one that sent Lalage's fetch to the Mauve Gryphon.

The Rescued Whale Tenant

The mate of the ship was skilled at what professors know as explicating a state of affairs. "When, like now, the wind quits blowing, anybody who doesn't like swinging an oar gets a chance to swim wherever he wants to."

As the breeze had deserted *Sumerian Queen*'s big square sail where several shark fins were slicing waves, I nodded comprehension, "Count on me to stay with you, though candor asks me to own that I'm not good at rowing."

The man's persuasive powers would have topped those of Edmund Burke, "Unless our friendship is to end within the hour, get good," he coaxed.

Learning to handle a sweep while recovering from the effects of a mickey kept me from feeling sociable that day, but on the following one I felt well enough to beef about my blistered palms and sun-scorched back to my oar mate, Luis "Trincafortes" Camoens. "To think," I then groused, "that when I was a tadpole, I wished I'd the nerve to wiggle to sea in search of jolly times."

I could spare breath for talking, as the stiff wind which was then heeling the ship put oat play out of order. My partner gazed at the waves bobbing along the lee rail before turning his port eye, which was the only one that let light in or out of him, my way.

"It's better to ship out when you're old enough to write about the drink, which is the only theme you'll find worth while, once you've got salt in your pores."

"Yeah, and you'd better be gull's eye accurate," a handler of the sweep in front of ours said, "For if you make one little blooper you'll get letters from fifty old tars accusing you of learning about deep water from the marines." Then he turned to give me a friendly nod. "I'm H.B., which stands for Homeros Beta to everybody but the clucks that insist I'm Alpha, too."

"I'm tagged It." While so saying, I rubbed a shoulder in a try to ease sore muscles but only succeeded in making sunburn madder than it was. "Do you feel that a writer should have to go through the drudgery of being an adventurer himself?"

Before H.B. could answer, his oar-mate spoke up. "I'm Mike Cervantes, It, and the way I feel is that the marks—I mean the fans—have a right to expect the author to be described in jacket copy as the kind of petrel an interesting book could pop out of. And it's wiser for the joe to supply the meat of honest poop; because if he doesn't, some publisher's flack will dish up a hashish dream that even a buyer of Erech Bridge wouldn't believe."

"Right," Camoens cut in. "Take that corn about Lucretius bumping himself off because his wife slipped him a love cocktail which gave him the willies. Any lad who's had a hangover worth remembering knows that you're in no shape to master the intricacies of a hangman's knot then. As for shooting yourself with the shakes, a man couldn't hoist a gun dependably in line with his ticker, even with the aid of a bar rag draped over his shoulder."

"You, too, have suffered," H.B. analyzed. "But to get back to publishers' puffs, how about the eagle that one of them said had mistaken the bald bean of Aeschylus for a rock and dropped a tortoise on it, to crack the shell and make the meat available? Birds were never a problem for writers before, but since then one with an unthatched dome hasn't dared stroll where bald eagles—Linnaeus named the species that after the one supposed to have knocked over Aeschylus—are likely to be met, unless he's wearing the hard hat he never used to need."

"Worst of all," Cervantes said, "was the fable cooked up about Shakespeare and some brunette." A wave washed inboard a seahorse which gave a grateful neigh when Mike handed it back to the ocean. "I admit Bill made it hard for the promotion boys by keeping what he was up to during certain years in the decent obscurity belonging to privy parts, but—"

"But that doesn't excuse somebody on his publisher's payroll that invented a hot flash for him and sonneted the tramp in his name," Camoens filled in. "Bill was the original clam about his love life; the one writer with sense enough never to tell where the body was buried; and they had to stick him with one of those cheap horn blowings where the guy tells ALL, whether he actually got to first base or not."

For a moment I wished I'd thought of saying as much to a mynah bird that had sniped at me with one of the same phony bullets; but H.B.'s next remark switched my mind down a different track. "Alpha's publisher thought a pathetic gimmick would grab the readers and bleated he was blind as a mountain oyster; so I had to be, too."

"That's not as bad as the caramel candy wished on Dante, of all hard cases." Cervantes could hardly make his point for laughing. "A fl-flack had him g-gooey about Beatrice when she was n-nine years old—an age when nobody but doting parents and starving lions can find any brat appealing."

"What did they do to you, Trinc?" I asked.

"Their publicity gink should have been a dime novelist." A bit of wind caught and flapped the patch over his right eye, as Camoens wagged his head. "He discovered Portugal's princess royal had a crush on me and transferred to her poems of mine written to dishes I'd actually dated. Then when I was in India he fixed me up with a beautiful Chinese slave girl; and if you think she was anything less than a kidnapped cousin of China's emperor, you underestimate the promotional mind. Anyhow that dream killed my chances with the real girl I'd left behind me, who slammed the door when she was once more before me."

Trinc brooded a moment prior to saying one more thing. "I wish some of that imaginative talent had been invested in thinking of ways of selling my books."

That pumped a guffaw out of Mike Cervantes. "When the first part of *Don Quixote* was supposed to go on sale in Madrid, my publisher threw a combination cocktail and autographing party in the Palacio Real, the idea being that if the guests got loaded enough, they could be talked into buying D.Q."

"By An, that's more mercantile gumption than I thought any publisher could muster!" Trinc's face showed he really was impressed. "How many copies did the drunks walk off with?"

"One, and if I hadn't been a little canned, I'd have skipped planting my John Hancock on that." Mike waved his maimed south paw, which he seemed not to have owed to writer's cramp. "The first customer objected, on finding that I'd sprawled my signature on Fed Dostoyevsky's *House of Death*. It turned out that Fed was supposed to be the literary idol of the moment and that D.Q. wasn't scheduled to be released for another two weeks."

"At least your publisher recognized that you and Fed were two separate people," Homeros Beta pointed out. "Now I'm not claiming that I'm better than Alpha, nor am I bowing to him; what I *am* saying is that we have different outlooks and strengths. He was a ruggeder character, and a sharper hand at humor, while I— Well, I'll sum it this way: I could never have created Nestor, that grand comic figure, and Alpha never could have shaped my delightful Nasicaa. Yet my publisher always tried to—"

"The wind's dying, so oars will again be swinging," the mate here raised his voice to predict; and, unwilling to spoil his record of always being right, I helped Camoens unship our sweep.

By the time my blisters were callouses and my sunburn a tan, I was enjoying rough work in good company. But I never got to drink with fine fellows in Dilmun because a week short of there a water spout hoisted our ship. Not built to balance on a walking salt water geyser, *Sumerian Queen* broke in two. As to where Trinc, H.B. and Mike surfaced after the crash, I can only say that I saw none of them while floundering in search of wreckage large enough to buoy me.

About to settle for a barrel holding some sort of stores, I spied the captain's gig bobbing unoccupied some rods away. With wind and waves operating to push it from me, overhauling it was slow work, complicated by confrontation with a mermaid.

I had met none during my tour of the Goof Stream, but when I turned to see what was tickling my left foot, I found a lovely specimen laughing at me. "What's your hurry, handsome?" she demanded.

I couldn't remember with clarity. Glancing toward the little rowboat, drifting farther away while I trod water, I felt it was somehow important to me. Yet when I looked again at water foaming about bare shoulders, it seemed ridiculous to prefer a wooden piece of flotsam.

"Have you anything on? I mean in the way of social engagements," I amended my question. Only by that time I wasn't talking just to her, for another sea-belle had slithered from aquamarine depths. "Ready is the word for me, but how do you go about it here?" I asked my newer acquaintance.

"You keep out of these waters, Sappho," number one snarled. "I lamped and vamped him first."

"Yes, but you haven't got what it takes to drown a man in love, Lola M.," the second said. "But if you'll get out of the way and watch my technique, you may be able to pick up some tricks that'll enable you to pull a fellow under next time."

"Speaking of dying in the drink," Exhibit A snapped, "as long as you took the trouble to drown yourself because Phaethon ditched you, the least you could do would be to stay true to him."

"All right, Gibraltar," Sappho came back. "How many of those five hundred degrees above fahrenheit poems of yours were written to the same slouch?"

"They never, any of them, bought their way into my bed, like that punk brother of yours, when he ransomed a strumpet in Egypt, crumpet." And with those fighting words, Lola M. reached for a fistful of hair.

As soon as they started mixing it—with flippers they used like the French do feet in *la savatte*, as well as hands—I remembered the gig and why I wanted to board it and struck out as fast as I could through a sea over which twilight had begun to settle. But I was afraid I had dallied too long until I saw the Evening Star and heard its owner's voice.

"Don't worry, darling; all mermaids aren't murderesses. So if you'll keep swimming right toward me, you'll find one holding the skiff for you."

Relaxing then, I swam to where I could see the pale gleam of a sea-belle's face with just behind it the dark blur of the little boat she was keeping from drifting out of reach.

"Here's the painter," Sappho said; and I knew it was by no accident that she had arrived to interfere with Lola M.'s deadly designs. "I fixed her so she won't be helldiving with any man until she gets over a shiner and grows back that widow's peak she thinks is so fetching," she certified my guess.

Sappho is the only mermaid I ever got to kiss, though I was too tired to make a good job of that. I barely had the strength to haul myself aboard, and as soon as I'd managed that, I stretched out and slept until Utu was well on his way the next morning.

There was hard tack and water in the gig and fresh air all around it. On this diet I lost as much dilettante blubber as Nebo could have wished. So I was feeling ready for anything when the gig was overturned by something rising roughly under it.

Dunked and finding my boat topside down in shoreless water, I made for the lolling tongue of an albino whale—probably the cause of the disaster but surely the only nonliquid item to be found—and crawled up on what I had thought only a temporary resting place. But when he closed his lips and hiccoughed, I joined men whose mumblings cast light on what was going on amid the encircling gloom. Of much to the same effect three quotes should suffice to give the general tenor.

"If Ishmael Melville could wring something tasty out of these glands and guts," one told himself, "a jasper who's read the same books he did, and, *his to boot,* ought to be able to beat his game and have a few chapters left over to furnish a running start for another classic; maybe next time about a rogue paramecium that's sworn to get square with a science prof that gave him a rough time under the microscope."

"You've got to have a symbolic rope to lasso and hogtie 'the big one,' but I'll have the critics buying *me* drinks," another said, "in place of having to shell out to buy good reviews from cauliflower heads whose literary education stopped with *Five Little Peppers and Who They'd Screw:* I mean *Whom,* of course."

"If I can just find one theme I can relate to all humanity, I'd have it made," the third mooned. "Joyce chose Hubbard squash and renamed it Ulysses after General Grant, but there must be plenty of other rubbish that'll serve just as well."

In the course of being digested by the whale I became a muttering monster hunter myself. "There's bound to be one bijou of a concept that I can turn into such a literary mountain that even Lalage's damned mynah bird will be impressed."

By that time on the threshold of the pylorus, I found that countless others were already engaged as I yearned to be. For gazing down the long intestinal hall before me, I saw that it was lined with desks at which sat wranglers of stylus and clay, brush and parchment, or typewriter and paper; and as they jabbed, painted or pecked, the authors were mumbling in chorus; "All you need is a key notion, and you can do the rest standing on your head."

As hypnotized by the hope of a razzle-dazzle book formula as any there, I would have undoubtedly become one of will o' wisp's destroyed dupes. But as I lifted my foot to cross the pyloric sill, a hand fell heavily upon my shoulder and jerked me back.

"Come on, trouble!" Ninshubur grated. "She sent me to get you, and you're going to be got."

"But whales!" I expostulated.

"There have only been three identifiable ones—St. Brendan's Jalisco, Moby Dick here and Jonah's that he likely gave a name only the Bible expurgated it—which is all that literature can afford."

Without symbolism to serve as rose-colored glasses, the inner workings of a whale failed to pass inspection. Suddenly not feeling well, I gulped.

"Let's go, Nin, if you know the password that will win us free of where I never belonged."

It developed that he knew an even surer method of arranging our exit. At the far end of the gullet Ninshubur hopped up; and when he came down with both feet, we got service which was extended to all in the whale forward of the intestines.

The others started swimming back to their happy balenic home as soon as they hit the sea, but I knew what my goal was while I was still tumbling through the air. For I had seen four swans which didn't seem to have changed a feather since they had nick-of-timed me away from Tim O'Lucian's bar, back before I had so much as met Nebo. In the driver's seat by the time I had climbed aboard, Ninshubur clucked to them, and won from the team the usual cheerful response.

"They're good birds," I said, when they had finished spiraling upward and were flying east, "but what became of *Belle of Heaven?*"

"Oh, that was a Sumerian concept of how she got around, but now we've got to keep up with the notions of other people."

I goggled at him. "You mean to say that there *are* other people?"

"Golly, you were in the gut of that sperm a long while!" But after so exclaiming, Ninshubur began to dribble bits of information. "When the Sumerians had worn themselves out, with help from attacking Elamites, Gutiums and Bedouins, she was through as Ininni but found openings as Shaushga among the Hurri, and as Ishtar among both the Hittites and Akkadians, who had set up civilized shop, with Babylon for capital. Then the Syrians got religion, and it created problems for her.

"You never brushed against any mermaids during your tour of the Goof Stream, because they didn't exist in Sumerian times," he next explained a mystery. "But some of the coastal Syrian cities that wanted her to become their goddess of love and whatever else she might care to supervise hankered for a mixed land and salt water deitess; so as Atargatis she became the original sea belle, It, and of course, could have briny girls created in her image. Ninshubur shrugged. "There were some people that didn't like the idea of a strain of fish in their goddess of love and, to accommodate them, she merely changed her name to Astarte and carried on business as usual."

I nodded although by then puzzling over a point of personal interest. "How the Nergal, or whoever has taken his place now that Sumer's up the flue, did you guess I was in that blasted whale?"

"By looking in all the likely places and falling back on E.A. Poe's theory of inductive reasoning." There was a pause while we both watched a dove of peace chase a hen and accomplish its mission. "I've sometimes wondered if Linnaeus spelled that name right," Ninshubur commented. "But to get back to inductive reasoning, you weren't outside the varmint, so you were bound to be in it. And I had to keep looking, because she wanted you found."

Thinking how near I'd come to being irretrievable, I shuddered. "I'm sure glad you kept trailing me, chum, but you haven't said why she was anxious about me at this particular time."

Instead of answering he pointed ahead. "There's a spot on the map of both of our pasts which I'd like you to look over."

Realizing the river in front of us must be the Euphrates, I began to look for other familiarities; for although I'd just been told that Sumer was a drained barrel, the implications of the message hadn't reached me. "Landmarks say we should be near Erech, but I don't see it," I complained.

"We're right over it," Ninshubur said.

Below us was a great mound of sand, from which the hulls of ruined buildings here and there protruded. In place of a water front crowded with shipping, there was a fen which looked to be teeming with frogs. Covered with scraggly brush were the sites of extensive grain fields, orchards and pastures. The only signs of present life were a structure and its cluster of outhouses some miles south of what had been the world's first epic city.

"Let's see what they know at the hostel, or whatever it is," Ninshubur suggested; and as I couldn't spit out the lump in my throat, I but nodded. For it wasn't the fiddler crabs of the Mauve Gryphon that I was harking back to; rather the place Ininni had picked as her headquarters, and the great adventure of sailing thence to prod the Second World awake—that marvelous exploit in which I had taken part and was yet to learn how to chronicle.

After steering the car to a river bank point in front of the inn, Ninshubur released the swans so they could browse. Then we strolled toward the building and its superimposed sign: "The Caravanserai, O.K., Proprietor." Evidently the landlord wasn't counting on a dry clientele, for suspended from his shingle was a plaque charged with this quatrain:

The taproom entered, do the generous thing
Nor fly upon a tightwad's single wing;
For, bird, the Cat of Time can close the bar
Before you're ever full enough to sing.

Action in the Critical Woods

True to the boniface's expectations, we did advance upon the mahogany, behind which was not only O.K. himself but another framed four-liner. This, however, proffered local history rather than advice:

When gay Ininni brashly harrowed Hell,
The wall between the dead and living fell;
So when she flung Dumuzi to the fiends,
Returning canceled his despairing yell.

"That's a little allegorical," O.K. admitted, "because actually she sicked the gallas on him up here, and they shagged him down yonder to Kur, as it was called then."

"Dumuzi was after my time," I told him, "as I left while Enmerkar was still on the throne. Why did she feel like steeping him in death for a spell?"

"Oh, they used to say that the gent who hasn't been to Hell hasn't enough flavor to interest a girl. The usual?"

"Sure," Ninshubur said. "What is it?"

"It always used to be Bourbon and ditch water, but there haven't been any ditches since Erech was wrecked and all the farms hereabouts folded up, so we scoop it out of the Euphrates and don't charge extra for any minnows or tadpoles that might be caught in the middle." O.K. put a bottle, a pitcher and two glasses in front of us. "Drink hearty."

"That's good whiskey, by—" Pausing there, I looked at Ninshubur enquiringly. "You've told me how she adjusted when Sumer crashed, but how did the other gods ride with the punch? I suppose that An is still the one to swear by, but I'd like to be sure."

"His case history is a sad one, It. You see, when Babylonia rose after Sumer sagged, the Babs changed An's name to Anu and let him know they were willing to call him the head of Heaven as long as he didn't try to raise his voice above that of Marduk, a pet god of theirs."

"Oh well," I said. "Presidents of the USAL get used to stepping down—although I suppose it hurts their feelings to find nobody thinks they're worth shooting any more. But you never hear them complain."

"It would have been well for An if he'd had their philosophy." Ninshubur slugged his highball. "Unwilling to play second fiddle in the Akkadian Heaven, he stormed out of it and into that of the Hittites, set on pulling the rank he didn't have on Kuwarbis."

"I don't know him yet, Nin."

"Well, the Hittite gods were mostly a decent lot, but they'd been bulldozed by this Hurrian, as he originally was, who was strictly bad medicine and had bought his way to the top without asking the Marquess of Queensbury what the rules were." Ninshubur drank up and mixed himself another. "To cut a painful story short, when the god we knew and respected tried to come it over this tough, they tangled, with the result that Kuwarbis bit Anu's testicles off, and swallowed 'em, too."

"Divinity's a chillier field than science," I said, when I'd thought that information over. "What happened to An's son, Enlil?"

"He switched to the Hittite Heaven, too; but after what had happened to his dad, he can't be blamed for tiptoeing; so Kuwarbis let him stay."

"Gods whose worshipping nations go under don't have it easy, do they?" After moodily sipping my Bourbon, I asked what I was half afraid to. "What about Nebo?"

"Except that they gave him a wife named Tashmit and insisted on pronouncing his name 'Nabu,' there was no change in old Neb's fortunes, It. Nor in Enki's, only they called him 'Ea' for reasons that might be clearer to me, if I were an Akkadi—"

He quit talking, because O.K. had turned on his bar's TV: "The rising of Aphrodite from the Aegean is covered by special correspondent Lucius Apuleius," the announcer said, "who interviewed the new Hellenic goddess on the salt water spot. Come in, Apuleius."

Lucius gave the usual buildup, beginning with the founding of Olympus and involving sketches of all the entrenched gods the new feminine recruit was expected to join. But finally, as dolphins ecstatically frolicked nearby, a lovely head popped from waves which knew better than disturb a newly set hairdo. As Ninshubur had traced her progress only as far as her tours as Shaushga, Ishtar, Atargatis and Astarte, I hadn't been prepared to find in "Aphrodite" any one known to me. Yet as I gazed at the screen, the face that always reminded me somewhat of Lalage's let me know that this new carnation was what she had wanted me to be aware of, and had sent Ninshubur to winnow the globe for me accordingly.

While that realization was dawning, Ininni's drapeless figure followed her features out of sea depths matching eyes whose lids fluttered at the knot of gods gathered to watch her arrival. Then she timidly discovered the waiting pink and white cockleshell, aboard which she stepped.

With a veteran correspondent's aplomb, Apuleius flung about her a filmy negligee, and from his own deftly maneuvered float commenced the ensuing exchange:

APULEIUS: "I'm sure I'm speaking for all here when I say you look like a million talents. Would you be good enough to make a statement covering your reactions to your appointment as the Greek goddess of love?"

APHRODITE: "I was simply overwhelmed when I found

that I had been selected, and I want everybody here to know that I'm as proud as I can be, clear down to my littlest toes."

APULEIUS: "And charming littlest toes they are. Now do you plan to make Olympus your regular place of residence?"

APHRODITE: "Oh, *yes!* Back when I was a teensy girl in pigtails, or long before Cronus made all this possible, by amputating the penis of *poor* Uranus, I used to dream of living there, but I never thought it would truly happen."

APULEIUS: "Well, hitching your wagon to a star takes hope for harness; and speaking of transportation, how do you expect to commute between Earth and Heaven?"

APHRODITE: "Being a sissy, I'm scared to death of boats, and horses, like Helios drives, so I've arranged to be drawn by swans, which are so quiet and gentle that I can identify with them."

APULEIUS: "With apologies to Bobbie Burns, if he's on the line, a swan ungentle could not be the swan of Aphrodite. To conclude this interview, would you briefly describe your program as a Greek goddess."

APHRODITE: "Lucius, if you don't mind my calling you that, my ambition is to add something new, and sincerely my own, to the life style of Olympus."

From time to time during the quoted chat, Ninshubur and I had been glancing at each other, dead of pan, but her closing words cracked us up. "Zeus and his crowd looked like they were really falling for that 'sweet young thing' line." Then I shook my head. "I don't see how Mummu could have turned out anything as far fetched as she is."

"Why don't you ask Nebo, or Nabu rather, about that?" Ninshubur wanted to know. "I've got a hunch you'll be hearing from him soon."

"As he's shown no interest in me since the last time I saw Erech, what makes you say that?"

My friend's shoulders hunched. "She wanted you here, so I moved you here, but that's all I could do; and somebody's got to show you how the Road runs when you leave the Caravanserai."

A barkeep named Saki having shown up, O.K. was free to show us where souvenirs of Erech were available for inspection and purchase.

"Most that come here wouldn't know a back scratcher from a croupier's rake, if I didn't coach them," the landlord said, "but as you're an Erech old timer, I may have some things in my combination museum and store which will mean more to you than stuff to impress people with the idea that you're a traveled sage."

While talking he was pulling out a drawer and finding a bladeless knife. "You remember Lugalbanda, that was Enmerkar's trouble shooter, who later wore his crown?"

"Yeah, Gilgamesh's father," Ninshubur said. "He was the one that carried a message to Ininni that Enmerkar was in a tight military spot; and, as I remember it, the good old boy made the run through wild mountain country all alone."

"So Ininni rushed the relief force that lifted the siege," O.K. nodded. "Well, this is the haft of the dagger he had with him then, but I can't let you have it, because I promised Walter Scott I'd give him dibs on any weapon of Lugalbanda's, or of Gilgamesh, some of whose trophies are on display there."

He motioned toward a showcase then being examined by a woman trying to enrapture her small boy with ancient history. "This is very educational, dear. It says that this big tooth belonged to Khumbaba, who was even bigger than the giant Tom Hickathrift killed."

"You mean," the kid shrieked, "the one Tom stabbed in the butt with the sword the king give him?"

"Had given him, dear. And please say *'derriere'* like the polite French do, in public at least. But I meant that Khumbaba was huger than even the monstrous one that Tom beat in a perfectly fair fight on his way to Wisbeach. And when the brave Gilgamesh had killed the horrid giant, he brought this tusk back so people could judge how big and terrible the brute really was. Look, dear."

"I will if I can have a hunk of jelly-roll right after," a promising extortionist screeched.

When they had left, so he could collect the specified pay-off, I examined what was in truth a formidable fang. I also read lines which told that its famous extractor had himself met defeat:

> *When Gilgamesh was hopeful to achieve*
> *The murder of mortality and leave*
> *All men removed from time as gods and stars,*
> *Ininni nixed the goal he would achieve.*

I read it twice before I was convinced it meant she had deliberately foiled the hero's try to stamp out death for Lalage and me. "How about that, Nin?" I asked, while impeaching the quatrain with a shocked finger. "Why would she have connived against life?"

"Because she was seeing the big picture, boy, and working for poetry, as always. Look; if they'd had tickets to eternity, what in Hades would all those virgins that Bob Herrick was trying to spook into coming across have cared when he fed them that 'Gather ye rosebuds while ye may' line?"

"You've a valid point there," I acknowledged.

"You mean she was thinking straight," he corrected me. "And how could Callimachus have written that grand elegy that opened with 'They told me, Heraclitus, they told me you were dead,' if everybody had life insurance that really insured life?"

"Point carried," I yielded.

"Now let's move up to epic," Ninshubur persisted. "What's the most powerful passage in the one about Gilgamesh himself?"

"Where Gil tries to bail Enkidu out of Kur, and finds death didn't issue his chum round-trip shuttle service back to life; and before you hit me with any specimen of stage tragedy, I'll grant it couldn't have existed, if she'd allowed the mortal dogs to be called off."

"Just remember her thinking is never orthodox but always on target," Ninshubur wound up his argument, "What have you got there, O.K.?"

"Something I found in the ruins of a waterfront bar and had reconditioned." The innkeeper took from a closet a triangular object lapped in a gazelle hide carrying case. "I figure some admired old poet must have died there and this was saved in his honor. Anyhow I thought it might be of interest to you holdovers from Enmerkar's day."

The thing turned out to be a harp built for carrying, not the concert hall. Like something in a dream, the instrument was familiar without telling me why. I was still groping for grounds warranting my warm feeling for it when a customer who'd just entered spoke up.

"Name your price and I'll pay it; for that's what I need to add a pre-Tin Pan Alley twang to the Harmony Hoodlums, as my band of sharp flatters is known." Undertaking to thrust a possessive hand between myself and O.K., the music master touched wood which resented the familiarity.

"Take your hands off me, sour milk!" the accents of Torna snarled. "I wasn't made to be fingered by a sub-grub."

Backing off as a buyer, the fellow became a claimant for damages. "This is a public place, and I've been subjected to defamation in it," he told the landlord. "Will you give me to understand what you mean to do about it?"

"Right on the button!" cheered the harp, when the galoot had been served as requested. O.K., on his part, commented on the upshot in his private fashion:

A moving mauley strikes, and having hit
An absentee of manners as of wit,
The noisy nuisance issues from a door
More circumspect than when he'd darkened it.

I, however, was by then looking from a harp I itched to own to the highway between the Caravanserai and the river. Footed either north or south, it stood for my next stretch of wayfaring; but though eager to be on the go, there was a question to be put before I could again follow the Road; and I risked placing a hand on the harp.

"Would you go with a hoper of no present standing?"

"By Angus of the Boyne, yes!" it rumbled. "You were Torna's friend, which is to say mine, when nobody else was."

I didn't think about how ownership would be transferred to me; that I took to be an inevitability. "I'll take him with me to sing of how she sailed in Belle of Heaven when the old world was dead and the young one not yet born," I told O.K. "Not that I have the science for handling a theme like that yet."

"Being a narrative poet is like putting on the right act as an eel or an oyster; you learn by doing." But Ninshubur's look as he said that told me that this was what Aphrodite now wished. "So long until the next drink, It," he then added.

He had turned to haggle with O.K. for the price of the harp, which growled, "Let's go," when I stuffed him back in his case.

My new companion felt good, riding my left shoulder, but I was still uncertain of my way, as I stepped out under scudding clouds. Northward lay the corpse of Erech, but to the south the way was prowled by what looked more like a wolf than a stray dog. In the absence of hippopotamus-murdered Vinegaroon, I didn't want any part of it, and struck upriver accordingly.

That lobo failed to make me happy by choosing to follow me; for I could feel him trotting up my spine, as I trudged toward ghosts I'd just as soon not rub against. And hardly more comforting was the figure in black I found seated in the wreckage of what had been Erech's great river-fronting gate. For though the hump of a harp was peeping over his shoulder, he looked like he'd been carved out of a Hallow-e'en night.

Still his tone was friendly enough when he looked up from reading matter. "Is that your wolf, or mine that I hadn't expected to meet short of woods that are supposed to flourish hereabouts?"

"Maybe this is the one; and if so, you're surely welcome to him. I'm not entitled to a wolf or any other claim to recognition as yet."

"For a writer that isn't always bad luck. Having just picked up mail forwarded from the old home town via the Caravanserai, I've examined some recognition I'd willingly transfer to you if I could." Laughing like a skeleton's finger bone grating against slate, he handed me the ensuing message:

> *Whereas it was duly motioned, seconded and passed that D. Alighieri should be given a fair and impartial trial in absentia, he was given such a trial, with the result that he was sentenced to be hanged if caught alive or dead anywhere near our fair and impartial city.*
>
> *Snelf the Guelph*
> *Executive Secretary*
> *The Florentine Vigilantes*

"They sound as tough as the ring-leaders of the New Stonehenge Faculty Club, when a member's let a rat out of the bag," I sympathized.

"Yes, but I've taken out anti-gallows insurance which I count on being effective as long as I stay on the lam." Stuffing his mail in his harp case, the outlaw rose and shouldered the instrument. "But there will be no squirming out from under, when *I* pass judgment on *them* and dish out sentences compared to which hanging's a mint julep. Are you acquainted enough with these parts to know where she made her pacesetting descent into the local form of the Inferno?"

As I started walking on again, I noted that the wolf was now trotting ahead. "There was in my day a vent called the Ganzir Hatch which was said to lead to Kur, but—Oh, oh, I knew those clouds weren't going to hold out on us, D."

When a desert turns on a squall it can do a good job. Wind blew us through sheet rain up the Euphrates to where the highway forked and signs told how. The one pointing along the river said "To Babylon 65 Polyglot Leagues" and the one aiming west read "To the Critical and Other Woods." I wanted to head for Babylon, as the footing was better in that direction, but a growl from the wolf sent me floundering along grass-grown wheel tracks already being followed by the wanted man from Florence.

"Now that the storm has taken its foot out of my eye,"

I told him, "I can see that this branch of the Road leads toward the Hatch of Hades that Aphrodite used when Ininni."

"And after her by Hercules and Orpheus, Theseus, Odysseus and Aeneas," Alighieri said. "My conviction is that I can do no less than follow suit."

"Good man to want to get in that line." Somehow I couldn't bring myself to pat D. on the back, fine though I liked him. "My own experience with confronting enormity was limited to braving the Goof Stream."

"An undertaking of honorable largeness," he was good enough to concede. "For if you go up against creation with the defeatist idea that it's bigger than you are, you might as well quit trying to be a real dog and join the Vigilante curs."

Woods which dusk had darkened were just ahead, and in their gloom the wolf barked with unexpected geniality. "That's his signal that he's found Virgil, able and game to guide me," D. said. "There's always room for one more in Hell, assuming you'd like to join me."

He was just airing his manners, while I was glad to have the excuse of truth when pointing out that I was committed to a different errand. Yet some minutes after he'd swerved north along a dim trail, I would have gladly swapped places with a nice warm Inferno. For then a mortally cold nose stole from behind and pressed one of my hands.

Like many another shock, this sparked understanding. "All right, Nebo-Nabu," I said, when sure fright hadn't murdered me. "Come out of it and tell me what you want."

"It's a wise writer—or in your case a scoreless pretender—who knows his own god's cast-off names."

Giving off the radiance of a watch geared for reading in the dark, a figure both new and familiar shucked the guise of a beast and rose to stand beside me. His features were handsomer and his body more athletic than I recalled, but there was no doubt as to his satiric expression or his bantering voice.

"Let me introduce you to Apollo, It; lord of prophecy and medicine, destroyer of mice—the Greeks believe in getting their money's worth in return for laying out for temples and so on—protector of groves, keeper of flocks, sender of plagues, terror of monsters and, oh yes, patron of literature."

I nodded grumpily. "I don't see how operating in any of those lines qualifies you to badger me as a wolf."

"What the Sumerians never knew about me but the Greeks did was that I was born on the island of Delos, whither lobos had carried my mother. As the wolf has since been the family totem, it was the natural form for me to adopt both for giving Alighieri his needed starting point in a dread forest and for guiding you to its annex, the Critical Woods. If you don't think you're in them, bide a wee."

He ducked out of sight then, but hoping to find a spot where it was dry and warm, I gave him no further thought. Next I tripped over a rope that was stretched across my path and sprawled, face down.

"We got one!" a rough voice chortled. "The fluke's packing a strumming thing."

Then I was jerked to my feet by wildly painted savages with human bones knotted in their hair; and for all my lack of experience I knew them to be man-eating book reviewers, capable of any brutality up to and including holding their own ignorance against you. "The water ought to be simmering now," one justified my forebodings, "so let's rush him back to camp and plunk him in while he's still alive enough to yell."

But another had had a more refined notion of cruelty. "Let's find out what he's written, and hoorah him about it while he's cooking. This gadget he totes around ought to be able to tell us."

He was taking from its case a harp that had been silent ever since being covered back in O.K.'s display room. Once it was clear of its case, though, it spoke with Torna's bold heart as well as his rusty voice:

Now we'll battle. Boldly rax
A hero's hand and snatch the axe
Of cluck that of our murder clacks.

The startled reviewer that held the harp jumped as if bitten by a boomslang and dropped the harp. But with new fight in me I caught the instrument that now told how next to proceed.

A trusty hickory at our backs,
Upheave the bit and blast the yaks
To grant them all the Reaper's pax.

So sang my ally, and so I acted. Leaping at a cannibal who thought all the initiative was his, I wrenched his tomahawk from him, split his head with it and put my back against what smelled more like a pine than a hickory. Far from finding fault on that account, however, the harp I still clutched with my port paw was gleeful.

That's the way to teach 'em facts;
Death's the best of brazen tacks
Hammered home with bloody hacks.

My rallying foes were getting ready to hack too, but at this moment Apollo appeared. "That will be all for both sides." After restoring the man I'd slain as only a god of healing could, he took the weapon away from me and gave it back to the revived savage. "You've done nothing to deserve notice yet," he said, "but she wanted you to have comprehensive knowledge of the Road, and being ganged by reviewers is essential to full scientific awareness."

"Killing one of those bastards was a real satisfaction." I patted the harp as I shoved it in its case again. "What do I do now?"

"You're not out of the Critical Woods yet." He gestured toward the trail. "Keep on, and with luck you may learn something."

A Night at Eldorado

Afraid of stumbling on another band of savages, I was cautious about nearing the firelight I finally saw ahead of me. Yet as the five men lolling about the blaze had the look of unhostile campers, I called to make myself known and crossed the intervening creek on a rickety rustic bridge.

Seeing I was shivering, a man rose to fetch me food and hot drink. Otherwise they took no notice of me, continuing with talk I didn't try to follow until I had emptied a plateful of venison and beans and was leaning back against a big log with a second half pint of strong tea in my fist.

"I'm not at all sure I understand you, Stagirite," a wearer of buckskin was saying at that moment. "Why do you contend that dredging a theme from the common trough of history promises better results than an author's reliance on his own god-given originality?"

"For one thing, I've met enough gods to understand that there's a lot of Indian-giving connected with Heaven." The speaker stopped stropping his knife on the sole of a moccasin he'd shed for that purpose and pointed the blade at his challenger. "You take a novelist that invents all his characters and situations, and what you get is a duck that's spending sixty per cent of his gun powder on explaining things to readers: who his figures are, how they skidded into the bind they're in et cetera—stuff that an author tapping history doesn't have to waste his capital on."

"So then he's theoretically able to devote all his energies to character interplay," a smoker said without taking a pipe from his mouth. "But authors tell me that history has been mighty stingy about offering themes ready-made for epic use. Can you—Who in Hades is out there, sneaking up on this camp?" he then jumped up to demand.

There was no answer from the dark in terms of words, but the sound of someone blundering through underbrush made it plain that no furtive approach was intended. Then a ragged figure staggered into the light and fell full-length between the men I'd been introduced to as Boileau and Croce.

"Water," he feebly begged. "Bourbon and water!" Yet the plea clearly drained the last of his forces; for he closed his eyes and made no further sound or movement.

"He talks rationally when conscious," the one called Lessing commented, "but we can't give him what he most needs until we reach that keg of Old Bonanza we cached at the edge of the woods. Anybody know him?"

Studying gashed and twisted features, I was only sure of who must have caught him. "His guardian angel wouldn't know him, if he's still got one," Croce said. "Those devils!"

"They must have been the kind of savages that enjoy the blood more than the meat," Boileau reasoned.

In another instant the poor fellow began to air his troubles. "They trapped me and they wouldn't either kill me or let me go. "And the friendly ones—or they said they were friendly—tortured me just as bad as the others."

"I think it must be Tasso," Apollo stepped from nowhere to remark. "I know some others who've been ruined by the so-called reconstructed cannibals that don't like a writer until they've given him fatty degeneration of the ego; but I can't think of any other author who was misused by that sort and the ones that hunt with envenomed darts, too."

"It *is* Tasso," Croce groaned. "To think we were boys

together, and I wouldn't have recognized a great man who was never allowed to get over romantic schizophrenia of the epic brain lobe and achieve what his talent entitled him to."

"Of course, he was very young when he picked the theme from a do-funny bush," Aristotle reflected, "but there in that title lay a craziness which would have shown up, if the case had ever been sifted in court. For neither the winning Christians nor the Moslems they stole it from were wanted by the thoroughly undelivered Jerusalemites, caught in the middle and clutching an honest deed to the city."

"It all comes of developing too early." Lessing looked up from tucking his folded jacket under Tasso's head. "Every young writer likes the idea of being a kid whirlwind, I'll grant, but lads shouldn't be allowed to try out for the big time. For they don't understand that all the skill in the world can't produce a legitimate masterpiece from a bastard concept—half history and half fairy tale in this case. But Torquato wouldn't have made that mistake, if he'd postponed his try to shoot the moon until he was old enough to understand that it required matter which supports poetry with what somebody called 'the quality of hardness.'"

"That was my capital friend, Hillaire Belloc," Boileau informed him. "But poor Torquato was sentenced to a palace—which would only be right for a poet if he was the janitor—where they bragged of colored TV in every room; so what could you expect?"

Coming to, and with eyes that spoke of lucidity for all the pain they reflected, the bard again begged for ministration, "Bourbon and water, or failing that, just a straight shot."

The pathos of that request emboldened me to brace the Olympian on a fellow writer's behalf. "Can't you do anything about that cry from the heart? One hooker shouldn't be much for a god to wrangle."

In spite of looking concerned himself, Apollo shook his head. "I can't regale him here in the Critical Woods, where the rule is that everybody must cope himself with whatever treatment he's dispensed, but—"

"You could trans-substantiate him," Aristotle suggested, "as Aphrodite did, when turning herself and Eros into fishes that time Typhon surprised her along the Euphrates."

"I was thinking of a bird, though none that fly at night would be appropriate," the god said. "Neither would any fish which that creek affords, but a goodly four-footer does frequent it, my friend. As a sportive otter, Tasso can gambol and go fishing that never got to do either as a human. Carry him to the stream any who will."

After we'd all toted him to the creek and dropped him in a spot over which Apollo stretched his arm, Torquato surfaced as a frisky otter and swam off down stream, where I judge he would find a place to go sliding with some slick otteress. But although we all knew he'd be happier now, the case made us all feel how chancy and subject to change without notice a writer's life is. We were therefore all moody when we returned to the fire until Croce spoke up.

"Apollo, couldn't you favor us with a cheerful song?"

"I will do that," the god agreed, and forthwith threw his head back and let his voice roll.

When Romulus [of Trojan blood, but fallen from the graces
Aeneas owned, because a wolf was not the best of nurses
For teaching polish], left Italia's wide and open spaces
And founded Rome, he had for Omar's wine, a wench and verses
No gust at all. And thus the leader, thus the churls he headed:
They wanted frugal homes in fields which they had dourly planted
And sturdy kitchen cows that they unsmilingly had wedded
Who never for a furbelow or frill had ever planted.
So there the clock had stopped for them, if left to peasant labors;
But other folk in Latium County couldn't stand the quiet

Of rustic life. And so it was to chasten flighty neighbors
That Romans formed a column and advanced upon a riot,
As stolidly and businesslike as when they teamed for haying.
But when they'd hushed a burg, they judged it best to stay its schoolers
And gravely scattered orders which the quick were soon obeying;
The dead alone successfully ignored insistent rulers.
But still the proverb 'when in Rome' provoked the corollary
Of 'when away from there.' When he'd encountered foreign fashions,
The absent Roman, in a word, was not the same canary
He'd been at home; and wine was added to the soldier's rations.
Yet still they marched to keep the peace, and found the pacing smoother
When piping timed advancing. Or a chanticleering varlet
Would raise a song, when music ceased, which proved alike a soother
Of tramping legionnaires. His lyric tutoress a harlot,
His harmony was not in praise of frugal rural striving;
But neither was he now a pig who'd pass again a filly
While lost in contemplation of the mule that he was driving.
The captivated capturer enraptured willy-nilly
Is not the picture quite. It's rather moth from caterpillar,
Attained in easy stages. For when Rome had conquered Hellas
As far as southern Italy, it was at least a miller
Which knew it shined to light, if not of personal brilliance zealous,
But Greece itself produced a dish that foundered ogling yeomen;

For flown by swans, there swooped upon them glorious Aphrodite,
Compelling them to worship her, So Venus her cognomen,
She ruled a race where Philistines were ousted as the mighty;
For Venus conquered every anti-cultural exhorter
[As when she posed in Milo, she was utterly disarming],
And hastening to crowd into the city's Latin Quarter,
The arty Romans poetized and sculptured her as charming.

Soon afterward, what with the forest air and exercise, I went to sleep where I was. And when I opened my eyes again, I found that Hark-hark the larkess had laid another up and doing egg. Sitting up then, I realized three other things. Apollo was nowhere about. The hunters had breakfasted and gone about their business. Squatting by the remnants of the fire was a man in short boots with long spurs.

"I didn't hear you ride in," I remarked.

"For the excellent reason that cannibals shot my *caballo* from under me." After giving me that explanation, he fished tawny strips of bacon from the spider in front of him and stretched them on a rock to let the grease drain away. "Admiring their own image, these Mazorcan savages prefer horse rumps to man; and while they were at their butchery, I managed to escape."

There was a harp in a weathered case hanging from a silver birch branch, so I reasoned it was all right to chirp for breakfast. "If you'll wait till I get back from a dip in the creek, I'll help you out with that bacon," I called over my shoulder.

I hadn't thought much about Economic Geography lately, but my knowledge of it sometimes cast surprising light into what would else have been dark places. While I was plunging and dressing again, I decided that only one man of the Road would think of dubbing hostile critics "Ear of Corn" cannibals.

"You must be Joe Hernandez," I said to a fellow whose

accomplishments by then included making flapjacks.

He expertly tossed a final one in the air before replying. "If I must be, there's no use fighting it; yet as a man who's had to skip town to keep from wearing a hemp cravat, I've got out of the habit of announcing myself to strangers." He put the by then crisp bacon and two stacks of cakes on a tin platter and strode toward the log I was by then straddling. "Sorry I can't place you," he said, while motioning for me to dig in.

Thinking of Egill Skallagrimson and D. Alighieri, plus now this lad, I would have given anything if I could have bragged of foes honing for my head or neck. So my voice was plaintive as I blurted out the embarrassing truth.

"I don't see how I'm going to do any good on the Road, because where I came from, nobody ached to kill me!" Grief didn't prevent me from following Joe's example by wrapping a flapjack around a bacon strip and munching the result. It was therefore a minute before I could voice a following thought. "I admit I haven't published anything to speak of, but—"

"You've put your finger on your fault right there. You can't expect to make any first rate enemies without working for them." Hernandez smeared the subject with a dismissing hand. "Which way are you heading?"

"From hunters I met last night I gathered that Eldorado is not too far down the—Hey, who threw that?"

"Dropped would be more accurate," Joe said of a knife that pinned a piece of parchment between us." As there's no shiv with an elkhorn haft from Pilcomayo to Tierra del Fuego, that note must be for you."

The handwriting being eccentric, it took a minute or so to decipher a brief note. When sure of what it said, I read it aloud to my breakfast-mate.

Olympus
4/18/75

My Dear It:

Due to being hastily summoned to a committee meeting, I left without instructing you to stop at the rock where she, as Nimuue, imprisoned Merlin so that he would be available for consultation by such surveyors of the Road as yourself. Just follow along after Eldorado and you can't miss it.

Your obedient servant,
Apollo of Helicarnassus

"He didn't say anything about the knife," Joe said, "so I guess you get to keep it."

"It'll come in handy if I meet any more reviewers." I yanked from the log a blade to whose haft the sheath had been tied and rose to belt it on. "Shall we go, as soon as we've laundered the kitchenware and stamped the fire to death?"

The way stayed faithful to the right bank of the creek during a full day's march, bringing us at sundown to the mining camp of Eldorado. That this was booming, signs at the outskirts were sufficient to prove: "Get your outside coat of gold and your inside coat of Old Philosopher's Stone at the Manoa," one advised. "See Twenty Golden Girlies Go It at the Golconda," a rival bill ordered.

Proceeding downtown, we passed 'the Golden Moose Call where Lonesome Men Get unlonesomed in a hurry,' whence a man dashed followed by a young woman all of gold except the pistol with which she let drive. "That'll learn you to call an eighteen karat lady of the evening a 'cheap chippie,'" she told a bleeding sinner I knew to be repentant because he started crawling toward the "Golden Reformed Tabernacle—Admission Only One Double Eagle for Contrite Hearts."

"This camp's too rich for us, Joe!" I despaired.

Luckily my anguished cry reached the bluff heart of a prospector who'd struck it rich. "Hola, men of harps, Eldorado has more than the tourist dead falls you'd be fools to drop money in even had you any. May I be privileged to demonstrate as much by taking you to Pen and Dagger?"

As he was cordial and we were in need of well-heeled cordiality, we were led to a combination bar and restaurant where good drinks were followed by good food and wine that hadn't been born yesterday. As for the conversation, it was rather a monologue with which this gusty frontier character enlarged his hospitality.

"They call me Voltaire for the incontrovertible reason that my true name is Arouet . . . Nino de Lenclos said a feel from me was worth one of her nine lives . . . The reason for the Geneva Convention is that they didn't know what else to call it by the time I was through blowing holes in that Swiss cheese . . . I was the best stage director and leading man that any of my plays ever rejoiced in, and my only regret is that I could never figure out a way to shine as the ingenue and clown as well . . . As I forgot to draw my own out of Joan of Arc, could I borrow that knife of yours for a worthy cause, It?"

A sport that had just called for another bottle of Burlesque 1755 was no one I felt like being stingy to. Just the same I was embarrassed when Voltaire walked over to a bird leaning against the bar and airily cut his throat.

This display of frontier high spirits convulsed others there, however. As for the slayer, he threw doubloons on the mahogany yelping, "Plant a boot apiece on the rail, boys, and drink to the soul I just rescued from a cesspool muskrat while she's still working her way out of his system."

"Glad to; but what did you carve this time?" a stickler for details called. "Was it another literary louse like Freron?"

"It was only a mathematician," the killer admitted. He waited for the rest of us to be served before scooping up his own glass, "But Maupertuis believed in the principle of Least Action and, by deism, I sure saw that he got it. Could I buy you a short one on the rocks, honey?"

Having extricated herself from Maupertuis by then, the dead man's shy little anima paused to give her liberator a grateful wave of farewell. "Thanks, but Pythagoras always told us girls we shouldn't drink with strange men anywhere but in the privacy of the back room." Whereat she flitted out the door and off to Limbo, there to vacation until it was time to enter whatever carnal shape was next in order for her.

She had hardly left when two more harp bearers came in, and Voltaire added them to our party. "Primas of Chartres and Krishna Dvaipayana," he introduced them on the way back to our table. But we'd hardly got seated when Hernandez was tagged by a rough and ready character.

"Hey, Joe, you old pampas mustang, I've been looking for you from Hell to breakfast. Ready to ride?"

"You bet, Martin," my sidekick said. "But a careful gaucho like me always insists on a horse—and in this case one for my pal, It, too. This is Marty Fierro," Joe said to me, "and he's got a swell scheme for ringing the noses of a bunch of mean bulls you'll be glad to be in on."

He had me sold, for I liked him fine and felt sure I'd be glad to side as well the rawhide laugher who'd ridden to Eldorado to find him. But just as I was about to commit myself to be of their company for whatever was afoot, a voice whispered, "While I like you for wanting to help your friends and share their danger, their expedition is nothing to her—and less to us."

The tones were such as to make me gaze about in wild astonishment. But my eyes found no woman in that stag company, let alone one with the lissome lines which the voice of Lalage had prepared me to discover.

"Ready to light out, It?" Hernandez said.

Now although nobody had ever counted on me to ride a winner in the Bourbon-country Derby or the Ryeland Preakness, I had braved the hurricane deck of a horse, and thought I could manage it again for cause. This is not what I urged, however.

"Primas," I fudged instead, "is an old Chartres crony I haven't seen since he and Golias and I used to throw Papal bull sessions together, and I can't hurt his feelings by skipping a reunion now."

"Understood," Joe said. After bidding Vol goodbye, he had one more word for me. "May there be not only cantinas wherever you go, but live ones to buy for you, amigo."

The Lake Where the Lady Lived

"I don't get you," Voltaire was saying to one of the newcomers, when I turned from that farewell. "You're going to cover the great war for the city of Hastinapura, and you plan to pen-name yourself Vyasa instead of plastering Krishna Dvaipayana on—What did you say you aimed to call your work about the Children of the Moon?"

"Mahabharata."

"It's a fine brass band title, but why don't you stick your real John Henry under it in neon lights like everybody does but Anonymous; and I've been tipped off that he's on the dodge to keep from paying alimony."

"I grasp your point," Dvaipayana replied, after tapping his highball. "But it isn't always safe for a great poet to leave his name in the vicinity of a great work. For if it runs short of characters, it's apt to draft the maker for any old bit part: look what happened to Valmiki while he was dishing up *Ramayana*. The first thing poor Mik knew he was in his own epic as a hermit—not only in charge of two snot-nosed kids but on the wagon!"

"No fooling!" Primas was shocked. "Isn't that against Grimm's Law?"

"Sure, but Congress didn't put any teeth in it, so it didn't keep Milton from flopping into *Paradise Lost* first person singular, interrupting a legitimate character who never forgave him; but what happened to Mik was worse, of course."

"As infamous as a play by Crebillon," Vol declared, "but let's talk pleasanter shop."

We did that for the rest of a good evening. I'd neglected to make any arrangements for the night, but Voltaire had a swell mansion he called Delices, where he invited all three of us to bunk, and whence he sent us on our way with good breakfasts to buoy us the next morning.

"The old boy's easy to get along with, if he likes you," Dvaipayana said, as we harpsters strode out of town along the Golden Thigh of Pythagoras Street, "but I heard chatter about him slipping a knife into a guy called Maupertuis, to teach him better mathematics."

"And he bragged of having butchered writers as well," I put in. "With the honorable exception of hari-kari committers, bitter rivalries infest all professions, but that method of expressing distaste for the work of another strikes me as extreme."

"Yet it's one of the trade's standard hazards," Primas chuckled. "Remember what Alec Pope did to about everybody he couldn't find in the mirror, or that didn't belong to his club. And Mike Cervantes romped all over Europe, just so he could get to wade in the blood of authors he had it in for."

"And it doesn't matter if an enemy's already kicked the bucket," Dvaipayana pointed out. "Aristophanes dashed off *The Frogs* so he could get to dance on the grave of Euripides while it was still warm with the tears of old Rip's admirers."

"Well, it's a tough business any way you look at it," Primas came back. "It's also the only one that *I* know of where you've got to be careful whom you pick to give the works to, or you'll wind up finding that you've done him a favor. Why some of the geezers Catullus drew and quartered were palookas that nobody would now know of, if G.V. hadn't harpooned them and jerked them out of Lethe."

Thus whiling away an hour or so, we came to a crossroads of six ways instead of the usual four. "'Visit Alexandria, where Euclid learned to proposition,'" Primas read out one of the signs. "'Your money back if your own obelisk finds nothing more axiomatic than it was before.' Any takers?"

"Too cryptic," I complained. "Try again."

"'Visit Thebes, where Semele found that a girl should always wear an asbestos nightie.'"

"Elementary," Dvaipayana growled. "Go on."

"'Visit Ghazni and inspect the charred spot where the Emperor Mahmud burned up after Firdousi epigrammed him for welching on his contract for *Shanama*.' Tempting but too specialized, I'd say, but how about 'Take in Hastinapura, coveted by both Indian branches of the moon's famous family.' Sounds like a real opportunity for a scop not afraid to think big."

Dvaipayana nodded. "That's where I will get off or fall off," he said, while unholstering a flask. "I have a bit of gathered-and-brewed-by-moonlight soma. Will you join me in one for the Road, birds of my songful feather?"

When he had gone on his epic way, Primas declared himself. "As Thebes was where Cadmus taught the alphabet to whoop it up, I can do no less than make a pilgrimage of tribute." Reading in my eyes that I didn't feel destined to go along, he produced a leather-covered vademecum, which looked as though it had inspired many a heartfelt lyric. "I have no soma but Caecinian has its virtues."

"I know it must have or one of your severe standards wouldn't promote it," I said, "but what kind of a grain or grape does it spring from?"

"From the highest and driest of all bard-aiding vintages, taste a song I can summon from not far away:"

Barkeep, lag a jereboam, lad,
Of old Caecinian, screw the useless cork
Dawdling in the path of progress, add
A stoup that might be nested by a stork,
Pour until the brim admits enough
And tack the tab upon Apollo's cuff,
Hollered Bobbie in a Lochlea dive,
Afire to raise the bail
To jump from feckless jail

In mere percept, a song that asked the drive
Falernian owns to fetch it forth alive.

The wine that Burns had so heartily endorsed proved, to no astonishment of mine, worthy of his praise. "Thanks and good hunting, harper."

Alone, I examined a sign reading, "To the Lady's Lake. Don't overlook the school where Lancelot was trained to make Guinevere and wreck the Round Table." The other ways all started out by arching over hills, but this one slanted downward along a rapidly flowing creek, and for no better reason I took it.

The way was wooded but by no means lonely. Whisperings and soft chortles were exchanged between the trees; and every now and then there would be a flash of rosy flesh, as a dryad shed her own bark and streaked to visit a neighbor.

Charmed by these social calls, I forgot what Apollo had enjoined me to watch for and would have breezed past it, had not I heard the clearing of a masculine throat. Startled, I stopped to scout the vicinity. To my right there were but trees, some tittering but none productive of nymphs. To my left the scene was the same, except for the creek and a boulder which stood on its nearest bank. It was obviously this that had made the first overture, so the next move was up to me.

"Are you free for consultation, Merlin, or am I supposed to make an appointment?"

"I wouldn't have flagged you down, if I hadn't guessed you a rover of the Road in need of pointers." Coming through stone gave the voice an impressive resonance. "What's troubling you, son?"

"Beyond the fact that I've a theme for which I haven't found the right approach or measure, I don't know, sage or wizard."

"You can call me both without stretching the truth or hurting my feelings," he assured me. "As for your problems, it may be that you're not in tune with the atmosphere of the times. Can you name the six noble gases?"

As that could be no poser for an economic geographer, I rattled them off in their proper aristocratic order. "Helium, Neon, Argon, Krypton, Xenon and—er—Radon. They were raised to the peerage in the eleventh year of England's George Fifth, and Neon was awarded the Order of the Seraphim by Gustav the Sixth of Sweden for its compassionate service in guiding to bars and beaneries guys who roll into towns late at night."

"So shine good deeds in a sleety, windy world," Merlin remembered. "Can you cite the six *ig*noble gaseous elements?"

"Well, things will probably get worse before we can hope for a breath of fresh air; but as things stand now, I'll stay with the collected works of the Lost, Beat, Rock-Hopped, Grass-Swacked, Roll-Sold, Fix-Nixed and Blissful-Pill generations."

There was a pause while he considered my reply. "That's close enough to show you've studied the situation," he decided. "You now have a right to brace me with regard to any specific point that has laid you a stymie. I'll solve the enigma provided she doesn't show up and rechannel my energies." The boulder rocked due to an underground chuckle. "I'm still a bit of a dog, you know."

"Yes, sir." I eyed the stream swishing by while I shaped my query, "Merlin, I've had a lot of coaching here and there; but nobody told me how to keep a verse narrative from sinking like a shot-riddled beer can, which it's bound to do, if you put the wrong English on it."

"Or Hurrian, Hattic or, most especially Hittite," the sage amended.

I could think of nothing pertinent to say until a nudge from my harp brought back a recollection of the song Torna spieled the night before I shipped out of Erech. "I'm afraid that, not counting rowdy behavior on the part of Kuwarbis, I know nothing about the Hittites except that they referred to her as Ishtar."

"Know nothing about the Hittites!" My admission shocked the wizard into his first display of irritation. "If you're planning a report on the Road and are as ignorant as that, you're loony! And that puts me in mind of how I can best speed you on your way—after first furnishing some needed instruction."

Nervous about having roused the red pepper of a sorcerer, I decided to clear out, only to find that something had gone wrong with my left foot. While I was staring at what had become a webbed claw, Merlin commenced chanting:

I carol of the keystone Hittite state,
The marvelous message center
Receiving with integrity the great
Traditions of the East and passing on
The tales of which its past was the inventor,
That spoke for hosts of nations gone
To young, dynamic Hellas,
Of new creation zealous
And building out of night another dawn.

Meanwhile what I had seen Enki do to himself on the ark went on happening to me. I was feathered to the knees—assuming I had any knees—as Merlin proceeded with his tutoring.

Akin to Medes and Aryans through the gods
That blew them to Asia Minor,
The credent Hittites reasoned that the odds
Would favor men who stretched their holiness
By welcoming each new theistic shiner
That tribes they fought had thought to bless,
Besides the native heroes,
Benign or primal Neros,
They saved for Greeks to greet and reassess.

And, dipping deep in Syria, this crew
Was Babylonia's neighbor
And plumbed the storied wealth that Akkad drew
From Sumer, dressed in wrinkles of its own;
They joyed in Canaan's lore and liked the labor
Of Ugaritic poets, prone
To celebrate Phoenicians,

For passing to the Grecians,
Along with tales Arabian wits had flown.

By this time fledged above the navel I no longer had, I counted on crossing Merlin up by flying away, as soon as I had wings. The flaw in that scheme, though, was that as my brain was still human, I had no notion of how to work pinions. So as birdiness crept up a wried neck, I helplessly listened to services performed by a vanished people.

So when Achaeans stormed the Hittite fort
Of Hattushas, they looted
A glorious cosmopolitan port
Of call for many nations' drifting dreams:
From Hurrian and Hattic skalds recruited;
Palaic and Mitannic schemes
Plus Luish were some treasures
In prose or melic measures
The Hellenes hammered into Western themes.

Not least of my concerns had been wonder as to what sort of ave I was becoming, but just as the wizard completed his chant, his transforming spell reached my brain. Then I knew I was a loon, and although I could fly if need be, that wasn't my first locomotive desire. At hand were inviting creek depths, so with the scream of a love-lorn werewolf I dove into them.

I was at first pleased to find how skilled I was at swimming under water, and next aware that I had a pressing hunger for fish. These were plenty, I found as I cruised downstream; but something was throwing my timing off, when I plunged to get one, for I kept overshooting perch, or what have you, that should have been easy kills.

Not being dumb, as loons go, I came to see that I was starving amid abundance because I hadn't learned to reckon with the pressure of the current. It pushed me at every instant, whether riding with it, turning to slash through it or bucking it in pursuit of game which understood its force better than I did.

A loon can have a pretty salty vocabulary, I discovered,

but after I got a tricky, fish-rescuing current thoroughly told, the watery grape vine brought me Merlin's low-keyed comment. "You wanted help with a narrative project in verse, and the first thing you have to understand about poetry when used for that purpose is that the measure adopted is like this stream's current in being an unchanging enormity which everything in it must accept or die of damned foolishness, as you're now on your way to do."

Being too hungry for repartee, I didn't answer back. Instead I flapped to a tree overhanging the creek and studied the problem by noting how fast things floating in the current or swimming in it passed under me. And the next time I dove for a fish I worked out an equation involving its speed, my own and the current's which netted me a tasty sun fish.

No longer afraid of dying of hunger, I could afford to be gracious and acted accordingly. "I take it all back about you being a two-bit son of a hellbender, Merlin," I said as clearly as a full mouth would allow. "You know your onions about stream fishing, and I bet you gave me a straight steer about narrative poetry, too."

My newly learned mastery ceased to be of any help, though, when I came to a lake's stillness about a half hour later. With no current to contend with, I was basing my calculations on the theory that it was yet a factor and making flubs all over the watery joint. And just as I became hot under my feathery collar—for a loon's temper has a short fuse—Merlin got to me again with some counsel.

"A lake's like prose, It; all the pushing is done by whatever it holds. If you'll just remember that you're now batting in a league which doesn't ask for split-second timing, you'll leave the loonatic fringe and catch something for a change."

If it hadn't been for that pun, I wouldn't have told the underside of my breath exactly what I did about a wizard whose advice added up to logic. As it was, I sulked and muttered until following his counsel netted me both a fish and good humor again.

"If the situation had been turned around, I might have made that crack myself," I laughed. Then, because a loon is good at that, I did it again. "Oh, oh—that's for me!"

Hoisting scut with that phrase, I dove to catch a lake

trout which, instead of trying to dodge aside plunged steadily deeper. "Go on, you poor dope," I grinned. "When you fetch bottom and have to level off, I'll dive along the hypotenuse, in place of following you around the other two sides of a triangle; and that'll be all for you until you win a new outlook as part of me."

When he did reach bottom, though, he found an opening I hadn't counted on and darted through it. My blood up, I followed him around first one sharp turn and then another. Had I stopped to reason, I would have seen that he must be heading upward again, but I was thinking only of the juicy quarry I was closing in on.

Yet just as, sure of seizing him, I opened wide my triumphant beak—I found I didn't have one. For it was as a man that I popped up in a well lighted indoor swimming pool, from which another of Pithecanthropus's godsons was in the act of hauling himself.

Stroking to the opposite side before doing likewise, I found a bench laden with my clothes and against which my harp leaned. Above it was a sign I studied while banging one ear to clear it of water:

> *Guests of the palace will please be so good as to take a shower before donning human raiment.*
>
> *Morgan le Fay,*
> *Owner of the Lady's Lake*

Conceding that I did have a gamey carry-over from loondom, I went where an arrow said I should, and found the late goal of my pursuit already soaping himself. After giving me time to adjust an adjoining spray to my satisfaction, he caught my eye and laughed.

"Sorry to have been the one to let you down, after having lifted your digestive hopes up. But as I was the only one available when Merlin telepathed word you were en route, the management drafted me as coney catcher. I'm Colin Clout, alias Ned Spenser, by the way."

"Yes, the harp case you noticed contains an instrument," I answered his look of enquiring interest; "but it's tight as a new shoe when it comes to helping me make anything, so I've been It for longer than I like to remember."

"We all go through that." Having let cold water pelt him, he snatched a towel from a pile on a rack and began trotting back toward the pool-side bench holding his duds. "I'll wait and introduce you to your host; for it's always problematical whether she'll be here."

True to his kindly purpose, Colin soon led me down corridors opening into rooms of royal glitter. But it was in no such plush that our march ended. Ogres have dens, and so did the man of this subaqueous house. Brackets on one wall supported a sword as long and broad as a bull elephant's trunk. From other wall spots the heads of a sea serpent, a unicorn and a fire-drake peered with toothy affability. Along with books and assorted drinking implements, a table held an upended human skull from which the stems of several pipes protruded.

Bending over this same oaken centerpiece, a two legged mammoth was giving a bamboo fly rod a fresh protective coating of shellac. "Count Ogier of Denmark," Colin said, when the big fellow looked up, "this is another fisherman, It by name. Merlin forwarded him because she wanted him to stop by."

"So the wizard obeyed an irresistable impulse to oblige," Roland's old comrade-in-arms chuckled. "A flunky's brought word that she's just checked in, so stick around, if you don't object to being caught in a high wind."

He had hardly raised that storm warning when Morgan le Fay came sailing into his arms. But from them she bounced, moments later, upon catching a glimpse of the scenery.

"Look at this Calydonian boar frank!" she said with a tragic sweep of her hand. "Gilgamesh and Hercules combined would have a hard time purging it of junk!"

"Then you could hardly expect me to accomplish that all alone," Ogier murmured.

She didn't take that offering of logic in good part. "It's not expecting too much, even from you, to put books back on shelves and to get rid of bottles, when you're through with them!"

"As an old soldier myself," he countered, "I wouldn't

feel right about ousting them just because their days of martial glory are done. And that books are better off on shelves, than where they can be reached without leaving a chair or an unchaperoned snort, is a superstition peculiar to the beautiful and charming."

"Don't try to soft soap me with an evasion a Sassenach in his cups would be ashamed of," she sniffed. "And didn't I tell you to get rid of that hideous fire-drake?"

"It seems to me that I once heard subdued murmurs to that effect," Ogier owned, "but with you away I was too lonesome to face forfeiting anything else."

"I have to leave sometimes, to keep from being driven as mad as Lilith by your sub-savage habits." Here she glanced at me with eyes that saw only a further excuse for upbraiding him. "But if you insist upon fouling your nest in a manner to bring a blush of regret to a hoopoe, couldn't you refrain from bringing a guest in here? It's bad enough to inflict your disgusting taste in decor on old and resigned friends of the family like Colin; but to drag an appalled stranger into your shambles—Whose skull is it that you've sunk to using as a pipe-rack, may I enquire?"

Picking the trophy up, Ogier peered at it reflectively. "It isn't big enough to be Brehus's, but it might be Loher's or Brunamont's. I ran across it while I was ransacking the cellar for varnish thinner, and brought it up for old sake's sake."

"Well, if you want a skull to keep your pipes in, for Pwyll's sake, get a fresh one somewhere. But don't ever again display an old, moldy one where aghast strangers—"

"But he can't be all the way a stranger," Ogier objected, with a nod toward me, "as Merlin flicked word that you wanted to see him, hon."

"Why *It, darling,* to think I didn't notice whom I was spatting about!" Morgan then cried. "Of course, I want to see you, and hear everything that's happened since I last talked with my lamb—at sea, wasn't it?—and spang this instant!"

The Transmitted Humagram

Surprisingly, after she had led me to a room resembling Ogier's sanctum only in having a floor, ceiling and the usual quartette of walls, Morgan proved a good listener. It helped, besides, that she was a schooled listener; for I needed but to name a person, place or situation to draw a nod which certified she was with me. Her eyes meanwhile appeared to be studying an invisible chart, and checking off points as I described my arrival at each.

"And now I'm here," I brought my explorations up to date, "which I understand was Lancelot's alma mater."

While I tried not to sound accusatory, a small flattening of my accent told her I was thinking about what the sign at the six crossways had said about the mentioned knight. Sitting up and turning her head, she got an 'All's Well' signal from a wall mirror before settling back in her chaise lounge. "Something had to be done to give Arthur's story a direction and climax, to keep it from just running out of wind like one of these dynastic series of novels. Then most of the surviving Round Table knights had to chop each other up for about the same reason that I couldn't allow Gilgamesh the immortality that would have disinheroed him. It would have been a shame to leave the R. Table a going concern until it was dozed over by a bunch of rickety old boys past leaving it for any adventure; but nobody except me considers these things."

"I never should have doubted you and don't very often," I muttered. Then, because I couldn't help it, I came out with what had been secretly troubling me.

"You thought I ought to come here—why?"

"Not for the reason of your doubtful hopes and uneasy fears, sugar." She drew a cigarette from a jeweled box on the taboret beside her, but waved me back to my chair when I rose with a view to operating her lighter. "Once upon your time you undertook to tell me that your amorous *nom de guerre* was 'Torpedo.' Do you still imagine yourself—with apologies or thanks to Beaumont—such a knight of the burning pestle?"

On the wall behind her was a painting of Venus granting Vasco da Gama empery of the sea while Trinc Camoens looked proudly on, and I made a business of studying it before replying. "At times aspiration is larger than achievement in fields other than that of writing."

I was hoping she would say nothing about my lobsterine flight from George Sand, and she forbore to do so, though a twinkle let me know she was aware of one reason why I was no longer plugging myself as a Casanova. "But you're not like that prissy cub, Hippolytus, whom I had to deal with because he declared himself a walking monastery."

She exhaled smoke which formed the initials L.F. before continuing. "In part you worship me because I remind you of one whom you have neither the power to forget nor the moxie to win."

"She keeps a bird I'd be incompatible with," I mumbled, "and as I was born a bachelor, marriage never crossed my mind."

"Not with anybody else," she agreed. "But for her you have a fine fatal passion for which death is the only specific." The idea seemed to please her more than it did me; for she smiled as she blew a tiny ring and thrust the fourth finger of her left hand through it.

"A perfect fit," Morgan then announced, "but whether I

do anything about it depends on how well you continue to serve me in your scientific capacity. You're bearing in mind, I trust, that class you're due to hold at a quarter of two?"

"One-forty," I furrowed my brow while so correcting her. "But so far I'm short of the data needed for your commission; and my harp must go into action somewhere, you know."

"Your time from now on must be spent to no waste purpose; we both understand that, dumpling." As she rose, so did I, but she waved me back to my chair. "And don't move," she admonished. "I'm going to transmit you past some relatively unimportant points; and for a humagram, I've got to know where your every fibre is, including your harp, which I wish you to hold in front of you."

For a moment she stood with the tips of her fingers pressing her eyes, while voicing a cantrip I don't remember because of suffering a dizzy spell which wound up as a blackout. When my head cleared, I was no longer in the Lake Lady's submerged palace. Rather I was dangling from something I couldn't see above a highway a couple of yards below.

Next I found that I was still clutching my harp and deduced that what had interrupted my flight was the snagging of its casestrap by some projection. I had not yet got as far as reasoning that if I let go of the instrument, Newton would see that I touched earth again, when a voice hailed me.

"You're not Cyrano Savien de Bergerac, back from a jaunt to the sun, are you?"

"No," I said, as I swung to eye a pair of walkers who had caught me in a position for which I didn't relish witnesses, "I'm E.A. Poe's Angel Israfel, up here practicing to despise a mere mortal's unimpassioned song. But as I'm through rehearsing, I'll join you groundlings, being a democratic if wildly well singer."

With that I let go of the harp and stood upon earth as promised. There my first move was to find out what had halted my humagramic flight. My harp was suspended from a finger of a signpost standing at a fork in the highway. Pointing down one branch was a hand reading 'Broceliande:

Ferry to Avalon.' Aiming along the better traveled way leading straight ahead, the sign simply read, 'To Troy.'

While I was working the harp-strap loose from this board, one of the two watching me stopped eating an apple long enough to register a complaint. "Road signs should be more definite or they're of no use to an enquiring mind. Every time I pass by here I am struck by the disappointing fact that this one utterly fails to specify *which* Troy."

"Is there more than one?" They were both harpsters, but the more bronzed of the two asked that.

"There should be," the tall apple eater argued. "In the United States of Artless Letters we boast of twenty-nine distinct Troys." He poked what was now mostly core in a vague westerly direction. "One Florence!" he snorted. "In the USAL we have founded and maintain a round thirty-four."

"It shows you're thinking big," the other admired.

"True." The speaker tossed the remains of his pippin to a waiting woodchuck that caught it on the fly with an appreciative grunt. "And there are other advantages to having multiple towns of the same name and fame. I will quote from Anonymous's *Ode to Usalia*, a deserved tribute to the USAL's muse:

How literary history would have altered,
Had sweet Usalia's land been all its stage!
Alighieri, when his fortunes faltered,
Would not have known an exile's desperate rage,
Expressed by curses, spewed in Tuscan torrents.
With ample alternates to choose among,
He simply would have picked another Florence
And happily his shingle there had hung.

When ordered from his city, with the rider
That if he stayed, he'd dangle from a rope,
Poor Villon found the world an ill provider
Of Parises, when fleeing as a mope
From that upon the Seine. But had by luck he
Been hatched beneath Usalia's kindly sun,

If banned from, say, the Paris of Kentucky,
He could have joined a Maine or Texas one.

Because his daughter, Julia, was a strumpet
Who treated men by legions to her tail,
Augustus Caesar undertook to trumpet
That Ovid must be ousted, and bewail
The Rome he'd forfeited in Pontic Tomi.
But in Usalia's happy realm a skald,
If booted callously from any Rome, he
Could find a hustling dozen likewise called.

"But we're not in Usalialand now," I said, "and must take the cards as they are dealt. In my case, gentlemen, I feel compelled to follow this road, whether or not it leads to the original Troy."

"In that case we shall have the pleasure of your company for a while at least, making introductions in order." The woodchuck's benefactor extended a hand. "I'm Ralph Emerson, akin to Ralphs Roister Doister and Coilyear through mutual Adamic ancestry. And this is Nizam-uddin Abu Mohammed Ilyas bin Yusuf, renowned in particular as celebrator of Alexander the Great."

"And you?" the latter asked. But reading embarrassment in my eyes, he slapped me on the back. "Your time will come, but for the present you might join a trade discussion the sight of you served to interrupt. Ralph here had opened by saying—Repeat the hogwash for It's benefit, chum."

"My contention," Emerson said, as I fell in step with them, "was actually a query, to wit: where does poetry get off in considering itself separate from other writing? Or to be more exact, what is the function of verse at all, in as much as the prose of any stylist has rhythm, even if not of katy-did assertiveness."

"Did you hear him reasoning like a bactrian camel?" Nizamuddin demanded. "But I'll return him an intelligent answer. Ralph, you are not being fair to prose if you join the mongeese who insist any imaginative and pleasingly worded passage is 'poetic,' regardless of form. Sure, good hands can wring beauty from prose; or even from a stone, when a sculptor is moved to extract her sea-risen likeness from it."

Emerson nudged me. "When your opponent makes what look like generous concessions, beware; but I've got to bite on something, and my apple's gone. What's the differentiating touchstone, burning man?"

"A verse pattern you're pledged to stick to, if it means making Eblis (Hell to you, heretic), and high water swap places." The heat Ralph had been kidding Nizam about had now broken out of wraps, and had him stabbing the air like gamblers on the finger matching game. "That form takes the place of Allah, while you're working for it. It owns you and dictates what you write. Shaitan can take *your* ideas, even if it means changing an entire episode, or revising the whole slant of the poem's story in order to be faithful to the incubus you've sold yourself to. I tell you, Ralph—and I love you, unbeliever though you are—the product of such a way of working is not what you write or *I* write, but a transmuting collaboration between the form and the enslaved author that squeezes all that's vital out of him, even if it kills the poor, despised son of a bitch. And that drained blood is not 'poetic,' Rumi; it's poetry!"

Looking to see how Emerson was reacting, I caught a wink from him. "It takes a lot of maneuvering to pry an honest answer out of some people," he remarked. "Ah, here we are. At least we're at my destination, and I'll be pleased if you'll both make it a stop of your own."

As we had rounded a sharp turn, we were abruptly in sight of a large, white building, its naturc declared by a sign on our side of the grounds about the structures. "Will's Wayside Coffee House," it announced. "Great Cham Tea a Specialty."

"Why at this time of day I've got nothing against the cup that cheers but never spiflicates, as long as that's the best luck in the dice box," Nizam said. But as we all veered to partake of this tannic refreshment, there was a shout from above.

"Hold it, bin Yusuf! You're wanted to cover a new campaign of Iskander's."

The cry came from the pilot of a flying carpet, who

brought his gaudy sky-kite within three feet of the coffee house's lawn, leaped out and steadied it with a practiced hand. "I grieve that emergency doesn't spare me time to introduce myself as more than Abu Hohammed ul-qasim ibn Ali ibn Mohammed al-Hariri," he said, "but to speed things up, I suggest that you just call me Al."

"Done, Arabian seller of poetic silk." It was clear that Nizamuddin was as hot for action as for argument. "Your message for me is what, Al?"

"Iskander is about to throw a pontoon bridge across the Oxus to pin down the main forces of Timur with that feint, while his left wing swings through the Karum Korum sands, to take the lame Mongol's army from the rear; and he wants you to cover that annihilating maneuver."

"Any place Iskander wishes me, there I'll be." Having tossed his harp aboard, Nizam stood ready to help the rug ride an upward thrusting wind current. "So long, Ralph. I'm looking forward to hearing word of you, It. Let's get this carpet on the road, Al."

"Fine fellows," Emerson commented, when the bards and their glider had whipped off north and east, "but not the type, I think, to enjoy the Great Cham's type of chai catai."

A mild April day having caused windows to be flung open, we commenced to whiff tea's aroma while yet short of the house's door. We were also regaled by the Cham's own flavor.

"The poets of Albion and its literary offshoots," he was rumbling, "have with rare exceptions been a shiftless lot, when it comes to exploiting the possibilities of the medium in which they profess expertise. For if industrialists had been as unenterprising, every Jim and Joan of us would still be clad in fig leaves—bound to us by molecular attraction, it must be presumed, in the absence of any girdle, belt or galluses shown in the extant illustrations of the vogue. Why I myself have devised, in pursuit of illuminating my contention, some thirty-five previously unused yet highly viable forms."

"Of fig leaves, Doctor?" some one asked, as Ralph opened the door to the coffee house.

"Of metric combinations!" the Cham thundered. "And when the scoundrels do employ a pattern of new promise, they like as not lack the fibre to be true to it. For if it calls for monosyllabic rhyme, and they can't extract such from a moment's cogitation, the culls will sneak in a set of dissyllabic endings. And this is perpetrated on the plea that there is no difference between masculine and feminine rhymes. Bah, sir! Anybody that ill schooled in anatomy is of too primitive intelligence to be allowed inside a red hot dish's boudoir, or the sacred precincts of Helicarnassus, either."

By that time we had passed through Will's main guest room and had reached an alcove holding a table and three men so far occupying chairs around it. "Ha, the sage of Concord," a long-nosed fellow grinned, "where the act most prized is touching off a blast heard all around Boot Hill."

"It," Emerson said, "this is Erasmus, the best skate ever to flash over the canals of Holland. The troll filling a saucer to slurp from is Rasselas Sam Johnson, the worst writer ever to win bays with a diamond-studded tongue. And that solemn-seeming scamp is Tully Cicero, who'll defend you for a handsome fee, should you ever need legal aid, or cut your throat with a saw-tooth epigram for nothing."

Having fared among sharp shooters at New Stonehenge, I knew better than to comment. "In as much as I appear to have stumbled into a seminar," I said in my best professorial voice, "would some onc inform me of the topic?"

"The Cham just slew the one we had," Cicero said, "chopping off its head after lulling it into a false sense of security by feigning it was open to debate."

"Never give listeners—an inferior human species—an even break." Rasselas Sam was filling with tea a saucer resembling a soup plate. "Hitherto I've but dealt with parochial matters tonight. But now that Ralph and his guest are here there will be no more trifling with affairs of less scope than the entire extent of terra firma."

As he drank with the gusto of a stegosaurus, sopping at

some primeval water hole, I could not promptly request clarification. "Have you any such massive subject in mind, Doctor?" I asked, when the echoes had quit gurgling.

"Ignoring Antarctica, homeland to only illiterate penguins, the area of the globe's non-marine surface is 52,352,883 square miles, plus forget how many acres." When refilling his trough, the Cham added several hefty pinches of snuff to jazz up its flavor.

"Of this area," he then went on, "something under 10,000,000 square miles have radiated literatures in the collected histories of lettered epochs. Due to the sempiternal collapse as well as rise of civilizations, the world's literate area has never surmounted 7,000,000 square miles—a figure attained in the nineteenth century of the Christian hypothesis—while the present poor showing approximates 5,000,000, or less than ten percent of the mentioned terrestrial area."

An inspiration was fighting for my attention, but I fought it off. "Does that include the recently recovered areas?" I demanded.

Having disposed of his tobacco flavored bohea with the resonance of a blowing whale, the Doctor cocked an eye at me. "Recovered from what?" he countered.

"From the hags of Erebus, I suppose. From oblivion or whatever had blacked it out, when I was younger, and even before my time, as I am given to understand." I hunched my shoulders. "One day I knew nothing about An and his universe of Sumer, but then he cast off concealing shadows and became the only arch deity worth swearing by. And even after Kuwarbis fouled him I couldn't forget his glory. I know the Hittites have triumphed, but—?"

"You do, eh?" The Cham dropped his saucer in his excitement. "You, sir, are hep. Where's my notebook, Tully? There's a fine new word for my dictionary." Finding his note repository in his own pocket, he jotted his invention down. "You're hep to the Second Renaissance, It, which jiggers—there's another swell word; I'm in winning form this April day of hers. I'm hep as a Hittite, than which there is no more to be said."

However that may be, I believe the Doctor said it for the next hour, but though present, I was not a member of his audience. Inspiration, in the form of a possible way to begin my projected tale of the raid on Enki had come back to fix me in the trance of Pygmalion, beginning to find the lines of Aphrodite in a block of marble.

A Surge Through Helicarnassus

Not counting dessert, I had put supper away when I next became conscious of any thought but my own. As the party was about to break up, the Cham was nailing down the topic to be discussed at the next meeting.

"The theme we'll start with will be the paramount importance of subject matter if a writer of seniority is to compete in popularity with the contemporary cubs of any given era. For if away from the friendly basketball court of his own times, so to speak, an author's got to play at least thrice as well as the young fellows the fans are in natural sympathy with to draw anything but a rain of pop bottles and a howl of 'haul the dead goat away.' As he cannot figure on mounting the grade sheerly by scribbling skill—for technical prowess has been reasonably common in many periods—he must depend on the signal worth of his thesis to hold the attention of moderns tolerant of radish of the horse from writers exploring their own tempora and mores, eh, Tully?"

"It's nice to be quoted, but just now I'd prefer to know what you're getting at beside that pumpkin pie you're hacking," Cicero answered. "Could you be more specific?"

"Why as Horace said of Alfred de Musset, it was a pity

that he never found a theme worthy at once of his verse mastery and the breadth of his awareness."

"It was a perceptive remark," Erasmus told the ceiling, "but it happens to have been made by Gil Chesterton, of rotund as well as blessed memory, with respect, Sam, to baronial Al Tennyson."

"Don't hold me accountable for the grotesque errors of fact," the Cham admonished. "What I quoted *should* have been said by Flaccus while appraising the other Alfred, but I disdain to quibble. The issue is that Apollo has been parsimonious about meting book subjects of the first order; a sticky wicket which can't be circumvented by ballooned rhetoric such as 'The splendor falls on castle walls.' As I can think of ninety-eight splendors without shifting from low gear, I wish to be told which one ambushed the castle and what was the origin of the feud. As for Chesterton, I will remind you that he was careful to say of Ch'a Ching: 'Tea, although, an Oriental, is a gentlemen at—'"

"The supposed topic was the validity of a moonshee's subject matter," Ralph interposed, "but as the stage has arrived, let's explore it at our next session, as you earlier suggested. Are you bound for Memphis, It?"

Earlier in the day Morgan had remarked that I had no time to lavish on side issues. "Is it on the main road to Troy?"

"No, but the sphinxes and minxes are worthy of a scholar's absorbed attention, and Tully and I are going to debate 'Man: Reality or Supposition' at the town hall."

In spite of those attractions, I chose not to risk swerving. As my friends could not proceed until the passengers earlier aboard the coach had been served refreshments, I left them dawdling over a final dish of tea and pushed out of White's. Within a hundred yards I came to a choice of ways, but I accepted the counsel of the sign reading: "Take in Troy and never mind the fact that its true name is Ilion."

The evening being an April one, the spring peepers were making such melody as Chaucer ascribed to birds; songsters in their own right, to be sure, but now competing with joyous trillers only by a sleepy peep or so. But to lay sooth on the line, I gave small heed to the music of either tired avians or talented frogs. For I commenced to be vibrant with the long sought measure to employ for my tale of how she, Ninshubur and I—squaring accounts with Enki, as far as I was personally concerned—had snaked civilization from the shipwreck rocks of sea-washed Eridu.

Going the peepers one better, I was trying to meld verbal sense with orchestration. Fortunately there was none to overhear and guess of me that I suffered from overexposure to the moon which next shone. For by then I was sorting phrases aloud, this moment triumphant, as one struck me as apt, and then despairing of a language ill able to mount meaning astride my metric vessel.

Green as I was at this, I had made but spotty progress at moonset—followed by darkness during which I lost the highway somewhere. For when the wolf's tail of false dawn brushed the sky, I saw I was on a but little traveled track. About to retrace weary steps, I caught sight of a billboard not too misty to impact this message:

"You are now in Helicarnassus. Don't fail to stop at the Flying Mustang Gatehouse."

Not sure a tyro would be welcome at this installation, I fell, upon my arrival a few minutes later, into four leaf clover. "I'm the thunderer's boy, Bacchus," a hearty voice said, when I'd put the door behind me. "Half of this poetic pitch is mine, though you'd never know it from the way Apollo beats his publicity drum. Had a rough night?"

Bone-reaching chill hadn't improved a dawn soggy with dew. "It seems to me," I said as well as chattering teeth would let me, "that I've had it rough ever since I met your partner, which was way back when he was Nebo."

"Yeah, he never cares what happens to his hard luck cases—all of 'em, as far as I can make out. But I'm not like that because I had a rough time myself, what with the old man turning the lightning on Ma." While he was talking, he was making a jug hic its cork. "This is Ole Hippocrene, guaranteed to do something to the taker, even if there's no malpractice insurance to compensate him if horsefeathers grow on him instead of Pegasus."

Although the glass he filled for us was no bigger than

the sort used for an old fashioned, I found that I couldn't empty it in less than three gulps and keep the top of my head on. "It did things for me," I announced, when sure I wouldn't lose my grip on gravity and float away. "Now where's that Muse a maker's supposed to have rallying around and inspiring him? I've got business with her."

"You're taking it big." Bacchus seemed pleased at the sudden storm of self confidence I owed tò Old Hippocrene. "But let's find out which of the girls you need, or you might ask prissy Polyhymnia's advice on how to let go with a belly laughing number meant for Thalia, and get your eye dotted."

"Well, what I've been trying to make a metric glider of is a bite out of history, not blowing it up or adding any Romantic razzamatazz, Dionysus, but—"

"In that case the jill for you is Calliope!"

The Muse who skipped down from quarters upstairs in answer to that bellow reminded me of Lalage except that she was friendly and interested in my welfare. "You warm yourself in the inglenook and tell me all about it," she directed, "while I fix you what a man of vision needs, if he's to go into action. How would two golden-eyed cackle-berries and a rosy slab of old ham inspire you, backed by hot biscuits, not afraid of blackberry jam?"

There was no withholding of confidences from a girl with those sharp perceptions. While she tossed the specified breakfast together with slide rule efficiency, I told her what I'd been mulling over all night; and after she handed me a stiff snort of Castalia, in place of fruit juice, I began to chant snatches of the work. Calliope pointed out some minor inconsistencies and suggested tightening the structure by ditching a couple of incidents which didn't help the cause of dramatic intensity; but mainly she approved of my scheme.

"As your plan sticks to the business of telling about an adventure that was a double-action caution, It, there's no reason why you can't wring a tale out of it which will qualify you as the journeyman of the Road you need to be in order to make the knowledgeable report she expects of you. Now after you've given what I've cooked a good home, I want you to go up to the guest roost and catch some of the sleep you muffled last night. Then I'll show you how to get to Troy without doubling back to where you lost the highway."

The trace she sent me on, with a kiss for bonus, led between the twin heights of Helicarnassus; and then I learned that Bacchus was telling more truth than I'd given him credit for. In one direction the cross-trail I then found led 'To Lycorea, Sacred to Apollo, Custodian of Bards,' and in the other 'To Tithorea, Votive to Dionysus, Master of Wines and Anything Else That's Headily Potable.'

But a geographical discovery which I normally would have hailed as a sign of how carefully the cosmos had been organized at this point made hardly a dent in my consciousness. For now when I formed phrases I meant to keep, or cast poorly shaped ones aside with haughty snorts, I was no longer forced to lean on my own unripe judgment. I had a Muse (the best one of all the nine, I was ready to shout), to go over my verses with me. And though she was never captious, she never soft-soaped me, either.

"That has a good, rousing ring," Calliope might say, "but wouldn't a bit of smoothing help?" Or if I tripped into bombast, she'd kid me out of it. "No, that's a glitterbug," I remember she once told me. "Throw the crawly thing away before anybody finds that on you, It."

She had, of course, given me dependable word as to how to arrive at Ilion alias Troy. Yet bound as I was to the events of the narrative I was spinning, I didn't spare much dream on the city of Homer A., Virgil, Dictys Cretensis, Dares, Benoit de Saint-More, Boccaccio and Chaucer—till all of a sudden it cornered the horizon, its vast walls and catellated towers outlined in gold by the sun crouching behind them.

Moments later I saw a poster, nailed to a giant sycamore, which raced excitement up and down my spine. "Open to All Bardic Comers," it said, "The Annual Iliac Eisteddfod, April 16-18, 8-11 P.M., at the Teucrian Art Center."

My good luck next took the form of catching up with an old timer called Ignotus, who'd written other good things but now had come up with *The Historye of Reynard the Foxe*.This was his entry in a contest he managed to get me admitted to, before seeing to it that I arrived in a relaxed mood. For, make no mistake about it, Troy was a swell town; and if I'd had any tin, it wouldn't have been good on any bar in that nook of the Phrygian woods, as long as I had a harp strapped to me. And Ignotus saw to it that I ballasted the hooch with a Phoenix a la Scamander dinner.

So I checked in at the Arts Center without the kind of load to make me bumptious, but with enough of one to keep me cool about competing with famous old hands, and judged by blue ribbon referees. For although Priam sponsored the Eisteddfod, the professionals actually in charge were Sam T. Coleridge, Saxo Grammaticus and old Cass Longinus.

I won't give all of that night's program, but Strasbourg's Gottfried offered that part of his masterpiece where Tristram—to keep from leaving any snitching toe prints—hopped from his bed to Iseult's. And don't ask me how come Mark allowed her bunk to be so conveniently placed; because I've never been King of Cornwall and don't understand all its obligations. Anyhow my pal, Ignotus, then harped of how Renart took unchivalrous advantage of Mrs. Isengrim, by sneaking up behind her when she was stuck in the mud, and of the mortal challenge flung him by the justly indignant wolf. Finally Adam Mickiewicz recounted the breezy wedding which healed the Baltic basin vendetta central to his *Pan Tadeuz*. But as Ignotus had reckoned a late but not closing spot was best for a man without a laurel leaf to his name, I performed first.

Nobody could accuse Coleridge of being short of words on most occasions, but as he was up against a lack of data when barking of me, he could add little to his sonorous beginning. "King Priam, Queen Hecuba, abducted Queen Helen, Crown Prince Hector, Crown Princess Andromache and Prince Paris, you lucky rascal, I take pleasure in presenting as this Eisteddfod's next competitor, It—of whom—er—you will doubtless, by the favor of Zeus, hear again. Meanwhile he will regale you with an exploit of hers in which he personally took part—no less a matter, indeed, than her retrieval of the Mes of civilization, happily including the one for poetry, unknown to the First World."

For a moment after Sam T. had left me the only one standing in that great hall, I thought myself stricken with lockjaw. Yet as I desperately drew my harp into position and struck a few chords from it in a play for time, it steadied me sotto voce.

"This is what both of us are for, so don't sell us out to funk. . . And don't sink the act by yelling, mumbling or spouting too fast for clear catching by the ears we're aiming at."

"Right," I whispered. Having thus found out that I had not been sentenced to permanent silence, I opened up and rolled the following forth:

THE CRUISE OF ININNI'S YACHT, BELLE OF HEAVEN

I'll sing of how the world was roused and given back its ghost
What time a god was rolled for holdings, song begrudged the most
Which had before been held by jealous deity from men,
Though cocks could learn to crow when craft was slipped within their ken.
But first the Belle of Heaven spoomed from Evening's Star to reach
A village by Euphrates, where I spied her from its beach
And watched her meet the water, needing yet another hand;
So in I dove to board her when Ininni waved command,
Who sensed that I'd be proud to pounce on parts unsearched before
And risk at beauty's bidding any trap in Fortune's store.

Otherwise performing pretty well, I had pitched my voice a shade too high. Calm, now that I had broken the ice without cutting myself, I deepened my tone while moving from the proem to a word about her errand as well as mention of the expedition's third party.

The raid commenced at Erech, when we made for Eridu
To win the Mes Ininni wished and thus our longing, too;
With Ninshubur as helmsman and me to man the sail,
We flew her pennon deep below the belly of a whale;
For Enki, keeper of the Mes, was warden of the sea
And sharks patrolled the stronghold which he'd builded craftily
Amongst the shards of grandeur done under by the Flood,
For Eridu was mighty when the world was first in bud;
And silver soared the portal, tall above the ruins there
While lapis lazuli were ashlars carved with sorcerous care.

Focusing till then above the heads of auditors seated about tables below the dais my own was on, I now dared to see how they were taking my outpour. They were listening, and I didn't think it was entirely due to good manners; for by the ghost of An—remembered by me if forgotten by others since Kuwarbis did that dirty job on him—I had a story to tell!

Yet having glanced, I sued the daughter of the moon inside,
Not sad to find that Abzu Keep was out of bounds for tide
And glad to learn that Enki knew that cruising in the chill
Which gripped the nadir of the sea deserved a flagon's fill.
But knowing rievers mustn't drowse, I didn't dive in wine
As Enki did, because Ininni seemed to find a mine
Of wit in all he said, and drinking small herself the while,
Insinuated every jolt engrossed his shine and style;

And when his conning tower buzzed alike a swarm of bees,
Her key was woe: "In Erech we are minus all the Mes."

There had been half a goblet of wine in front of me when Coleridge summoned me to stand and deliver. Under cover of harp strokes forming a sort of intermezzo between strophes, I scooped the glass up and annexed the contents. I guessed that to be bravura the crowd would take in good part, and as a ripple of mirth sustained me, I went on to tell how she had lashed the normally cagey Enki to the mast.

The sobs she bravely strove to rein were torture to a heart
The grape had rendered tender. "What, you're short of every Art,
Design for Living, Fateful Bent and Handicraft, my dear?"
He thundered next. "I want the Mes, the whole set hustled here!"
Now Isimud, his factor, wasn't stewed and was astute.
"I counsel morning after thought before you grant the fruit
Of all your inspirations, sir." But Enki banged the board.
"She's sad, and I won't have her sad; the Mes at once!" he roared.
"And stow them in the darling's boat." "You're sweet," Ininni said.
"I know I am," said Enki, slowly sliding toward the bed
He found beneath the table, where I judged his slumber sound;
We didn't wait to listen—home the laden Belle was bound."

Priam's lads and lasses seemed delighted with the euchering of Enki, so I permitted myself a smile.

Yet speed was rather our desire than in the rate she logged;
She wallowed with a cargo piled so high it all but clogged
A boom that answered sluggishly to every tidal tack
Required when beating upward through a sea not wholly black
Because Ininni's star, that ushers in the dawning's sky,
Was shining through. She surfaced and I bailed the daisy dry.
But scarcely had I stowed the scoop when purple monsters rose,
All bulging eyes and thrashing arms and beaks for mouth and nose;
With Isimud to sic them on, they thronged about the ship,
And while Ininni girled the helm, we broke their scaly grip.
"He craves his Mes!" cried Isimud, the second time they swarmed.
"He swore them gifts, and we will see his promise is performed."
Ininni called while steering for the choppy channel mouth
Which signaled the Euphrates there was bucking sea-ward, south
From feathering Sumer green again, the tender hue of spring.
"Be wolves of war," she bade us. Then we wielded spear or sling
And knives as well for closer work; so some we warped away
With whizzing stones, and some we stabbed whose claws essayed to stay
The reeling Belle. Aye, seven times in all we fought them off,
Before we gained the river, source of painful wheeze and cough

For monsters weaned on seaweed; and because of their default
Their drover called the chase a loss. Our wounds for prideful salt,
We coaxed the doll to stem the stream, and watched the western rand
For signs of Erech's clutch of huts and twisting lanes of sand.

I felt I had been right in making one episode of flight and the successful fending off of pursuit, in place of treating these in separate strophes. With the action thus condensed, I could afford to follow it with a more leisurely treatment of the upshot, which my audience now settled back to learn.

At noon we made our landfall and lugged the Mes ashore
That once had fostered cities in forgotten times before
The Deluge drowned the world like a kitten in a pool.
We split the liquor Ninshubur, a lad who'd been to school,
Had thought to add in Abzu to the loot from Enki's hall
Ininni'd won, and watched rejoicers answer to the call
The Mes she issued each wahooed. Then Nanna's daughter flowed
To smile at me, her fist the gang about a hidden lode.
"Now Ninshubur will bide with me, as that's in long accord
With cosmic writ, but what have you in heart as a reward?"
She queried me. "For what?" I asked. "I did but what I must
Because you wished it, Evening Star and Morning one, and just
As beautiful at either hour, and more than all but you;
I've been rewarded, haven't I?" "Thus much I thought you knew."

Her speech wasn't finished, when I paused for a run of harp chords, but a small break was due between her offer of a guerdon and her actual award—through me to all mankind—of a bittersweet magic theretofore worked only by gods. I tried to put some of the knowledge I had come by on the Road in the tones delivering her continued words.

"Since nothing's been your seeking, you'll receive the best and worst."
She opened then her hand to show the talisman it nursed;
A bit of clay a tiny bird had trod when it was wet,
It seemed, before Cuneiform had captured me and set
Its seal upon my pulses. Then the fancied tracking bird
Revealed itself the wonder of melodious light—the word
Now apt for rhythmic beaming. So I won the worst and best
Of Mes; and while the hearties who were meted all the rest
Were building high, or smithing swords, or digging deep to steer
The river into fields where there'd be barley for the beer,
I hammered metric tools in trim, if wearying the sledge
And scorching was the forge I fed to fetch the needed edge,
Or timbre true to every sonance, thunderous or slight,
If harsh as city sacked the theme or lucky-wooing bright."

Having got that far without stumbling, I waved a triumphant hand in sign of striking into the valedictory. For this, involving as it did all the hard but prized sledding leading up to and away from her yacht that I'd boarded, my tone was elegiac.

The Belle's been idled since I turned a smith of Nebo's forms

And trudger of the Road, despite deprival, loss and swarms
Of insolent deputies of death. Yet still I joy to think
Of how we sailed, when destinies were flat as spikeless drink,
And battled back from Eridu in lading with the Mes
Which made of empty, torpid men the swiggers to the lees
Who'd build to please Ininni, or wreck for smiles from her:
The essences of gleam and gloom to match the mix of myrrh
And aconite she'd handed me, because I was her man
And served her once in Erech, where the Second World began.

Nice people those Trojans were (except for that Paris gold brick that ratted on his wife, Oenone, who was an all-right girl, according to Ignotus), so they gave me a hand that clouded my eyes with so much mist that it took a couple of wine bumpers to evaporate it. Not that the ovation was so wild as to promise me a prize—nor did I expect to come near doing so when vying with ranking Road roosters. But I had crowed to the top of my capacity and found ears which knew I had faked nothing, which was all I asked.

I felt so good, in fact, that when the Eisteddfod was over I went out to get plastered. And though I accomplished my mission, I neglected to take out bon vivant insurance, with the result that a certain melancholy had replaced my gaiety, when I awoke next morning in the back room of a dive called the Discord Apple. But being a harpster, I was staked to whiskey sours and as much breakfast as I was game for at a beanery next door.

Then I had to have plans for the future, though that seemed a lot to ask of a man who wasn't sure there was a future. Anyhow I found myself slouching through the Scamandrian Gate, determined to stick with the highway I found under foot until an interesting direction finger pointed me away from it. But as I was passing a grove of bay trees, while still in the suburbs of Ilion, a familiar figure left its shade and stood waiting for me.

"Why, hello, Nebo—I mean Apollo." Although I hadn't found him an easy companion in either capacity, I was glad of anything that might take my mind off the ashes of my joy. "I might have guessed you'd be in the vicinity of an Eisteddfod."

"I thought I'd better be on hand to guard the leaves of my laurel orchard against ambitious poachers, George."

On account of my condition I paid no attention to the fact that he addressed me by name for the first time. "Probably you didn't notice, but I was among the entrants." Trying to keep from babbling of my big moment, I failed. "The crowd didn't use their hands just to sit on either."

"The Iliacs are as renowned for their courtesy as for their ability to corner trade markets," my god said. "Still such people wouldn't act as if they felt they were being well served, were that not—with one exception—the case. What kind of 'liquor' did Ninshubur share with you, following your Apocatastasis to Erech?"

A son of science, I fielded Aristotle's six cylinder word for "return" without choking on it, while my memory slid back an estimated eighteen hundred years. "It was ale, and strong—stingo, in fact."

"Why in the name of the white hot hinges of Hades didn't you state that then?" he demanded. "The function par excellence of poetry is to tell readers or hearers what any action, feeling or substance is *like*—and not leave visualization up to empty or perverted imaginations. An abstract term such as 'liquor' defines nothing, and could as well be an Angel's Teat Cocktail as the honest booze Ninshubur actually pinched from Enki, while the latter was as dead to the world as a stuffed alligator in the window of a padlocked junk shop."

I gasped admiringly. For centuries I had been trying to think what Enki had reminded me of, when he'd lolled on the floor—still trying to grin entrancingly for Ininni's benefit—and here Apollo had hit it with one fired from the hip shot. Yet his graphic comparison could not, as I reasoned, have popped from pure intuition. Somewhere and some-when, he must have seen a dusty saurian dreeing its weird, as shadows closed about a bankrupt crame in a city's dingy by-street; and held the picture suspended in recollection until the moment arrived to fit the image where no other belonged. But while I was deciding that the faculty at work was the paramount poetic trait, I was forming a reply to the charge of failure to be vivid.

"I goofed by not naming stingo," I admitted. But when I did, I felt it was a mighty small fault for which to boo a work I was proud of; and as a man wearing morning after rue, I wasn't slow to air my irritation. "You know, Apollo, I have a hunch that being a god of writing, like being a critic, is a sight easier than producing the stuff. I bet that if *I* was in your niche, I'd be more like Bacchus; and would pitch in to help a fellow now and then in place of upstaging him all the while.

I thought that a complaint that smacked of heresy might make him sore enough to destroy me—a notion that didn't chill me in view of how I was feeling. As often before, though, I hadn't known where to find him, so what I drew was a laugh and a nod.

"When you were on Mercury with my earlier incarnation, George, it was too crowded an occasion to allow you to grasp more than a few limited advantages. Now I know you have that class at New Stonehenge to preside over at 1:40; but by taking the short cut via my planet, you can be sure of promptness, with time to spare for features which include an illuminating view."

That Second Trip to Mercury

When Apollo again called me George rather than It, I realized that he did so because he no longer reckoned me a trifling apprentice. By my public performance at Ilion I had qualified for a licensed traveler of the Road, and its supervisor was accepting me as such.

It made the difference between going to Mercury first class and being lugged there as the piece of baggage I'd been on my first visit. This time my conductor gripped my right arm with his left hand, jerked his free thumb skyward to get the elements in tune with his will, and up we went like a pair of rocketing woodcocks.

"What's the formula?" I asked. "Or is that a celestial secret?"

"No more than any other mathematical solution," he promised. "You have to know the orbit of Mercury with relation to that of Earth, of course, as well as the orbital inclination of my planet with respect to the ecliptic."

"A whacking seven degrees," I nodded, "and then?"

"You simply assign a letter with its proper coefficient to each of the factors and divide by our travel rate of two and a half times the speed of light." A fine companion now that he no longer felt the need of hazing me, Apollo raised friendly eyebrows. "How's your hangover?"

Startled to find that I no longer had any part of the willies, I risked shaking my head. "It's gone away," I whispered. "What happened?"

"You shed it when you left the earth's magnetic zone; heavy excess baggage like that isn't allowed in interplanetary travel, George."

"Newton had some good ideas." But then I recalled my narrow escape on the way to Aldebaran. "Are there any Stratospheric Sirens to watch out for?"

"There's no room for them." The god from Delos maneuvered us around an asteroid the size of Moby Dick. "As soon as we're out of Earth's magnetic field, we'll enter that of what I still can't help from thinking of as 'Nebo.'"

Where we set foot on what I, too, had difficulty in viewing as Mercury, was not this time the hot and smoky shop where I'd been hammered into shape to begin facing the rigors of poetry. It was rather beside Le Vieux Dieu An, such a sidewalk cafe as old Rugby Hornspoon had dreamed of finding at Chartres.

At the moment its three patrons had pushed the demitasses of mid-morning refreshment aside and were deep in discussion. At sight of Apollo, however, two of the arguers rose and beckoned, while a third turned to call for the services of a hovering *garcon*.

What he brought us was coffee that couldn't be compared with that dispensed by Tim O'Lucian at the Crossroads, but the conversation was of a nature to make me forget what I didn't have and to relish what I did.

"Sophocles was saying to Aeschylus," Ted Watts-Dunton explained when we'd been introduced and the waiter had done his thing for all five, "that he was sorry to observe what he called 'the cornballing of poetry' by making characters in plays and epics blat the notions of their authors instead of allowing speech freedom."

"To which Aeschylus rejoined what?" Apollo asked.

"Before he could comment in any way," Ted answered, "I cut in and told Soph his remark was the first thing he'd said or written which made me think he was getting old."

Aeschylus helped himself to a brioche. "And now," he

suggested, "you might tell us what prompted your statement."

"Why," Watts-Dunton chuckled, "it's a sign of mounting years when one ascribes to his younger days the general practice of virtues which were actually as rare then as they have ever been."

"I'm not given to bragging of 'the good old days' in most respects," Sophocles objected, "for my eyes tell me the girls are just as pretty as ever, while my palate declares that the Bourbon, wine and ale are, if anything, superior to those enjoyed in bygone years. In the case of the scops I knew in former times, though—"

"You're lending them credit for abilities they didn't have and wouldn't have desired," Ted finished for him. "Do you know how many first amendment dramatists there have ever been; I mean those above using characters to blow their makers' horns?"

"Well, there's Soph himself," Aeschylus put in, "and Will, that's directing rehearsals in the theatre across the street."

"Plus you; and that's high, low, jack and game." After gesturing as though flinging down a winning hand at cards, Watts-Dunton looked at the Delian. "Have I minimized, or withheld from the list any that belonged?"

"Your tally jibes with the one kept at the Flying Mustang Gatehouse." Apollo shrugged. "Gilgamesh aided by Heracles and Paul Bunyan couldn't have kept the egos of Corneille and Johnson out of their dramatics. The air castle builders, like Calderon and Kalidasa can't reasonably be excluded from their own exquisite dreams. As for Euripides et al., they can't be persuaded that the stage is not a lecture plat—"

"Perhaps I *was* looking at the theater of my younger days with starry eyes," Sophocles then confessed, "but we ought to consider that Ted's dictum covered Calliope's skalds as well as Melpomene's."

"There was no objectivity in Milton," Aeschylus mused. "It's plenty clear that if God had decided that eating an apple was nothing for an adult deity to throw a vengeful fit about, John would have jumped into the Edenic garden and personally bum's rushed Adam and Eve out of it."

"Virgil was in his epic like Flynn, according to an aphorism coined by some USAL pundit," Sophocles remembered. "If we knew what Flynn was in, the picture would be clearer; but no matter, the statement can be allowed to stand. As for Firdousi, Camoens, Dvaipayana and Valmiki, none was a detached bird capable of looking at a narrative sun with an eagle's unsquinting eye."

"So the narrative palm must be split between Homer's Alpha and Beta," Ted said over the cup he was lifting, "for having the craft never to wedge between readers and their tales."

"I think D. was within his rights in egoing his account of how he followed her to Kur," I said. "But how about Chaucer? He could spin a yarn without spreading himself all over it like a dropped ostrich egg."

Apollo sipped the last of his coffee. "But he might be called the Einstein of poetry, for his objectivity owned no absolutes but was rather relative to narrators of his creation. If you, too, are finished, George, I'd like for you to see what's going on at the theatre across the way."

Arrived, I look down through a Greek amphitheater toward an orchestra peopled by but two men. "When you lead the gang in again," the guy with a script was telling a listener, "do it with the slouch of a body that's glad of not being top-sergeanted by what's upstairs."

From a program Apollo found in the air, we learned that the director was Avon's head swan and the drama old Obiter Dicta's *Man Unfenced In*. The protagonist was, of course, Book-Boozer, genially played by Don Marquis.

The prompter, Poquelin Molière next slipped out of a wing, courteous with information. "We are now at the crucial part where Book-Boozer reaches the realization that his essential self is located only where his mind is. This awareness Obiter has developed chorally through the usual interplay between strophic and anti-strophic performers. Can we have them run through the routine again, Will?"

According to the program the chorus featured such names as Mac Plautus, Hal Ibsen, Maury Maeterlinck, Carp de Vega, Bill Gilbert, Carl Goldoni and Cal Kalidasa. These were the only ones the Delian had time to peg before the air waves started crackling with the question of whether a man is where his head has the moxie to fly to, or if he's stuck where his feet bog him down. While posing this problem, the chanting dancers moved with the alertness of men struck by the lightning of a challenging idea.

Where are we, when we're sheerly off the base
A false geography assumes our post,
And tags us tangent to a point in space
We neither light with life nor dim as ghost?
By accident of unrelated drifting
Our bodies, semi-animate at most,
Are actless, whether shoes are still or shifting.

That brought the actors to the far end of the orchestra. There they reversed their field while brooding over the issues raised.

Our feet nor stir nor stance them. So what time
Is morning's two when ticked beside a fetch
In Baghdad, while his self unravels crime
From Poe's detecting flair. Required in Paris,
He boards a flyer rockets couldn't catch,
His husk abiding constant as Polaris.

When the first semi-chorus made way for the other half, Apollo pointed out Bob Greene, Jule Slowacki, Fred Schiller, Ed Rostand, Gus Strindberg and a few others I can't now remember. They, too, evinced a growing awareness of mind's independence of fleshly slow-pokiness.

Suppose us Hans, a Copenhagen cit;
Who are we, when we've left our land and flashed
To antique worlds that no such nouns befit?
The news and views of temporal zones we've crashed,
So help us Cadmus, confiscate our being;
And all our checks are passionately cashed
In bygone banks, from now our essence freeing.
Wherefore we're not the slaveys of the age
Presumed our Bastille. Pouf! There stand on shelves

And in our closets saws to shred the cage;
Let those who buy it live the lie themselves.
Perhaps tonight we'll merge with Mommur yonder
Which Oberon rules, her son that czars the elves
And owns a wine to make a walrus ponder.

Obiter Dicta was putting his fire across, for I had hitched forward to perch on the buttockal skin of my seat by the time the united chorus pranced back and forth, shooting out sparks every time their collective feet stamped.

A walrus, quotha! Why if such an oaf
Can box a riddle, we could be the Sphinx
Or Oedipus expounding why a loaf
That's patterned after lumpish missing links
Can be so various and skill-provided
That he can skate on discontinued rinks
And still engage the locus whence it glided.

But, stonily, we're mum on sorcery;
A canny advocate of laissez-faire
Determined no corrupt bureaucracy
May short our circuits of electric air
And ground us by confounding, rank misreadings
Of man's sublimest scientific flair:
His gift for double-entry life proceedings.

I'd have stayed, in hopes of seeing the rest of the play, but Apollo tapped my shoulder. "As the demichoruses were a little ragged about working together, Will's going to put them through that routine several more times. Besides, there's a view I want to show you, George, together with some men who have the leisure to talk to you that nobody here will until first night is behind them."

The way we then followed wound through trees I could like without naming them, steeped in air as winning as a desert's after rain. And walking on Mercury was more like bouncing, because there was less gravity to fight than on or in Earth.

"You've got an A-one planet," I congratulated the Delian. "I bet Roadsters could do better work here than in common surroundings."

"The importance of his environment to any such is real," Apollo owned, "but it's got to be tailored to the individual. The best place for a writer is where he can turn out a crackerjack piece of work; and sometimes jail is the only answer to the literary hopes of lively lads who can't be pinned down to the grind of daily composition by their own will power."

"But those were extreme instances," I argued. "All things being equal as all men are not—Heracles could doubtless beat me at Indian wrestling; but they'd put him on the Indian list if he tried to drink Bourbon with me, not having inherited a hand me down head for it—stimulating air must be more inspiring than the flat, heavy kind."

"It's useless to tell air what it must do," Apollo insisted. "And a bracing one's as little to the purpose as a nuptial bed without a bride in it if a maker isn't ready to—But there are the gentlemen of Pieria I hoped we'd find."

They were seated about a table under a vine-climbed ramada whose western rim looked out on space. Nor were any of them strangers, for though they all shouldered harps, I had sat at their feet before the Road was any part of my thinking.

None reminded me while Apollo murmured introductions; so I made a business of paying the debts owed to openers of vistas leading out into light. "Although aware of your finesse as a writer, Dr. Goethe," I said, when I'd filled the empty chair indicated, "I took a course of yours in biological morphology, which I learned to appreciate anew when I myself was translated into several forms of marine life."

"A pedagogue's best reward," he smiled. "Were you ever an auditor of your current neighbor, Michel Montaigne, D.D.S.?"

"Doctor of Delightful Skepticism. Your outlook, sir, is the only thing I can think of which saved me from the digestive pressure of a whale that had waxed abominably stuffy."

"One is appalled by these blubberous baleens," Montaigne mused. "And yet when thrown among chubs or pilchards, one perceives the dwarfism they are shying away from, and sneaks a feeling of charity even for lummoxes. At my right, by the way, is the dean of scientific wilderness flitters, Dr.—"

"William Bartram, or 'Puc-Puggy'—the flower seeker—as an Indian among my fellow students named him. When I was recently at an Eisteddfod of which the chief judge was Sam T. Coleridge, Doctor, I recalled how highlights of your forest hegira were interwoven amongst his *Ancient Mariner* and *Kubla Khan.*"

"There are rivers in that sylvan sector of the USAL which are as mysterious as the sacred Alf, while overhead yawn antra formed by arboreal giants which—"

He stopped because Apollo put a friendly hand upon his arm. "Here, accompanied by the Pierian Spring nymph, Scientia, comes one you stand in less academic relation to, bard—if truly to be a bard was why she sent you to me, George."

On the long Road leading to Troy the knowledge of which I was fundamentally in search was lost sight of in pursuit of an essential experiment. Now as I saw with what careless aplomb Lucretius bore the harp peeping over his shoulder, I knew that my own was not naturally part of my equipment. Yet I was happy at sight of him as of few met in the course of my journey. For if I had sat at his learned feet in earlier days, I owed him much that was warm besides being true.

"Carus, if so I may call you now," I greeted him, "it's been a Carolina coon's age betwixt drinks."

"That's a coon this naiad is about to shoot out of his tree." He was a twinkler rather than a laugher, and a smile was more of his eyes than his lips as he flicked a finger at my harp. "For keeps, George?"

"He had to act so, and even to believe it, to fulfill a contract," the Delian cut in, "but I'll tell you more about him, when Scientia proves she's as good as she is beautiful."

A Map of the Literary World

You could tell that Scientia was a naiad rather than a dryad because instead of a tree she wore slacks and a sweater that fitted her like a well tailored birch bark fits a birch. Anyhow she looked from one to another of us, then clapped her hands six times. At each meeting of roseate palms a bass-ale glass full of a midnight blue liquor appeared in front of one of my companions. My own rookie's share, though, arrived in one of those tall Austrian tankards such as good old Ignotus must have slugged from when writing *Nibelungenlied* and *Gudrun*.

While I was pursing my lips to sip a sample of a new drink, however, I was astonished by a kick in the shins from this gravely attentive beauty. "Read the directions!" she commanded.

As often happens in the case of these Austrian tankards, a motto in embossed letters ringed the one I held. Hence, by turning the vessel completely around, I became possessed of this message:

Partaking of Pieria, play it bold,
Or stay the slave that you yourself have sold;

Drink wide and deep, as wisely counseled Pope,
Or seek a tamer spring from which to tope.

So while the rest were trying to make a small dose of familiar stuff last, I drank like Seithenyn ap Seithen on Mardi Gras. And while thus I was attending properly to business, Scientia left. But I kept drinking, and feeling my envisioning powers expand, until the Delian felt me ready for the vista he wished to acquaint me with.

"May I call your attention to the unique view of Earth this eerie proffers, George." Here he gestured toward what had before been emptiness west of the ramada. "I had to wait until your home planet revolved until it could be seen to the best literary advantage."

Gazing where he'd directed me to, I saw a huge stretch of the world on display with the vividness of a geodetic survey relief map. "Holy cats!" It wasn't a particularly well chosen phrase for either a poet or a scientist, but it was the only one that volunteered.

His bleak smile was not meant for me but for bitter realities. "What I may seem to have owned has so seldom been my property long, that it might be said that every time I gain a sphere of enlightenment in one area, so much—or more—do I lose elsewhere."

"Lose how?"

"Aw, I'll get a pretty good literary nation rolling, and all the neighboring countries, that couldn't tell prosody from an egg beater want a piece of the incidental civilization you need to rev it up and start it flying. So they move in, drink the bath and sell the baby to an organ grinder that's lonesome for a monkey." Apollo's shoulders sagged. "Or a nation will be conquered and lose its pride like watered liquor. Or political or theological dictators will decide that only greeting card verse can be written. Or grasshoppers or invading sand dunes may flummox me. Look, I'll shade with the brown of autumnal decay areas where my writ used to run and where it has ceased to within the memory of living man."

"I'm a living man; try me out," I suggested. But while

I was examining the melancholy results, I saw four birds I'd met before.

"She thinks of everything," the Delian said, breaking out a smile, too. "Now I won't have to give you transportation so you can meet that class."

A few minutes later Ninshubur arranged for the team to browse and joined us in studying Apollo's map. "What about now deserted areas that used to be full of literary beans?"

"I've touched on them, and I'll take them up shortly again; but first I'll dispose of the reading matter never never lands." The Delian made sweeping motions which turned large areas as blank as virgin typewriter paper. "These, because of too much cold, heat, rain, drought, rock, bog or whatever, have good excuses for having no literary history; but these that I'm smearing bird-seed grey boast conditions promising light—which is not going to shine as long as majorities cling to the darkness of non-literary tongues."

"Yes, and if you ever pointed out that that's what's the matter with them, newspaper sob sisters of one sex or another would be comparing you to Kipling and meaning no kindness by it." Montaigne chuckled. "You'd think he'd slaughtered more innocents than Herod and Phin Barnum combined, in place of contributing more crackerjack items to dictionaries of quotations than anybody but the swan that Ninshubur here never got around to harnessing."

"It's odd to reflect," Goethe said, "that all old Rudyard did to arouse the implacable hatred of generations was to state a truism. In a minor piece of his he noted that instructing folk in need of it has been sandy sledding since Dewey retired from Manila Bay to louse up the library system and to launch the screaming meemies of Progressive Education."

"To get on with my map," Apollo said, when he turned to face the world once more, "the global area where writers still retain the priceless freedom to break their own necks has shrunk to eight per cent of terrestrial square mileage—and that has occurred in an era when mechanical progress has theoretically promoted expansion on a generous scale. Yes, George?"

"But there has been a marvelous development in that area which you promised to deal with later," I prompted him, "and which you saw to it that I investigated at some length."

A colt hippogryph strayed into the ramada at that moment and the Delian sent a not yet fledged hybrid scampering off by means of a pebble he plucked from the air and tossed at the trespassing little beast. "Suppose you describe what you have in mind," writing's god suggested.

"Well, I haven't given it a name before, but it's the New Double-action Renaissance promoted by us scientists more than by you authors." Startled at what I'd said, I paused; but convinced that I meant it, I plunged ahead. "It was brought about by archaeologists, paleographers, cryptologists and sapient rummagers of everything from bat-plagued castle lofts to curse haunted burial vaults in order to fetch back to ken the bodies of literature that had been long taken into account no more than a golf ball sliced into a wasp's nest."

"Even if George had a hat on, I wouldn't say he was talking through it," Lucretius offered. "Was Gaelic Literature realized when I was a lad? Not a bit of it! I couldn't have told MacDatho's pig from the anonymous one pilfered by Tom, the Piper's erring son."

"Sumer was just a primitive spelling of 'summer,' lacing a Thirteenth Century lyric with quaintness, till I was a junior in college," Montaigne remembered. "I knew that Babylon had been built by her daughter, Semiramis, naturally, but I couldn't have named as Akkadian the language of the *Enuma-Elish* creation epic, of which Babylonian creation I blush to say I'd never heard."

"I acquired my doctorate without guessing that Akkadian, Hurrian as well as Hittite renditions of *Gilgamesh* could and would be found at Hattushash," Goethe supplemented. "As for Ugaritic, Himmel! If you had asked me to define it then, I would have hazarded that it was a spiked milk drink, like Kumiss or Bulgarzoon, rather than the lingo of the literature Phoenicians weren't supposed to have."

"This Double-action Renaissance, as George not inaccurately names it," Bartram remarked, "slides the formally ancient Graeco-Latin epoch up into the Middle Ages—pouting now because they haven't anything to be in the middle of and have no choice but to make book with Modern Times. Moreover, the entire structure of letters is now bulwarked with a new foundation of origins, trends, sources and allusions. Couldn't we have the map adjusted to include all those new but old parts?"

Once Apollo had done that, I stopped feeling puzzled, because I could see where I'd been and how other parts could be reached. "Ah," I said.

Ninshubur, who up to then had noticed me only by his nod when arriving, now spoke up. "Ready to get back to Earth, boy?"

"Directly." In reality I was ready to leave then, but I didn't know how to voice my leave of my ex-god.

"You can see why she thought a new survey of the Road was in order," he now observed.

"But why did she get a microbe-tomahawking scientist to undertake it?" Goethe complained.

I was opening my mouth to snap that I'd never drunk the blood of a microbe in my life, when Apollo spoke again. "Why do you think she did it, George?"

"I reckon it was because she wanted some one to take a look at it that could see what it was, which she'd never get out of a dozen harp-happy authors."

"I don't suppose you could," the Delian astonished me by agreeing. "What is the Road, man that hasn't left it yet?"

Recognizing it as my farewell to him, I took my time about that one. "It's the one continuum; all that's left behind when an old empire falls down a man-hole, and all that's ahead when a new one—er—"

"Pops like a champagne cork," Ninshubur offered, "out of some cosmic crack that nobody knew was loaded."

"Thanks," I said.

The Delian's only comment was to squint at the sun. "Time won't permit the one for the Road I would otherwise offer," he decided. "Harness your swans, Ninshubur, and take this foreign friend back to where he can function as best his native bents permit."

A New University Discipline

I had hardly more than said goodbye to my revered old friends than it was time to step off the western rim of the planet that had been Nebo and into the waiting car. Sensing that my wheels were spinning too fast for words, Ninshubur drove the team in silence for a while. But when we were clear of the pull of Mercury and beginning to feel that of Earth, he prodded my ribs with his elbow.

"She'll want you to publish a report as well as spiel it to her. What's science got to say about the Road that anybody will want to read?"

"Plenty," I promised, "but I'll have a better organized idea after I've ad libbed a lecture on the subject at the class that's coming up."

"Speaking of which," he suggested, "you'd better crawl out of duds that haven't been in fashion for umpteen centuries and don the outfit I lifted from a gent's shop whose keeper thought it was closed in the wee small hours. Just pitch the boxes and your old rags over the side. Outer space won't hold it against you."

"Let's hope the gents' shop keeper is equally tolerant."

I admired the weave of my new jacket. "You sure picked top quality."

"She'll want you to look your best," he reminded me. "The usual?"

"Do I look like a heretic?" But though I lightly quoted a Sumerian wise crack, I had a serious problem to solve. "You know, Nin, I'm going to keep Apollo's knife. But I can't let a restless harp that I'll never wander with again froust in a storage closet with such souvenirs of outworn loves as a cracked curling stone and a moose head lacking one eye."

"Let's think about what would be right for it," Ninshubur said, when the swans had finished trumpeting agreement, "but first do you see what I ogle, besides a couple of highballs?"

As I lifted one from the tray affixed to the dashboard, I could see a light blue something a few thousand miles ahead and scudding toward the world on more or less the same flying lane as our own. "If scientists hadn't agreed that it was an unidentified object," I replied when I'd studied the dingus, "I'd call it a flying saucer."

"As it might be what we're looking for, let's catch up with it." After clucking to the swans with more than usual sharpness, my companion spoke again. "Take the case off the harp, so it can have a voice in the dialogue I'll try to promote."

In an hour or thereabouts we had caught up enough to be hovering just behind and a trifle to the left of the gizmo. The harp, which I'd unveiled had previously been silent, but then it spoke in Torna's at once hoarse and hearty tones. "Where are you trying to find your way without me, lost men from sorry parts?"

Those that he spoke to were not the green men of irresponsible fiction. The face of the pilot that rolled down the window and looked back at us was white as milkweed down.

"We're robbed poets, looking for Necrocantica." The voice was faint but had the carrying qualities of a stage whisper. "And we heard that province of else forgotten songs was on Earth."

"As that's where most of mine are drifting, I can show

you that it's light years north and east of the world, if you take me along." Abreast of the outer space craft by then, I was able to toss skeletons a harp that had one more word for me. "While I'll never understand why anybody would want to retire from it, when it's a cinch to run into blue ruin anywhere along the Road, I'll still get a laugh, George, out of good dreams that show you sinking a hatchet in the potato of that oofus-goofus book reviewer."

My eyes filled with tears. "It was you that put me up to it, buddy." But right after that the queer looking machine switched to a new course and darted off like a laser beam.

Moody at having cut my personal link to the Road, I was silent until Ninshubur jarred me with a second elbow dig. "Do you find anything familiar, kid?"

"I can see what writers mean by 'ageless university towns upon which the hand of time rests as lightly as a roosting humming bird,'" I said after staring. "New Stonehenge hasn't added or lost a rock."

"One of the things that isn't changed is that a prof is expected to gas when he gets on deck," he suggested. "Are you oratorically ready?"

"Aw there'll be nothing to rattle a silver tongue at but a bunch of kids that April has stricken with buck and doe fever."

"Roust out of your jimjams," Ninshubur advised. "As she wants you to cop a blue ribbon with whatever you're fixing to unload, you can bet she'll have you audited by someone able to boost your stock. But first let's see how she's socking it to the heifers who would be bulls."

The swans dived toward the campus, and I saw they were heading for a window of the co-eds' gym, open to give hundreds of lunching women the benefit of spring's refreshing air. But when we'd skinned inside, it was clear that post-luncheon speeches were in order. For alone on a platform at the far end of the building Venus was holding forth.

From the lectern on which she was leaning she raised a hand to deal us a greeting, without ceasing to scorch her audience with such a look as she had turned on Isimud when refusing to help Enki Indian give the Mes. "It's sheer jennyassinity," were her words meanwhile, "for supposedly adult femes to wish to borrow Peters to play Pauls."

Behind her dais there was a spot big enough for well adjusted swans to meet the floor without damage to either. "Thanks for the lift, Nin," I then whispered; and after giving each cygnus an appreciative pat, I slid out one of the gym's rear exits.

As the chapel clock pegged the hour as 1:28, I didn't have to sprint to reach the Geography Building with minutes to spare. But the calm I was thus able to parade nearly cracked when I met the Dean of Arts and Sciences just outside my classroom. As an encounter with him was reckoned as equal to passing under a ladder warded by nine black cats, I fed him the old oil.

"Can I oblige you in any way, Doctor?"

He smiled like the king cobra he was. "By delivering the report of which I've heard such glowing forenotices, my lad."

I was still in a daze owing to that sugar cookie from an unlikely source when Dr. T. Wilson Woodwind and his brace of assistant university presidents steamed through the door. I didn't know the campus chief had guessed I was alive; but he beamed at me as if I was a tycoon he was about to shake down.

"I'm told you've got a bibliophilic treat for us," a geezer I believed to read nothing but stock market reports staggered me by braying.

Then I was steadied by recalling Ninshubur's bet that she would paper the house with a useful claque. "I have hopes of pleasing you," I mumbled as if I didn't dream he'd been drafted.

When I was rolling out a stand freighted with a pad of unmarked maps of the world, such as I had formerly used for my Economic Geography classes, the Budget dragoon and a sounder of more deans filed in. Of students there were none, though while I was alternately watching the classroom clock and the door, a few took scared looks at the gathered university brass and fled as if Fran Thompson's *Hound of Heaven* was nipping at their heels.

An unexpected entrant, doubtless on campus to give readings from some of his plays, was Aristophanes. A regular of the same ambush before he'd become famous and I studious, he was a welcome revenant from auld lang syne. He was also a needed one, for seeing how edgy I was, he took a seat in the front row and lipped me a message: "Don't mind the sabretoothed tigers, George; once they've eaten you, it doesn't hurt a bit."

Bucked by that wisdom, I had no tremor in my voice, when the 1:40 bell clanged the order to use it. At least I didn't until I almost slipped on ice that hadn't been there until I began cranking out words.

"As all here know," I teed off, "I've for years touted Economic Geography, nosing out where diggers had upchucked natural resources and trying to make a comprehensible pattern of the result, when I didn't know what the Kur—or rather where the *cur*-rent of civilization actually welled from."

Landing dead, I needed to be cued by somebody before I could jump to the next square, and Aristophanes came through for me. "Back home," he reminisced, "we always figured that it welled from booze."

"You came pretty close," I patted Athens on the head, "but that was too limited a view. There are a couple of other contributing factors anyhow. You've got to have a country that the people can wear in all weathers, and you've got to have Mummu so they'll know their way around."

"Around where?" the Dean of the Engineering School asked. He was fidgeting with his slide rule, but I was rolling now, and was out of reach of hecklers.

"That's a very good question, Doctor, and I'll gladly give it a frank answer. Around all disasters owing to the restlessness of gods—until the collapse of Heaven furnishes them with far more serious problems than how to heckle men."

"What could disturb the serene omnipotence of Heaven?" the Dean of the Divinity School wanted to know.

I thought of telling him what happened to the potence of An, when he met Kuwarbis, but decided to generalize. "It's best to say that when new supernatural powers become dominant, those they replace don't fare so well. Need I remind you of what befell Olympus?"

A gold tooth illuminated his grin. "We sure knocked those rascals for a goal, didn't we?"

"You clobbered 'em all right; but if that hadn't happened, the countries which commissioned them as gods would have been chopped out from under them first instead of getting chewed up later. But it doesn't matter what Heavens will crash, as long as there's room left in the sky for her star and Nebo's Aldebaran."

If that statement bothered the Head of the Astronomy Department, he never got a chance to say so because just then Ninshubur opened the door for her and Lalage. I wasn't the only one that stared. That pod of academic whales gave them both the glad eye and started to flock around. But a goddess who'd raided Hell just to see what would happen wasn't about to panic.

"Shoo!" she said, with a crumb brushing gesture. "I'll let you know when I want any of you near either of us."

Without a glance in my direction, Lalage sat down in the very back row and opened the copy of the New Stonehenge *Megalith* she was carrying. "What's a word in four letters for a fish of no particular character or convictions?" she asked Ninshubur, while drawing a pencil from her purse.

I wasn't such a chub as not to take advantage of the disturbance. Reasoning that everybody had lost track of my actual remarks, I put on a gratified smile, as I answered a question nobody'd had sense enough to ask.

"Why, yes, Doctor, I agree with you that where and when civilizations connect with the Road makes a fascinating study."

Venus now spoke from her seat next to Aristophanes. "It might help you, in the way of clarification, if you'd employ the map under the blank one, George."

Praying she wasn't kidding, I flipped back the outline of the world displayed on the stand and found one outlining the view from Mercury. Bucked by a discovery I might have foreseen but had not, I charged my bellows and let my voice roll even where a crossword puzzle was the preferred game.

"In briefly describing Literaria as now constituted, I am happy to bestow tribute on our distinguished guest, without whose enterprise the seeds of culture would be sproutless in an undersea storage bin while a world forever barren of universities—and allowing only the drudgery of grubbing for a living—turned drearily on an axis which couldn't have cared less if sheepskins could find no higher occupation than being wrappers for woolies."

I had that crowd in my pocket then. After freezing with horror at the thought that they might now be doing time as roothog-or-die tribesmen, they cheered the breaking of the blockade thrown by Enki and every other sticky wicket the Road was somehow snaked past. Only one would have been difficult for me to explicate alone: the low down on the important other half of the first Renaissance apple—disregarded as though there was a worm in it by those who had never looked it over. I might have passed it up myself, if I hadn't noticed the presence of the New Stonehenge poet-in-residence, but the juicy water pipe he was smoking called my attention to him in plenty of time for me to ring him in smoothly.

"Hi, Ahmed, old boy." I marked a point on the map and beckoned to him. "Step up and give me a hand by telling what story themes charged into Constantinople under arms in 1453; for I don't have to cite what the Greeks lammed west with."

A good fellow, Kemal Pasha-Zada joined me as requested. "I'll have to back up a little and tell of the bardic cross-breeding which took place before we Turks of the Ottoman branch got to toot the Golden Horn," he told Prexy et al. "You see, gentlemen, even after Persia was conquered by Alexander, the since magnificently active muse of that nation stayed passive until Allah the all-providing sent Arabs a millennium later to give Iranians a new shellacking. Besides the necessary scimitars, the invaders brought a talent for lyric verse and a knack for narrative known to all adorers of Scheherazade."

Without losing the pointer I'd turned over to him, Ahmed lofted his hands. "Who can but follow in stunned amazement the pains taken by destiny when furnishing a poet with a subject in precise key with his powers? I—But your pardons; I do not come into the picture yet. When the smoke of friction between two great peoples had settled, it was revealed that *la belle dormante,* the lovely Persian muse, had awakened complete with her own traditions and a genius for narrative verse as well as personal song. In the course of the journey of which she told me something this morning," he then said to me, "did you chance on Abu Nizami?"

"Does a colophon mean a cavalry charge?" I wondered. That was swank, but I wasn't passing up any literary card at that moment. "When I last saw old Abu he was taking off for trans-Oxus parts on one of the nattiest flying carpets I've ever seen."

"That must have been when he was covering the campaign against Tamerlane." After helping to build me up with that remark, Ahmed picked up my question about the literary baggage of the Turks when they took over Constantinople as Istanbul. "We wrote of Iskander, or Alexander, too; and like Nizami again, we dealt with Khosrau and Shirin, those lovers supplied us by Persian tradition. Yet there was a third theme of the Iranians that we also favored: one the Arabs had brought with them when cutting their way through Egypt and Palestine. The passion of Yusuf—Joseph, you'd pronounce it—and Zuleyka was treated by no less than the Paradisiac author of *Shanama,* whose doubtless crummy true name Allah the compassionate was too good a scout to reveal. And all these story subjects were originally developed while we Ottoman Turks were illiterates who couldn't tell a divan from a piece of furniture, or a collection of Arabic or Persian poems from a couch."

"Who schooled you?" the Dean of the Education College enquired.

"Old fashioned teachers like Genghis Khan," Kemal smiled. "They chased us into the main literary traffic stream, where we got hungry for Constantinople, and started two Renaissances, counting our own." After tapping Istanbul again, he handed the pointer back to me. "For there in Europe I found realization in an Africo-Asiatic subject, ripened hundreds of years before in a region I'd never visited.

Is there any other way in which I could serve you, George?"

"M-m-m. Yeah, you might sketch the history of why the lines Johnnie Racine strung his swell plays on were named for a general who never got elected to the Academie Francaise."

"I believe I can nutshell that in a *mufred*—extempore epigram to you—if you'll recall that French bards storied in tirades, or rugged four beat measures, before finding, as Crusaders, the longer, smoother lines first perfected by Persians concerned as little with the Holy Land as Sut Lovingood with curds and whey." With that he plunged his daemon in thought, whence it rose with this summary:

> *"Iskander's tale a Saracen aired on Palestine's warring scene;*
> *A Gaul adapting story and measure, named then Alexandrine."*

About to quit me in favor of his water pipe, the poet whispered a query. "Who's the houri sitting in the back row?"

I shook my head, not because I didn't know but because I couldn't understand why Venus had arrived with Lalage in tow. "All I can tell you is that she's got a bitter-tongued mynah bird. Next time we hit a bar, boy, the bourbon's on me."

After the lift he'd given me, bringing the Road up to date was a breeze. Meanwhile, by sticking to the unpadded truth, I'd given an outline of exactly the sort of book she wished to see in print. Knowing I'd done all I could I fed her a chance to go into action when I signed off.

"As the classroom clock says the bell won't ring until nine minutes from now," I said, hoping to look as guileless as the electric eel that had wrecked my trust in sweet young things, "I wonder if any here has a question."

"I have but not of you." Venus rose to stand beside me and face gazers that now included Lalage, as I noted out of one gratified eye's corner. "George having demonstrated the worth of a wonderful new extension of learning, how soon are you going to add it to your curriculum, Thaddeus?"

You could have searched me from Abzu to Ziusudra's

ark without finding who 'Thaddeus' was; but Prexy T. Wallace Woodwind owned up, and sang like a skypipit when he made that admission against interest. "George has a honey of a gizmo to sell, so I don't see why he can't be switched from whatever he's peddling now. As soon as he's ready to shoot, that is."

Considering who said that, I felt that the gryphons had agreed to stand back and let me scoop up the gold I'd located but I hadn't reckoned with the budget's bodyguard. "If added to the schedule," this gallstone barked, "the course would require a paid leave of absence for Doctor Puttenham, so that he could provide the now lacking textbook. And that would force New Stonehenge to hire a substitute to handle his Economic Geography stints—which it could only afford at the cost of forfeiting scholarships for the football team's third string tight-end, and that sober one the coach is grooming as a secret threat."

Prexy frowned. "They're both Ralph Henry Barbour 'for the honor of the school' athletes, or we'd never have recruited them; but without scholarships for them and their sweeties, paid for pads, walking around money and a new car apiece they'd quit us colder than an Eskimo whore's heart, wouldn't they?"

"You could even say colder than a barefoot Antarctica penguin's tootsies," the budget's Cerberus gloomed.

I thought the cause of Literary Geography was as lost as poetry was before Odin screwed that giantess, but the diplomat who'd talked An into giving her a yacht to streak around the cosmos in merely raised a hand and crooked a beckoning finger at Woodwind. "Come here, sugar," she said.

His bow tie didn't need straightening, yet she gave it a couple of tugs and finished with a pat on the cheek that nearly swooned him. "Now I understand better than anybody what responsibilities you bravely carry, and act as if they were nothing; but as I also know how wonderfully resourceful you are, I don't want you to go away until you know how you're going to finance George's course, or courses rather."

"I'm thinking," Prexy said. And he was, too, beginning

by putting the squeeze on me. "With the summer vacation looming, you won't need more than one semester to reel off your Lit. Geo. text, will you?"

"Not if I could take off today," I horsetraded. "The rest of the Geo. Dept. ought to be capable of taking over my teaching load by splitting it into ten equal parts of thirty-six extra minutes each per week."

"As that doesn't seem too much to demand of esprit de corps," Woodwind nodded, "I know a got-rocks who'll be flattered to have a professorial chair named for him, but I can't get to the hyena until next fall, because he's banked all his boodle in Switzerland while he's in stir. Play it cagey while you're away, George, and don't get tied up in any jackpots where the windows are too high to jump from."

Love Is Like the Road

While Prexy was leading a doctoral parade past a door I couldn't use without asking Miss FitzHorace why she was on hand, I was reflecting that my classroom was on the fourth floor and I had no parachute. "Some paper work will hold me here indefinitely," I therefore said to Venus, "but let me say that I have no words to tell you how grateful I am for what you've done for me."

"You in turn have carried out an assignment for me," she remembered, "nor am I a short sport. Escort George's charming reward in this direction, Nin."

I suppose Ninshubur followed orders by coming with her, but all that I was conscious of was Lalage strolling toward me, as indifferently as she had nth times done on the campus or streets of New Stonehenge. The confidence that had buoyed me when I'd rammed a great project through to acceptance by killer whales was as missing then as on all similar occasions. Reading me like a book with a disappointing finish, she spoke to herself while passing me.

"It's strange that now he's become a sailfish he acts as though he were still a chub."

There was, however, one difference as to this encounter.

Unless jumping from a window reared at such a height as Prexy had advised against, she could proceed little farther and there, to dispose of me, stood with her back turned. Having gazed at it despairingly a moment, I cast Venus a look of appeal.

"Quit funking the amorous jump like a virginicus oyster," she lipped. "Is she your girl or isn't she? If she is and you're not game to give her the all forever pitch, there'll be no use inviting you to drop dead, because in that case, you're there already."

Her blazing eyes reminded me, for the only time in my experience, of the fire-eater Tim O'Lucian had said she was; and I saw she'd wipe me off the map as cheerfully as she had fixed the wagons of Gilgamesh and the Round Table lads. But I didn't get sore at her on account of seeing that love was different from science; it was like being on the Road, in fact. If you weren't a yak, you did what was called for and never asked what it would get you, which was probably nothing anyhow.

So philosophizing, I bit Cupid's bullet, which is what he has instead of the arrow superstition arms him with. Slowly doing an about face, that is to say, I leaned over a cold shoulder, and after clearing an ear of copper tresses, filled it to this effect:

Sweet Lalage, my harp's unstrung;
But if you hark my heart,
Melodiously you will be sung
As vireo evening woods among,
Unpublic in its art
Yet yielding to a heedful ear
A harmony—the counterpart
Of mine when you are near.
I've learned in five millennia on the Road
That beauty linked with salt is where I've owed
A headlong love of which I'm so the thrall
I beg to wed you, mynah bird and all!

"I'll tack your name on the list of applicants," she yawned. That's when Venus chewed fire again. "You've just listened to the applicant that matters, ninny! He's just about to take off on his honeymoon, by the way, and he's not going brideless. Give George the plane tickets, Ninshubur."

"They're waiting at the air field. All Mr. and Mrs. Puttenham have to do is to step up and claim them."

"They'll be in a position to in a jiffy." She was smiling again now. "Stand with the happy couple as witnesses, Ahmed and Aristophanes."

Without objecting, An knows—or did when he had everything that belonged to him, including his buttons—I thought I owed it to the family honor to have things done properly. "We can't be married without a license and some kind of priest."

"Marriage isn't license, it's liberty," she corrected me. "And what can any mere flamen do that I can't perform? Face me, both of you; and take his arm, my dear, in the confidence that marriages I preside over stick for at least one lifetime."

It hadn't occurred to me that Lalage couldn't always out-cool cucumbers, but now she came down with a bride-to-be's jitters. "You can't railroad me without I get my hair shampooed and set! I've got to be at home tomorrow when Aunt Editha calls for the mynah bird I've been keeping for her! I can't leave the University without returning Alph Daudet's *Tartarin de Tarascon* to the library! I can't traipse off to any old wheres without getting someone to water the petunias I've planted in a window box! And without an armful of lilies of the valley I won't promise to love, honor and sass him or any other man in need of a frock coat and zebra-striped pants!"

"All those are reasonable requirements," Venus soothed her; "and reliable Cupidos will attend to such matters as can't be taken immediate care of here." After touching me and throwing a cloud around Lalage and herself, she reached out of it to put a hand on Aristophanes as well. "I almost forgot to clap a trance on Stoph, so he won't have a laugh convulsion at what's happening to you," she explained, while merging with impenetrable mist once more. "Being old school, Ahmed will be no problem."

Turning into a wearer of formal duds, such as I'd never

seen outside of an illustrated Nineteenth Century novel, was much like being transformed into a loon. As had happened when I was worked on by Merlin, the process began on the ground level. My brown shoes became a modest black—obviously curried, that is, but with nothing that could be mistaken for a flashy USAL shine. While the stripes that crawled up my trousers were too thin for a zebra to brag about, there was no other comparison that I could think of which would fit that pattern better. I had a bad moment when my belt melted, never having learned to trust galluses, but disaster didn't strike; and I soon boldly sported a marble shirt front and a cast iron collar, plus two tails to the devil's one.

The by then vanishing cloud showed my fiancee in white frills and lilies I suppose came from that valley she didn't name; but I had no leisure to admire her, as Venus pulled Aristophanes out of his trance and marshaled the wedding. "Ahmed, pass George the ring you'll find inside the front fold of your turban. Lalage, give Stoph your bouquet to hold until the rundle's on your finger."

She said other things before the ceremony was over, but I chiefly recall her last instructions to me. "George, take Apollo's sheath-knife out of your breeks' waistband and put it in an inside coat pocket. That's right, honey; *because from there you can snick it across a throat in a hurry, if a critic or something asks for it!*"

About the Author: "Courtesy of John Caldwell and Alice O'Neil McCorry Myers, I was born on January 11, 1906 in Northport, Long Island, where I was named for John Myers, my grandfather, the extra Myers, sparing me a dynastic "II" as per race horses, czars and yachts.

"After conning books at St. Stephens, Middlebury and the University of New Mexico I spent a year traipsing around Western Europe and part of another following the Danube from Vienna down to the Black Sea.

"On this side of the Atlantic I wandered, shouldering a knapsack, drank Prohibition under the table and functioned as a newspaperman in New York and Texas. Finding more fun than profit on the Pacific Coast next, I dug in as an advertising copy writer after skedaddling back to Manhattan. Thence, for a change of chores, I joined a pair of cronies who had squatted on one of the Sea Islands of South Carolina. The idea was a back to the soil stint, but as wild woods hogs guzzled our crops, we throve only by trapping them, stoking them with corn and marketing them as pork.

"Hog ranching didn't represent my true bent, however, so I returned to New York and hung out my shingle as a writer. But in due course the Army beckoned, with the consequences that I put in five years as an enlisted man and officer of the Armored Force during World War junior. Soldier's compensation took the form of meeting Miss Charlotte Shanahan while I was stationed at Fort Knox. Married in 1943, C. S. Myers and I now live out in the chaparral cock country north and east of Mesa, Arizona, within visiting range of our two daughters.

"Aside from writing while in Arizona I have taught it at Arizona State University, where I also conducted a writer's conference and assembled a Western Americana collection for the University Library."

John Myers Myers